Acclaim for the authors of

A Western Family Christmas

MILLIE CRISWELL
"Ms. Criswell's charming characters
work their way into your heart."
—*Romantic Times Magazine*

MARY McBRIDE
"Mary McBride is a natural born storyteller."
—*Affaire de Coeur*

LIZ IRELAND
"Ms. Ireland has a true gift of creating
extraordinary characters that stay with the reader
long after the book is finished."
—*Rendezvous*

DON'T MISS THESE OTHER TITLES AVAILABLE NOW:

#580 IRONHEART
Emily French

#581 WHITEFEATHER'S WOMAN
Deborah Hale

#582 AUTUMN'S BRIDE
Catherine Archer

* * *

A Western Family Christmas
Harlequin Historical #579—October 2001

Dear Reader,

The holidays are fast approaching, and Harlequin Historicals is delighted to bring you the first of this year's two Christmas short-story collections, *A Western Family Christmas,* by three of our best-loved authors, Millie Criswell, Mary McBride and Liz Ireland.

From *USA Today* bestselling author Millie Criswell comes "Christmas Eve," the story of a lonely spinster in Colorado who's sworn off celebrating Christmas, and the handsome drifter who blows into town during a blizzard and helps her rediscover the joys of the season.

Author Mary McBride brings us a touching tale of love and redemption in "Season of Bounty," when a Civil War doctor turned ne'er-do-well gambler wanted by the law finds happiness in a small Kansas town and the arms of a widowed shopkeeper.

And last but not least, we get a romantic comedy from the talented Liz Ireland. In "Cowboy Scrooge," a spunky would-be mail-order bride finds herself the guardian of three bratty orphans instead. Watch the sparks start to fly when they arrive on the doorstep of their cantankerous cowboy uncle!

We hope you enjoy all three of these wonderful stories of Christmas in the Old West! And in November be sure to look for our collection *'Tis the Season,* three enchanting tales set in medieval Europe.

From our family to yours, have a wonderful holiday season!

Sincerely,

Tracy Farrell
Senior Editor and Editorial Coordinator

A Western Family Christmas

MILLIE CRISWELL
MARY McBRIDE
LIZ IRELAND

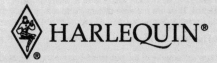

HARLEQUIN®

TORONTO • NEW YORK • LONDON
AMSTERDAM • PARIS • SYDNEY • HAMBURG
STOCKHOLM • ATHENS • TOKYO • MILAN • MADRID
PRAGUE • WARSAW • BUDAPEST • AUCKLAND

ISBN 0-373-29179-5

A WESTERN FAMILY CHRISTMAS

Copyright © 2001 by Harlequin Books S.A.

The publisher acknowledges the copyright holders of the individual titles as follows:

CHRISTMAS EVE
Copyright © 2001 by Millie Criswell

SEASON OF BOUNTY
Copyright © 2001 by Mary Myers

COWBOY SCROOGE
Copyright © 2001 by Elizabeth Bass

This edition published by arrangement with Harlequin Books S.A.

® and TM are trademarks of the publisher. Trademarks indicated with ® are registered in the United States Patent and Trademark Office, the Canadian Trade Marks Office and in other countries.

Visit us at www.eHarlequin.com

Printed in U.S.A.

CONTENTS

MILLIE CRISWELL

Millie Criswell didn't start out to be a writer. Her greatest aspiration in life was to tap-dance with the Rockettes. However, when that failed to work out, she put pen to paper and has authored twenty bestselling, award-winning historical, category and contemporary romances. She has won numerous awards, including, the *Romantic Times Magazine* Career Achievement Award and Reviewer's Choice Award, and the Maggie Award from Georgia Romance Writers. Millie has two grown children and resides with her husband in Virginia.

CHRISTMAS EVE
Millie Criswell

As an author I feel blessed to have
such loyal, dedicated readers, who have followed
my career path from historical, to category,
to contemporary, and now again to historical.
"Christmas Eve" is for all of you,
with my heartfelt thanks for your support
over the years. Happy Holidays!

Chapter One

Four Weeks Before Christmas, 1887

"Morning, Miss Eve. Getting an early start on your Christmas shopping, are you?"

Blue eyes narrowing slightly, Eve Barlow heaved a sigh of pure displeasure. "Now why would I indulge in such a worthless pursuit, Mr. Purdy?" she asked the well-meaning but nosy shopkeeper, trying to remain polite though she felt anything but.

Mathias Purdy, though relatively new to Cedar Springs—anyone who'd lived in the close-knit community less than ten years was considered a newcomer—knew very well how she felt about Christmas. Everyone in the whole town knew that she hated having anything to do with the holiday. Ebenezer Scrooge had nothing on Eve when it came to "bah, humbug" and keeping Christmas in her own way, which was not at all.

Most were smart enough not to press her on it. Most. But not Mathias Purdy, who made a valiant effort every year about this time to change her mind.

"Me and the missus are holding a small gathering this coming Saturday evening. Lida Sue Willis and Grady Boots—they're engaged now, you know—are going to lead us in song for the upcoming caroling event to be held at the Methodist church come Christmas Eve. Sure would be nice if you could join us."

Withdrawing a dollar bill from her reticule, Eve passed it to the owner of the mercantile. "You did say one dollar for the book, didn't you, Mr. Purdy?" It was the latest novel written by Emily Jean Bartlett, former dime novelist turned biographer, and Eve was quite anxious to read it. Next to baking, which she adored, reading was her favorite pastime.

With a look of disappointment at the woman's stubbornness, the shopkeeper nodded. "Yep. I'll get it wrapped up for you, Miss Eve. Won't take but a minute."

While Mr. Purdy tended to her purchase, Eve moved down the long glass case filled with gloves, hair combs, ribbons and the like, to the box of lovely glass Christmas tree ornaments sitting on the countertop.

The red and silver globes sparkled in the overhead light of the kerosene fixture, enticing in their beauty. For a moment she was transported back to a happier time, when her parents were still alive, when Christmas was still for dreams and childlike ambitions. When life hadn't been filled with so much unpleasant reality.

The Christmas holidays brought only sad memories for Eve, despite the fact she'd been born twenty-eight years ago this coming December 24—Christmas Eve, hence her name. Her mama thought Eve had been blessed for having been born on the Lord's birthday, though Eve felt anything but. Nothing good had ever come from Christmas, and she was convinced nothing good ever would.

"Them ornaments are mighty pretty, aren't they?" the older man commented, setting Eve's package down on the counter. "I'd be pleased to give you one as a gift, Miss Eve. You can decorate your tree with it."

Counting silently to ten, Eve reminded herself that Mathias Purdy was only trying to be kind, and she forced a smile, thin though it was. "Thank you, Mr. Purdy, but I have no use for ornaments, trees or any folderol associated with Christmas. I'll spend the holiday reading, as I always do. Reading, reflecting and enjoying my solitude." In fact, she intended to spend the next four weeks doing just that, until the blasted holiday season was over and done with.

She had plenty to keep her busy: new curtains to sew for the guest bedrooms, letters to write to her elderly cousins back east, and maybe she'd do a bit of baking. She had several new recipes she'd cut from the *Ladies Home Journal* that she wanted to try. The time between now and Christmas would be filled with purposeful pursuits, not wasted with a bunch of sentimental nonsense.

Scratching his balding pate, Mathias Purdy looked clearly perplexed and quite frustrated that he couldn't convince the young woman to come around to his way of thinking. "Don't seem right, you spending the holiday alone, if you don't mind my saying so, Miss Eve. Mrs. Purdy gave me strict instructions to invite you to Christmas dinner. Told me not to take no for an answer this year. She'll have my hide if you don't come. And though that hide is wrinkled and pretty wore out…well, I'd sure like to keep it.''

"Please thank her for me, but I must decline. Please extend no more invitations or gifts. I don't wish to be rude, but that's how I feel. And I'm not going to change my mind.'' She couldn't have made her feelings any plainer on the subject, even to someone as persistent and single-minded as Mr. Purdy.

Removing his spectacles, the older man polished the glass with the edge of his white apron while he spoke. "Don't seem right, your staying by yourself, but I'll keep my mouth shut. Don't expect Mrs. Purdy will understand, though I'll do my best to explain why you ain't coming to share dinner with us. I know she'll be disappointed. Sarah sets a great store by Christmas.''

Eve didn't expect anyone to understand her feelings on the subject, but she did expect them to respect her wishes. "Good day to you, Mr. Purdy. I'd best get home before the snow starts falling in earnest.'' A glance out the front window told her that the light snow, which had begun as a dusting this morning, had increased and was accumulating quickly.

"Stay warm and dry, Miss Eve. And if you change your mind about the dinner, the offer's always open. You've got several weeks before you have to decide one-hundred percent.''

With a small wave, Eve shut the door to the mercantile behind her, sucking in the cold Colorado air, then made her way down the splintered boardwalk toward the two-story white clapboard house she called home.

Her parents had bequeathed the house to her upon their death. It would be ten years this Christmas, ten lonely years since Alma and Kyle Barlow had been killed in the train derailment of the Denver Pacific Railroad. And not a day went by that she didn't think about them, miss them.

As a young woman of eighteen, it had been a difficult adjustment to meet life on her own, to support herself and find her way. Not much had changed in the past ten years. She was still lonely, still at loose ends, though she put on a brave front for others to see.

Eve wanted no pity from anyone. She'd received a heavy dose of that six years ago when her then-fiancé, Daniel Stedmon, had left her stranded at the altar on their wedding day—Christmas Eve day to be exact.

Thinking back on Daniel's bland personality and penny-pinching ways, the man had probably done her a favor by running off as he had, but she hadn't felt that way at the time. She'd been devastated, humiliated, and wanted nothing more to do with men. A woman didn't need a man in her life, she'd told herself many times. Eve wished only that she could believe it.

Spotting Florinda Cooper entering the post office across the street, Eve released her maudlin thoughts and waved at the older woman, of whom she had grown quite fond. Florinda was the town's postmistress, and had been since her husband passed on three years back from the influenza. She admired the older woman for picking up the pieces of her life and going on. Florinda had spunk.

For the most part, Eve had done the same, until the

holidays rolled around to remind her of how different
her life could have been. She knew better than to
dwell on "ifs" and "buts," but she did so just the
same. Humans were forever sticking their tongues to
a canker sore, just to make sure it still hurt. Drawing
up the pain from time to time at least made her feel
that she was still alive.

"Get yourself home, girl," the postmistress ordered in her normally bossy manner, her wrinkled
cheeks chapped red from the cold. She was bundled
from head to toe in a man's heavy wool coat and
work boots. Florinda liked dressing in her husband's
old clothes; said it made her feel closer to him.

"It's going to snow something fierce, mark my
words. I can feel it in these old bones. Wouldn't surprise me atall if we have a full-fledged blizzard before
nightfall."

"I'm on the way home now, Florinda," she
shouted back, glancing up at the leaden sky, which
looked more ominous by the minute.

Situated northwest of Denver, Cedar Springs was
nestled at the base of the Rocky Mountains and was
no stranger to inclement weather and massive
amounts of snow accumulation.

The snow was falling in earnest by the time Eve
pushed open the gate of the white picket fence surrounding her property, which was located at the east
end of town. Some of the pickets needed repairing,
the paint on the house was chipped in places, and all
of it was in dire need of a fresh coat; but none of that
seemed to matter when the pink tea roses bloomed
against the fence, and the large crab apple tree gracing
the yard gave off its sweet fragrance in spring.

Eve's home had been the one constant in her life, and she loved it. It was the means by which she supported herself. Taking in boarders during the year supplemented the small inheritance her parents had left her. The exception to that was the period between Thanksgiving and Christmas, when her home was closed off to travelers. No one was allowed to intrude on her solitude then. And she made no exceptions.

Through the heavily falling snow, Gabe Tyler spotted the two-story house at the edge of town and guessed this was the boardinghouse to which the owner of the hotel had directed him.

He hadn't figured on staying in Cedar Springs for any length of time. He'd planned on having a hot meal, maybe playing a few hands of poker at the saloon and then heading on.

Drifting was what he did best now.

But his horse had been spooked by a jackrabbit two miles outside of town and had pulled up lame, and a blizzard had a way of changing even the most predetermined plans.

Cedar Springs's only hotel had been filled to capacity when he'd tried to procure lodging there, as were the other two boardinghouses he'd visited. He hadn't counted on the Christmas holidays and all the extra visitors in town. Not that he had a whole lot of choice in the matter, circumstances being what they were.

The prospect of sleeping in the livery didn't appeal, even though his horse, Barney, found it quite to his liking, so Gabe decided to try the last remaining boardinghouse in town, though he'd been warned that the proprietress, a Miss Eve Barlow, wasn't the most pleasant or hospitable person at this time of year.

Gabe prided himself on his friendly demeanor and winning ways with women, especially the older ones, so he felt very confident that he could sweet-talk some aging spinster lady into giving him a room.

Trudging up the path to the house, Gabe had a bit of difficulty pushing the gate open. The snow had piled high against it, making it hard to move. Light shone warm and welcoming from the windows, so he knew someone was at home.

At the door, he banged the brass knocker a few times, stamping his near-freezing feet, blowing into his gloved hands, then pulling up the collar of his sheepskin jacket to ward off the frigid temperature.

The door opened, and Gabe thought he might be suffering from snow blindness. The woman framed in the doorway was anything but old, and she sure didn't look like a mean-spirited spinster. She was blond, blue eyed, and though her figure was obscured by the shapeless dress she wore, he could tell she was nicely rounded in all the right places.

"May I help you?" she asked, all businesslike and proper as she adjusted the crocheted shawl around her shoulders.

Gabe cleared his mind to the matter at hand and nodded. "Yes, ma'am. I heard from the owner of the hotel that you have rooms to let. I just got into town and—"

Lips pursed, like she'd been sucking a tart lemon dry, the spinster shook her head. "I'm afraid you've been given erroneous information, sir. I don't let rooms during the holiday season, and everyone in this town knows it.''

Porcupines had fewer barbs than this prickly woman. ''Yes, ma'am, that's what they said. But I was hoping you could see your way clear to changing your policy, just this once. My horse pulled up lame. And as you can see, there's a blizzard blowing like a sonofa—'' Her eyes widened, and he amended, ''Pardon my manners, ma'am. I've been on the road too long.'' Eight years too long, to be exact.

''I'm sorry, but the answer is still no.'' She started to close the door, but Gabe stuck out his foot to form a wedge, preventing her from doing so.

He figured he deserved some kind of award for keeping his temper in check. Miss Eve Barlow could try the patience of a saint. And he was no saint! ''Pardon me for saying so, ma'am, but that's not very hospitable of you.''

Spine stiffening like a steel poker, Miss Eve Barlow obviously didn't like being accused of lacking in manners or civility, which was too darn bad. Because where Gabe came from, people didn't turn away folks in need. And he was definitely in need.

She brushed back the stray blond hairs that had escaped her chignon, and Gabe was reminded of corn silk. Corn silk, honey and...

''It is not my fault, sir, that you chose to drift into Cedar Springs during a blizzard, and that you rode your horse so hard the poor creature pulled up lame. Now I must ask you to leave. Good day.'' She slammed the door in his face so quickly, and with such force, that he barely escaped with his frozen toes intact.

"Sonofa—! Tight-lipped, coldhearted old maid," he mumbled, before turning around and retracing his steps back to town. He didn't take kindly to anyone accusing him of mistreating his horse, especially a stiff-necked spinster, who probably didn't know one end of a horse from the other.

Not one to be dissuaded, and certainly not one to stay out in the elements any longer than he had to, Gabe headed to the Silver Queen Saloon to ask a few questions, and hopefully find someone who might be able to help him convince Miss Sourpuss Barlow to change her mind.

Damn, but the woman was contrary! It was no wonder she wasn't married. Not that he put a great store in that institution himself. Not after Marilyn Trusslow Tyler, his deceitful former wife, had taken their two-year-old son and run off with the child, along with his best friend and co-worker, Benjamin Fontaine, leaving Gabe with nothing but heartache and painful memories.

Nope. Gabe had no use for marriage. But fatherhood was a whole different matter. He missed his boy like crazy, had searched for Robby high and low these past eight years, to no avail. But he wasn't giving up. He'd stay on the road as long as he needed to, spend whatever it took, until his boy was found.

Chapter Two

"You say she slammed the door in your face?" Hiram Walker shook his head, slapped his hand down on the bar and laughed out loud. The freckles on the redhead's face looked even more pronounced. "That's Miss Eve, all right. She don't cotton to anyone staying with her during the Christmas holidays."

Gabe tossed back his whiskey, then said to the bartender, "And why is that? Is the woman a heathen, or just plain nasty?" After meeting her, he figured the latter.

The bartender refilled his glass. "Nope. She's a God-fearing woman, goes to church most Sundays. But she's got her ways, some peculiar thoughts on things, and she don't like Christmas, due, I suspect, to the fact that her parents up and died on Christmas, ten years back. And Miss Eve especially don't like boarders this time of year. Shuts that house up tighter than a virgin's thighs."

Well, isn't that just peachy? "But I need a place to stay." He was going to be up the creek if he couldn't find one.

"I could probably put you up with one of the working girls, if you've got the money to pay. Doubt they'd put you up outta the goodness of their hearts, whores being whores, you understand?"

Remembering the appealing warmth of the boardinghouse, the fresh, clean scent of the woman who ran it, Gabe shook his head. When it came to sharing a woman's bed, he was pretty discriminating, which probably accounted for why he hadn't shared one for quite some time.

"With the weather the way it is, there's no telling how long I'll be here. And I don't relish living with a lady of the evening, even one nice enough to share her room. Thanks, anyway."

With a shrug, Hiram continued mopping up the bar. "Suit yourself." He glanced up then, smiling at the nattily dressed man who had just entered the saloon. "Hey, Mayor! How's things?"

Gabe cranked his head to stare in the young man's direction. The gentleman who waved back couldn't have been more than twenty-five, which seemed rather young for someone to be holding such an important position. "That's your mayor?"

"Yep. Burt Moody's young, I'll give you that, but he's doing a right good job here in Cedar Springs. He's even come up with a plan for garbage collection. Don't that beat all?"

Yes. It did. And Burt sounded like someone who just might be able to help convince the stubborn Miss Barlow to rent Gabe a room. With that thought in mind, he headed in the man's direction.

A short time later, Gabe and Burt Moody were

walking down the street toward the Methodist church, chatting like old friends.

"Can't hurt to have a minister with us when we approach Miss Eve about her boardinghouse policies," the mayor said, stepping around a pile of fresh horse droppings and frowning. Burt had tried to institute a law requiring horses to wear diapers while in town, but the measure had failed with members of the town council.

"We pride ourselves here in Cedar Springs on being hospitable to strangers. Our town motto is Come One, Come All, and it just doesn't look right when one of our citizens turns away a stranger in need."

"I appreciate you offering to help, Mayor." Ever since Gabe had mentioned that he was one of the Boston Tylers, an influential banking family, young Burt Moody had fallen all over himself to be accommodating. It seemed Burt had political aspirations beyond being mayor of Cedar Springs.

The Tyler name had always opened doors on both coasts, though Gabe rarely mentioned the connection, unless he was in desperate straits.

Like now.

Eve had just taken the last batch of oatmeal-raisin cookies out of the oven when the front door knocker sounded several times in quick succession.

"Who on earth can that be now?" she muttered, wiping her hands on the pristine white apron that covered her shirtwaist and navy serge skirt. Not another stranger looking for a room, she hoped, though she had to admit the last one had certainly been handsome, even if he had been rude and overbearing.

Hurrying to answer the summons, she opened the door a crack to discover Reverend Brewster standing on the porch. Henry Brewster was Cedar Springs's Methodist minister, and her clergyman, and she hoped he wasn't calling to take another collection for the Widows and Orphans Fund. She'd given half a dollar at last Sunday's service, money she could hardly afford. Standing next to him was Mayor Moody, whose former profession as a Bible salesman had brought him to town several years ago. Odd that they should choose to call upon her today, she thought. The weather wasn't exactly conducive to socializing.

Opening the door wider, she was dismayed to discover the handsome drifter standing behind them, and the pleasant smile she wore melted. "Hello, gentlemen," she said, hoping she didn't sound quite as peeved as she felt at the moment, because she was pretty darn irritated.

"Sorry to bother you, Miss Eve," the reverend began, pulling off his hat to reveal his balding pate, "but we were hoping we could come inside and have a little chat. It's mighty cold out here, and my bones just aren't what they used to be." He looked over her shoulder with undisguised yearning toward the cozy lamp-lit interior.

"Of course. Where are my manners? Come right in. I have a nice warm fire going in the parlor."

"We hope you don't mind, but we've brought along a friend," he added. "Mr. Gabriel Tyler, formerly of Boston."

Her smile was as sour as vinegar when she greeted the stranger, who now had a name. "Come in, Mr. Tyler. I see you've brought reinforcements with you this time." There was not an ounce of welcome in her voice.

Gabe nodded, not at all embarrassed by that fact. "Yes, ma'am. Desperate men take desperate measures," he replied.

Once the gentlemen were seated in the parlor on the floral chintz-covered sofa, Eve removed herself to the kitchen and filled her best china pot with coffee. Arranging her oatmeal-raisin cookies on one of her mother's rose-patterned plates, she carried it out on a polished silver tray, setting it down on the table in front of them.

No one was going to accuse Eve Barlow of lacking in manners again. Inhospitable, my foot! she thought.

"These were just baked, gentlemen, so please help yourselves."

"Mighty kind of you, Miss Eve," Burt Moody said, licking his lips as he reached for a cookie. The Cedar Springs mayor had a serious sweet tooth, as could be attested to by the matchmaking mamas in the community, who had taken the young bachelor under their wings, supplying him with every type of confection available in the hope that he wouldn't remain a bachelor for long.

To date, Hetty McMartin's pecan pie was heading to the top of the list, and everyone expected Burt to choose her daughter, Holly, as his intended.

"I won't take up any more of your time than necessary, my dear," Reverend Brewster said. "But it's come to my attention that you've turned away Mr. Tyler during a blizzard, and I've come to see if you won't reconsider your decision about renting him a room.

"Mrs. Brewster and I would offer the unfortunate man a place to stay, but we've got a full house, what with the children and grandchildren home for the holidays. I'm sure you understand."

"I've already informed Mr. Tyler of my position on renting rooms during the holiday season," Eve stated, unwilling to make eye contact with the dark-haired stranger, though she could feel his deep blue eyes boring into her. He was even more handsome than she'd originally thought, now that she'd gotten a closer look at him.

Daniel Stedmon had been handsome, too, she reminded herself, trying desperately to ignore the fluttering in her stomach and failing miserably.

"Christian charity doesn't go by the calendar, young woman," the clergyman said, and Eve's cheeks blossomed pink in embarrassment.

"I—"

"Ma'am," Gabe interrupted, "I wouldn't have bothered you at all if there'd been any other means open to me. I was offered a room at the saloon, but my good Christian conscience just wouldn't allow me to accept." He did his best to look innocent, if not downright pompous.

Eve was surprised by the man's revelation but tried not to show it. Most men wouldn't have turned down an opportunity to share a whore's bed. Maybe there was more to Gabriel Tyler than met the eye, but she doubted it. Men, being men, were mostly cut from the same cloth.

"No indeed, young man," Henry Brewster said to Gabe. "You did the moral thing by coming to me. We don't condone what goes on upstairs above the saloon, but until an ordinance is passed preventing that sort of unseemly behavior, there's little our good mayor can do about it. Isn't that right, Mayor?''

"Quite," Burt said through a mouthful of cookies.

"Perhaps if women were treated as equals to men, gentlemen, they wouldn't need to work on their backs to earn a living."

The reverend gasped, then coughed into his hand, while the corners of Gabe's mouth twitched, though he remained silent.

"You are probably right in what you say, Miss Eve, but now is not the time to debate such a provocative issue," Burt stated. "Mr. Tyler's problem is most pressing, and we'd like you to aid us in the solution of it. He comes from a very prominent family, and I am quite willing to vouch for his good character."

Burt didn't even know the man, but he was willing to vouch for his character? That was rich, Eve thought, noting the intractable expressions all three men wore. She heaved a sigh of resignation. "Oh, all right. Mr. Tyler can rent one of the rooms, but I insist that he be gone by Christmas Eve. I want no one staying here then. And he must agree to live by the rules of this house."

Reverend Brewster was all smiles. "Splendid! I knew you'd come to the right decision, Eve, and I'm proud of you for it. Your soul is once more secure."

For some reason, Eve didn't find much solace in that.

Grabbing a handful of cookies off the plate before he stood, the young mayor shoved them into his coat pocket. "These cookies sure are good, Miss Eve. I'm taking some with me. Hope you don't mind. And thank you. I'm sure Mr. Tyler is very appreciative.''

Gabriel Tyler's expression was more smug than appreciative. In fact, it looked downright victorious, which irritated the heck out of Eve, who hated to be outdone by anyone, especially in her own home. ''You'd best fetch your things, Mr. Tyler,'' she told the drifter. ''I'll go upstairs and make sure your room is set to rights.''

''Why, thank you kindly, ma'am,'' he said. ''I left my saddlebags on your front porch, in the hope that you might change your mind. I'll just go and get them.''

The nerve of the man to be so certain! Eve thought, biting back the rude comments on the tip of her tongue. Bidding the Methodist minister and Cedar Springs's mayor goodbye, she waited while her new boarder retrieved his belongings, hanging his sheepskin coat on the oak hall tree. As soon as he returned, she said, ''Please don't think you can get around me as easily the next time, Mr. Tyler. I very rarely go back on my decisions once my mind is made up.''

''A rigid mind is a sad thing, Miss Barlow. One should always keep an open mind and learn to be flexible. Life is much more pleasant that way.''

She chose to ignore the rebuke, though it galled her to do so. ''Dinner will be promptly at six o'clock. If you are not seated at the dining room table by then, I shall assume you are not hungry, and you will not be served. I maintain a schedule, Mr. Tyler, and have good reasons for all of my decisions. And I assure you that I do not make them lightly.''

''Duly noted, Miss Barlow. Now, would you care

to show me to my room? I need to take a bath, wash this trail dust off and change my clothes. Only my horse smells worse than I do at the moment, I'm afraid.''

''A bath!'' She nearly choked on the word. He wanted to take a bath? To get naked in her home? ''Mr. Tyler, I—''

He arched a brow. ''Is there a problem, ma'am? You do have a bathing room, don't you?''

''Of course I have a bathing room. I take a bath every day, as a matter of fact, but I'm just not sure that...well, that it would be seemly for you to be undressing in my home when we're here by ourselves, and—'' She knew she sounded irrational—most of her boarders bathed—but most of her boarders did not look like Gabe Tyler.

Gabe threw back his head and laughed. ''I can hardly take a bath with my clothes on, now can I, Miss Barlow? And I wasn't suggesting we share the bathtub.'' Though the prospect was quite intriguing. It might be interesting to see just how straitlaced and prim Miss Eve Barlow really was beneath her corset and stiffly starched petticoats. In his experience, still waters ran deep. Even those in the bathtub.

Her jaw unhinged at the very idea. ''I should hope not. I have a very good reputation, Mr. Tyler, and I intend to keep it.''

''Well, your reputation is safe with me, ma'am.'' For the time being, at least.

She gasped, clutching the cameo at her throat, as if it were some talisman that could protect her from this man. ''You presume much to speak in such a fashion, Mr. Tyler. Any more of that kind of talk, and

I will be forced to evict you from this house. And don't think I won't. Reverend Brewster and Mayor Moody will do you little good the next time.''

"I apologize. I'd heard you were a spinster, and I just naturally assumed that you were a—"

"Mr. Tyler! I'm warning you."

Gabe grinned, then took the key out of her hand. "Did anyone ever tell you how pretty you look when you get riled up, Miss Barlow? See you at dinner." He disappeared through the door and was gone, leaving Eve staring openmouthed after him.

Chapter Three

"May I ask you a personal question, Miss Barlow?"

Eve looked up from the pot roast on her plate, her eyes wary. "No, you may not, Mr. Tyler. I think your earlier comments were of much too personal a nature."

Why did some men think they could get around a woman so easily? Because they could. Eve answered her own question, thinking back to how Daniel had taken advantage of her naiveté, how he'd broken her foolish heart, then left her to become the object of pity and gossip.

"How come you don't like celebrating the Christmas holidays? Talk around town is that you hate it, like in that Dickens novel. Though you're much prettier than Scrooge. Mighty good pot roast, ma'am," he added, throwing her completely off. "May I have a touch more?"

She handed him the platter of meat, potatoes and carrots, and watched him smother it all in thick milk gravy. The man had a hearty appetite, and she was pleased that he liked her cooking, even if he was obtuse.

"Are you deaf? I just told you—"

"Look, we got off on the wrong foot, I admit that. But now that we'll be living together, for the time being," he added when she opened her mouth to protest, "I think we should try to get along. I thought maybe if I knew something about your background, it'd help me to understand why you're so prickly."

She banged her glass of milk down on the table, and it nearly sloshed over the sides. "I am not prickly, Mr. Tyler. Normally, I am quite an even-tempered, agreeable person, but..." She swallowed, wondering how much she should confide. "But this holiday season gets to me, puts me out of sorts. A lot of terrible things have happened to me during the Christmas season, and I just dread having it come every year. Now, are you happy that you've pried that out of me?"

Leaning back in his chair, he studied her. Her complexion was flawless, like ripe peaches and newly churned cream. The glow from the candles she'd placed on the table illuminated her dour expression, and Gabe wondered if she ever smiled. He thought it would really be something to see Eve Barlow smile, as pretty as she was.

"How old are you? You don't look old enough to be a spinster. Most spinsters I know are ancient, dried-up old prunes."

"Well, I assure you that they didn't start out that way. And if you must know, I am twenty-eight, or will be come Christmas Eve, and certainly old enough to be considered 'on the shelf,' as they say."

His eyes widened. "Ah. I wondered about the name. Thought maybe you'd been named after the biblical Eve." She was certainly tempting enough.

"My mother thought it was wonderful that I was born on the eve of the Lord's birthday and wanted to honor him by naming me for it," she explained, hoping that would be enough information to satisfy his curiosity. Noting that he was finished with his supper, Eve stood to clear the dishes, surprised when he followed her into the kitchen, carrying his own plate.

Most of the men she knew wouldn't lift a finger to do what they considered to be women's work. Apparently Gabe Tyler wasn't most men.

"If you've got a towel handy, I'll dry."

"I don't normally make my boarders do chores, Mr. Tyler. But I appreciate the offer just the same."

"These aren't what you would call 'normal' circumstances, ma'am. And call me Gabe," he said, reaching for the linen towel hanging on the rack by the sink. After taking a moment to consider his words, she handed him a plate.

"So, you were named for the holiday. What else happened to make you hate it so? Most women are beside themselves during the Christmas season. I just find it interesting that you're not."

She gritted her teeth and counted to ten. "You don't intend to give up, do you?"

"No, ma'am. I'm sure you know by now that I'm a pretty persistent fella when I put my mind to it."

She harrumphed loudly, wiping moisture from her cheek with the back of her hand. Even though Eve had indoor plumbing, she always added boiling water from the teakettle to make sure the dishwater was hot enough. "A nuisance, you mean?"

He shrugged. "Some would say that. So, are you going to tell me or not?"

"My parents were both killed on Christmas Eve, ten years ago." She found herself relating to him the story of the train derailment, how she'd been left alone to fend for herself. But she didn't reveal anything about being jilted at the altar. She had her pride, and she didn't want Gabe Tyler's pity. Some things were just too personal to share with strangers. And despite the odd fact that she felt quite comfortable talking with him, he was still very much a stranger.

"Tough break. I'm sorry you had to go through all that."

"I'm a lot stronger than I look, Gabe." She tested the name on her tongue and found she liked it. "If folks would just respect my wishes about Christmas, everything would be fine."

"Hiding from things doesn't make them get any better, Eve, if you don't mind my saying so. I can call you Eve, can't I?"

She smiled—the first real smile she'd smiled in days, and her whole face lit brighter than a sunny day. "I believe you just did. Why don't we go into the parlor and have coffee and dessert. You can tell me all about your life, and how you came to be a drifter. I'm sure there's a story behind that. Turnabout is fair play, after all."

Settling himself in the dark green leather wing chair by the fireplace, Gabe placed his feet atop the embroidered footstool, wondering if Eve had done the sewing. His former wife wouldn't have been caught

dead with a needle in her hand. Of course, he suspected Eve and Marilyn had little in common, except
their gender.

The domesticity of their present situation didn't escape him. Eve sat on the sofa with a pile of crocheting
on her lap. All they needed to make the scene complete would be him in a smoking jacket and pipe, a
cat or dog resting at his feet. "Got any pets?" he
asked. You could tell a lot about a person by the
animals they kept.

Eyes filling with sadness, Eve she shook her head.
"I had a cat, but Desdemona died last year. I've been
thinking about getting a dog…to keep me company."
She realized he'd neglected her request to relate the
details of his life.

"Not fair. Don't go changing the subject, Mr. Tyler…Gabe. You said you would tell me about your
life."

"Not a great deal to tell, ma'am," he said, sipping
the hot, strong coffee and biting into the piece of apple pie she'd left on the table next to him. "I was
born and raised in Boston. My father and uncle own
one of the largest banks in the city, and I went into
the family business after graduating college." He had
a Harvard education, for all the good it had done him.
Those days, that person he once was, seemed like
another man's life, not his own.

"You were a banker?" She was astonished by the
revelation. "And you didn't like it? I think it would
be fascinating to deal with all those numbers, live in
a big city like Boston, and go to college. I can't believe you like drifting from place to place when

you've got family, roots, and a profession to practice.''

"It sounds great on the surface, but I found the banking profession stifling after a while. I was cooped up in a dingy office all week, my hours regulated down to the minute, and I had to deal with some very disagreeable types of people. But that's not what drove me from Boston.''

"Really?'' She paused, fork in midair, to ask the question. "What did?''

He fidgeted in his chair, clearly uneasy about what he was going to reveal. "I was married. The marriage was arranged between my father and his best friend, Marcus Trusslow. It had been decided while I was still in my teens that I would marry Marilyn Trusslow, Marcus's daughter. At the time I was too young and stupid to object. Marilyn was agreeable—the Tyler fortune was large, after all—so we eventually got married.''

At his admission, her eyes widened, and she paused to digest what he'd revealed. Gabe Tyler did not seem like the marrying kind of man. He certainly didn't seem like a banker, which meant there was a whole lot more to the man than met the eye. She filed that thought in the back of her mind, intending to take it out later, when she had more time to sort it all out.

"Is your wife dead then?'' she asked finally. "Is that why you left Boston?''

"She's dead to me. Marilyn left me. She had an affair with my best friend, then took our two-year-old child and ran off with the bastard.'' His eyes dulled with pain. "I haven't seen my ex-wife or boy since.

But I've been looking." And when he found her, there'd be hell to pay.

Eve gasped aloud. "How horrible for you! I'm so sorry, Gabe. Is that why you drift, in the hope that one day you'll stumble across them?"

He nodded. "I've hired private investigators from time to time, when I can afford it. Friends and family send me tips on Marilyn's whereabouts, but by the time I'm able to follow up on them, she and the boy are gone. No one seems to know what happened to Fontaine. I hope he's dead."

"I can't believe anyone would do such a terrible thing." Even being left at the altar wasn't as bad as having your spouse steal your child from you. And his wife had been unfaithful to boot.

What kind of woman was Marilyn Tyler to have behaved so badly? And why would any woman leave a man like Gabe Tyler? she wondered, then mentally chastised herself for thinking about him in those terms. Though he did have the bluest of eyes and hair the color of obsidian.

Handsome is as handsome does, her mother always told her, and she'd do well to remember that, especially after the way Daniel had treated her.

"You must have been devastated to lose your son."

"I'll find him someday. I'm never going to give up hope that I will. I think of the Christmas season as a period of hope, renewal and opportunity. Unlike you, I think that all things are possible during this time of year, when men's hearts are more likely to be open and people are generous in spirit. I've tried to put aside my bitterness, in the hope that God will reward me with giving me back Robby. It's foolish, I know, but that's how I feel.''

"I admire you for that. Thanks for sharing your story with me. I don't know how you've managed with the heartache you must have endured all these years. I—'' She almost confided about Daniel, then decided not to. One sad story an evening was about all she could handle.

"It's old news now. Like I said, I've tried to put it behind me. Dwelling in the past can only make a body bitter. And I lived the first few years after Marilyn left bitter as hell and hating everyone around me, even those who loved and tried to help me.''

"You had your reasons.''

"True. But when you hurt those around you, the reasons don't seem so important anymore. It's a wonder my brother and sisters are still talking to me.''

"Do you get home very often?''

He shook his head, trying to mask the sadness he felt. "I haven't been back since the day I discovered my former wife's perfidy. My father never forgave me for abandoning the bank, and my mother sides with him in all things. I'm in contact with Zachary, my brother, and my two younger sisters, Beth and Susan. They write to me from time to time, keeping me abreast of the goings-on back home.''

Eve's eyes got a faraway look in them. "I miss my family so much. I have a hard time believing that anyone would willingly give theirs up.''

"I didn't see that I had much choice. Boston society was stifling. After Marilyn cuckolded me with my best friend, I became the laughingstock of the social set. I was either the butt of jokes or the object of pity. I didn't want to stay around and be either. And I had an even better reason to leave—I had to find my son."

Staring into the flames of the fire, Eve heaved a sigh and said, "I guess neither one of us was very lucky in love." She didn't realize she'd spoken her thoughts aloud until she heard Gabe say, "Don't tell me you were married, too?"

Her cheeks flushed pink, which had nothing to do with the warmth of the fire. "I'd rather not talk about it, if you don't mind."

"So you were married?"

"Really, Gabe, you are the most annoying, persistent man I've ever met." And that included Mathias Purdy, who was pretty darn persistent.

"Don't see what the big secret is. Couldn't be any worse than what I've just confided."

"I was left at the altar," she blurted, and his mouth dropped open. "Are you satisfied? I was standing up there, wearing my mother's bridal gown, bouquet of roses in hand, the organist playing 'Oh, Promise Me,' and Reverend Brewster holding the Bible and waiting to proceed. The groom-to-be never showed up."

Noting the unshed tears glistening in her eyes, Gabe unfolded himself from the chair and went to sit beside her on the sofa. "I'm sorry. That must have been brutal. How old were you?"

"I was twenty-two at the time and filled with starry-eyed optimism that everything was going to be perfect between Daniel and I." She shook her head. "I was stupid and naive. I—"

He wrapped his arm about her. "The man was a total jackass, in my opinion, to have let someone as fine as you get away. You're much better off without such a spineless bas…creature. I realize now that I'm better off without Marilyn, too. And if it wasn't for my son, I wouldn't give a tinker's dam or spend another minute thinking about her.''

The arm around her shoulders was warm and comforting, and Eve was very tempted to give in to her tears—Gabe had been kind—but she wouldn't. Bad enough she had confessed her horrible story to a total stranger and allowed him to see her vulnerability. He must think her totally pathetic. Shrugging off his embrace before she made a complete fool of herself, she said, ''Thank you for your words of consolation, but it's getting late, and I have some sewing to catch up on. It's time for me to retire.''

''I sense there's more you haven't told me about your being left at the altar, something you don't like sharing with anyone.''

She heaved a sigh. What was the point of trying to hide the truth? He'd probably hear it from someone in town anyway. ''My wedding was to be held on Christmas Eve day. So you see, I'm not enamored of the holiday, for a multitude of reasons. If December 24 never rolled around again, I would not be sorry. I have no use for Christmas and, for that matter, men. Good night.''

He watched her go, wondering if she still loved her former fiancé, the man she called Daniel. By the devastated look on her face, he'd guess yes. And for some unfathomable reason, that just didn't sit well with him.

Chapter Four

The following morning the snow was still falling heavily and accumulating at a rapid rate. Eve had promised to bake cookies for the children of Reverend Brewster's congregation—it was something she did every year, telling herself that they weren't exactly Christmas cookies, but winter cookies instead—and she needed to purchase eggs, milk and butter from the grocer before she could get started. Though by the looks of the snow piled high on the ground, nearly a foot now, she wasn't going into town, or anywhere else for that matter. At least, not anytime soon.

Gabe hadn't put in an appearance as yet this morning, and she wondered if he was a late sleeper. She hadn't slept past five o'clock in years, having found that early morning was a good time to catch up on things like correspondence and reading. And she liked watching the sun rise, all fresh and new, and listening to the birds chatter happily on a spring morning.

A loud noise from the parlor caught her attention and she hurried in that direction to see what had caused it. The last thing she expected to find was Gabe with his head up the fireplace opening.

"What on earth are you doing, Gabe? You'll get your clothes filthy if you don't come away from there this instant." He was dressed in worn denim pants and a blue chambray shirt, and he filled out his clothes very well. His chest was wide and muscular, as were his arms and thighs. He had the body of a man used to doing a hard day's work.

Crawling out backward, Gabe wiped the soot from his face with a red bandanna, leaving streaks everywhere he touched. She fought the urge to assist him. "Just checking to make sure the snow hasn't blocked the flue. We'll be eating smoke if that happens. And I'm going to clean out the ash while I'm at it, so the fire will burn hotter."

"Really, that's not necessary. I'm perfectly capable of cleaning the fire box myself. I've been doing it for years, as a matter of fact." Though not as often as she should—it was such a ghastly chore—but she didn't expect, or want, him to do it.

Eve prided herself on being self-sufficient. She didn't need any man doing for her. If she relied on no one but herself, she was never disappointed.

"That's not a job for a woman. Besides, I like to make myself useful. And seeing as how I can't do much else, with the weather the way it is, I might as well help around the house."

Not having a strong argument for such logical reasoning, she said, "Well, since you put it that way…thank you. I appreciate your help. I'll just go in and fix breakfast. Do you like pancakes?"

He grinned, and it fairly took her breath away.

"Yes, ma'am. And it's been a good while since I've had any. By the way, I neglected to tell you last night, but you're a great cook. That apple pie you made was the best I've ever eaten."

Her cheeks warmed at the compliment. She hadn't cooked for a man, with the exception of the boarders, since Daniel. And he was a puny eater at best. "I appreciate your saying so. I love to cook and bake. It's kind of a hobby of mine."

"Well, you're darn good at it. I'll just clean up this mess, wash up, and be right in to help you."

"Oh, that's not necessary. I—" The stubborn look he flashed stopped Eve in midsentence. "All right. I know there's no use arguing with you when your mind's made up."

"Thata girl. Now go fix breakfast. I'm starving."

In somewhat of a daze, Eve walked into the kitchen. She wasn't used to having anyone, especially a man, talk to her in such a familiar fashion.

The boarders she took in were usually quiet, reserved and kept to themselves. As a rule, she didn't give strangers the run of the house, preferring to keep them to a strict schedule. She rarely had much interaction with her guests. It was the way she liked it. Or had liked it. Because having Gabe around was proving to be quite diverting. She hadn't conversed so freely with anyone in years.

And that scared the bejeezus out of her.

Gabe was a drifter—a drifter with a painful past, who was on a mission to find his son. He wouldn't stay in Cedar Springs long. Once the snow cleared he'd be gone, and Eve would be alone again, talking to no one but herself. She guessed it was her own fault. She pushed people away, never allowing anyone to get too close for fear of being hurt. But she did miss witty repartee, and even getting into a healthy argument now and again usually proved quite stimulating.

Having a conversation with Daniel had been like pulling teeth. He was always so introspective, so quiet. Now that she'd had time to reflect on their relationship, she wondered what on earth had possessed her to take up with the man in the first place. Her own company was far better than his had ever been. He certainly wasn't anywhere nearly as gregarious as... She shook her head, not willing to go there.

Eve knew the reason she'd accepted Daniel's proposal. She'd been lonely after her parents had passed away. Lonely and afraid of living the remainder of her life alone. Of course, she'd ended up doing that anyway.

Hurrying into the kitchen, she pulled a slab of bacon from the icebox, cutting several pieces off and tossing them into a hot cast-iron skillet. The meat started to sizzle and sputter at once.

She was mixing up the pancake batter when Gabe walked into the room, and she could smell the musky scent of his cologne, mixed with smoke from the fireplace, before he actually approached. "Coffee's in the pot," she said without turning around. "Help yourself. The bacon's almost done. And we'll be eating soon."

Pouring himself a cup of the hot liquid, he seated himself at the pine table that had been covered with a faded red cloth. "I like watching you cook. You're so efficient in your moves. I never could figure out how a woman could juggle so many things on the stove at once without burning everything, the way I do. I'm a terrible cook.''

Laughing, she turned in his direction, and he nearly fell off the chair at how beautiful she looked. Her hair had been left long, pulled back from her face, and was fastened at her nape with a clip. She wore a stiffly starched white shirtwaist and serviceable gray skirt, and could have passed for a schoolmarm. But her prim appearance only served to whet his appetite even more.

He doubted Eve Barlow realized the effect she had on a man. Despite the fact she'd once been engaged, might even have had her reputation compromised by that jerk-of-a-fiancé, she had a virginal way about her. Innocence shone in her pretty blue eyes.

But was she innocent? And was she virginal?

There was a lot more to the spinster than he'd first thought. Passion, certainly. Gabe hadn't seduced a woman in a very long time, but he was certainly thinking along those lines now.

Having Eve warm and willing in his bed would be a pleasant way to pass the time until his departure. But he would only make love to her if she was willing and not looking for anything permanent. From the sounds of it, she didn't have much use for men, had probably sworn off marriage, so he thought their coming together might just be what the two of them needed in their lives right now: a dalliance with no strings attached.

''Goodness gracious! Why are you staring at me like that?'' Eve's face flushed as red as the gingham curtains hanging at the window. ''You've got such a determined expression on your face.'' She felt as if he could see clear down to her chemise and drawers.

He smiled enigmatically, placing the platters of food she handed him on the table before pulling out her chair. "Do I? I was just thinking about something interesting, something I want to do." He shifted in his chair, hoping she didn't see how his thinking of her had aroused him.

"Care to share?" She passed him the platter of pancakes and watched as he forked five onto his plate. It was said that a man who possessed a healthy appetite for food usually had a healthy appetite for—

"Syrup?" she asked quickly, brushing loose strands of hair away from her face and taking a deep breath.

What on earth was the matter with her? She'd never reacted so strongly to a man before. Even Daniel had never made her heart flutter so madly. So why then did Gabriel Tyler have this strange effect on her?

"These are mighty good pancakes, Eve. Guess you know the way to a man's heart is through his stomach."

"I—I've heard that saying, of course. My mama used to say the very same thing, which is why she wanted me to learn how to cook."

"Well, she did right by you," he said, changing the subject as he reached for another piece of bacon. "You got anything particular planned for today?"

Sipping her coffee, she took a moment to answer. "I need to go to the grocer to buy staples. I make cookies for the church this time every year. The children who perform in the annual Christmas pageant look forward to them, and I don't want them to be disappointed." Eve adored children and regretted that she didn't have any of her own. A child could take up a lot of space in a woman's heart.

"You're not talking about making Christmas cookies, are you?" he asked, his expression as eager as a ten-year-old boy's. "Because if you are, I'll haul you over to the grocer on my back, if need be, so you can buy whatever it is you need. I'll even pay. I've got a real hankering when it comes to Christmas cookies." One of the things he missed most about being estranged from his family was not being able to share in the traditions of the holiday season, like his younger sisters baking cookies.

Her eyes widened then, noting his smile, she responded with one of her own. "I've got boots and a warm coat, and it's not that far to the grocer's, providing Willis is open." She was sure he was. Willis Adams prided himself on the fact that his store was open 364 days a year, Christmas being the only day he closed, mostly due to Mrs. Adams's insistence. He had a sign in his store window declaring it, so she doubted a little snow was going to prevent him from turning a tidy profit.

"Maybe after we're done buying the groceries, we can go out in the front yard and put up a snowman. I haven't made one in years."

Her jaw unhinged before she snapped it shut. "A snowman! You're not serious?" But she could see by his boyish expression that he was.

"Sure am. Didn't you used to make them as a kid? My brother and I had contests to see who could make the very best one. Beth and Susan acted as judges, and the snowman that won was rewarded with a whole plate of cookies. Of course, *I* ate the cookies, not the snowman.''

''Well, yes, I have, but—''

''Good. Then it's all settled.''

''My hands feel like two icicles,'' Eve said, scooping up another ball of the frozen snow and adding it to the pile in front of her. ''I don't know how I let you talk me into making a snowman. It's a very impractical way to spend an afternoon. And I still have dozens of cookies to bake.'' Oh, but she was having so much fun. In fact, she couldn't recall the last time she had enjoyed herself as much, and she had Gabe to thank for it.

Despite the heartache and misfortune Gabriel Tyler had been dealt, the man had a zest for life, making the most of every moment. *''Life's too short not to enjoy yourself,''* he had told her on the way back from the grocer's.

Gabe rushed to Eve's side, grasping her hands and pulling off her gloves. ''What are you doing?'' she protested, trying to pull her hands free.

''Let me see your hands. I don't want you getting frostbite.'' Before she could protest, he took her icy hands and brought them to his mouth, blowing his hot breath onto them. Eve began to tingle all the way down to her toes, and she fought the urge to pull back. The act seemed far too intimate for total strangers, but oh, it was delicious. It had been a long time since a man had paid this much attention to her. Daniel had not been the demonstrative type.

''There,'' he said, rubbing her hands between his own until he was satisfied she was warm. ''Is that better?'' His eyes filled with concern. ''If you're really too cold, we can go inside. Maybe what you need is a hot bath.''

The image of them in the tub together suddenly flashed through Eve's mind, making her entire body suffuse with heat. She shook her head to rid herself of the provocative thought. ''No! I'm fine. Besides, I think my snowman is going to be better than yours, and I want the chance to prove it.'' And she needed the diversion desperately.

He laughed and flicked the end of her nose. ''No way. There are cookies at stake, woman, and I'm determined to win.''

''Well, your balls are a bit lopsided.''

He jerked his head around to see what she was staring at, looked down at his crotch and then, deciding she was talking about the snowman and not him, chuckled. ''I'm not done yet, so don't start getting smug on me. I'm not a man who likes to lose.''

''Well, then I think you've met your match, Mr. Tyler,'' Eve retorted with a grin.

They worked for twenty more minutes on their respective snowmen. Eve draped an old shawl around her snowman's shoulders, deciding to turn it into a snow woman instead. She was tempted to give her snow woman breasts, just to see Gabe's reaction, but she thought it too unseemly. She didn't have the courage to be so daring, but sometimes, like now, she wished she had.

Gabe stared at both sculptures and shook his head. ''Darned if I know who won. Both look pretty good to me.'' His snowman wore a black bowler hat and an old pin-striped wool vest that Eve had procured from the attic, and that had once belonged to her father.

Wrapping her arms about herself, joyful in the moment, she smiled happily. "I declare the contest to be a tie. We both shall have cookies, and lots of them. I may even throw in a glass of milk for good measure."

"Hot damn!" Suddenly without warning, Gabe scooped her up in his arms, ignoring her startled shriek, and continued trudging toward the front door.

"Put me down this instant, Gabriel Tyler! Have you lost whatever sense you were born with? Someone might see us." She looked about to see if anyone had noticed his outrageous behavior. "I am a decent woman with a good reputation, and I won't be made the laughingstock of—"

"So what if they see? I'm just being a gentleman by carrying a lady in distress to her front door. I imagine your toes are about frozen by now. And if anyone does dare to say anything, I'll punch them in the mouth. How's that?"

He lost his footing and lunged to one knee, and Eve wrapped her arms about his neck to keep from falling. His eyes met hers, and for a moment neither spoke, then she cleared her throat and the spell was broken.

"Thank you. But I think you have ulterior motives in wanting to get me into the house."

Surprised by the accuracy of her comment, Gabe wondered rather guiltily if they were thinking along the same lines, though he rather doubted it. "Do I now? And what would those motives be?" Surely she didn't have an inkling of how much he wanted to carry her upstairs to his bed and make passionate love to her for the rest of the afternoon and evening.

"Cookies. You want me to start baking for you, don't you?"

He set her down on the porch, the lump forming in his throat very unfamiliar. "You saw clean through me," he replied. "Cookies are utmost on my mind."

Chapter Five

Two days later, Eve glanced out the front parlor window to see if the snowfall had abated, and was surprised to find Florinda Cooper trudging up the snow-covered walk.

What on earth was the woman doing out on such a dreadful morning? she wondered, hurrying to the door to find out, all the while hoping no one she knew had died.

She pulled open the door just as the woman was about to knock, admitting a blast of frigid air, which fairly took her breath away. "Florinda!" Eve smiled through her puzzlement, noting how red the woman's cheeks were. "You must be frozen. I'm surprised to see you out and about on such a nasty day." The snow was still falling at a rapid rate, and the dark clouds, heavy with moisture, promised no end in sight. "Come in."

"You know we postal clerks are a hearty lot," the postmistress said good-naturedly, stomping her feet to clear the snow off her boots before stepping across the threshold into the foyer. A puddle of water formed at her feet, anyway. "I've got a letter here for your boarder, Mr. Tyler. It's got a Boston postmark, so I figured, based on what's being said about him around town, that it's from his family." She reached inside her heavy jacket and produced an envelope.

"Would you like some hot coffee? You must be chilled to the bone. Mr. Tyler isn't up yet—" which was odd in itself "—but I'll be sure to give this to him as soon as he awakens." She placed the envelope in her apron pocket for safekeeping, wondering if it contained news of his ex-wife and child. The notion filled her with unease, for she knew it would mean Gabe would be leaving sooner than either one of them expected. Placing her hand over her heart, she covered the sudden dull ache.

"Late sleeper, is he? My husband George used to lounge in bed, especially on a cold morning. It took a lot of hot coffee and a swift kick in the behind to get that man going in the morning." Eve began to shut the door, but the older woman shook her head.

"Can't stay, Eve, but I thank you for the invite. I've got lots more letters to deliver before this miserable day is said and done. The Christmas holiday always brings out the correspondence in people. You'd think they could spread their writing out during other times of the year, instead of trying to get it all in at once."

Florinda's comment reminded Eve that she hadn't answered her aging relatives' last missive. Her New York cousins, Bitsy and Tootie Malloy, would worry if they didn't hear from her soon. And even though she'd explained numerous times to the cantankerous old spinsters that she didn't have the time to correspond over the holidays, they continued to write, making it clear that they expected an answer, Christmas or no Christmas.

"You be sure to come back when you've got more time and we can visit," she told her friend. "I made cookies for the church, but I always keep some back for company. I'll be happy to share them with you."

The older woman smiled gratefully. "Will do, honey. You stay warm, you hear? Now you'd best go and kick that handsome man of yours outta bed before he gets a good case of laziness and you can't cure him of it."

Cheeks filling with color, Eve stiffened. "Mr. Tyler is not my man, Florinda. You shouldn't say such a thing. I wouldn't want anyone, including you, to get the wrong idea."

"A woman my age can say just about anything she pleases," she replied with a chuckle. "And I can hope, can't I, that some Christmas miracle will happen and you'll find someone to love, someone who will love you back?"

Eve made a face of displeasure. "There's no such thing as a Christmas miracle." Or love, for that matter, she was certain, based on experience. "Thanks for the thought, but Mr. Tyler will be moving on as soon as the weather breaks." Her heart squeezed again.

Reaching out, the older woman patted her hand, and the leather from her glove felt rough against Eve's skin. "I'm a firm believer in the powers of the Almighty. You may not have experienced it, due to all the tragedy you've seen in your short lifetime, honey, but I'm living proof that the good Lord works in mysterious ways."

Eyes widening in disbelief, the younger woman shook her head. "How can you say that, after losing your husband of forty years?"

"Yes, I lost my darling George, and a dearer man has never lived. But I gained me a job outta his unfortunate demise, and I'm feeling useful for the first time in years. At least some good's come out of it."

"But—"

"It's hell getting old, and having people trying to put you out to pasture before you're ready to go, hon. I didn't want George to die, but I ain't looking a gift horse in the mouth, either. You gotta take what life throws at you and go with it, or else you may as well curl up and die yourself. And I ain't ready to do that. And neither are you."

Watching the woman disappear down the walk, Eve was perplexed by Florinda's unusual way of looking at things. People coped with tragedy in their own way, she guessed. Or they didn't cope at all.

Taking the envelope out of her apron pocket and noting the return address indicated Zachary Tyler, Gabe's brother, she knew he would want to read the correspondence as quickly as possibly.

Wondering why he hadn't yet come out of his room this morning—she had peeked at his door three different times to find it closed—she hurried up the stairs, hoping to be the bearer of good news.

Outside his room, she paused, biting her lower lip in uncertainty. Should she knock? Should she disturb him and possibly wake him from a sound sleep? He may have read late into the night, or perhaps had a bout of insomnia and was trying to catch up on his rest.

And what if he thought she had some ulterior motive in coming to his room? Men tended to think along those lines.

Indecision gnawed at her for several more moments. She finally decided that, if the shoe were on the other foot and it had been her letter he was delivering, she would want to be informed at once. She knocked three times in rapid succession. When there was no answer, she knocked again, puzzled by the continuing silence.

She knew full well that Gabe hadn't left the house this morning. She'd spent a good portion of the early-morning hours looking out the parlor window, day-dreaming about…him.

Eve knocked again, harder this time, then pressed her ear against the door, but there was still no answer. It was then she heard the low moan. And then again. Alarmed that something might be terribly wrong, she opened the door a crack and peered in to find Gabe still lying in bed.

The sheets were twisted around the lower half of his body, and he was moaning and thrashing about, as if he was in the throes of a nightmare, or in great physical pain.

"Gabe? Gabe, is everything all right?" she called out from the doorway, not sure if she should enter. He answered with a low moan.

Tiptoeing in, until she was standing right next to the bed, Eve looked down and drew in a breath. Gabe was naked from the waist up, and the knowledge that he was probably just as naked from the waist down brought a large lump to her throat, as well as some lascivious thoughts that were totally inappropriate, especially considering the circumstances.

Now is hardly the time for such improper thoughts, Eve Barlow!

The man was bathed in sweat, his face blotched red, and his eyes were shut tight against whatever ailment had him in its grip. Unable to stand by and see anyone suffer, she reached out a tentative hand to touch his forehead and found he was burning up with fever.

"Oh, Gabe," she whispered, wishing old Doc Stevens hadn't died last month of a heart seizure. Cedar Springs had yet to replace him, and they had no doctor to call upon in an emergency.

Rushing into the bathing room, she filled an enamel basin with cool water, grabbed a washcloth and some towels off the washstand, and returned to his bedside.

She would nurse him back to health herself, Eve decided. She wouldn't allow Gabe to fall victim to that wretched Christmas curse that continued to plague her.

Fortunately, she had a copy of *Dr. Chase's Recipes*, which covered a variety of medical conditions, including fevers. She would consult it to figure out the best course of treatment to take. And she would do everything in her power to make sure Gabriel Tyler lived to see another Christmas.

Seating herself on the bed next to him, she refused to think about the impropriety of the situation, running the cool cloth over his chest and down his arms. He moaned, and his lips moved slightly, as if he was trying to say something. Leaning over him, she moistened his lips with the damp cloth. Suddenly he grabbed her, pulling her down to his mouth, and her heart started pounding in her ears.

"I'll never forgive you, you faithless bitch, for stealing my son from me. I hope you rot in hell."

She was alarmed at first, until she realized he was delirious and talking about his ex-wife. Threading her fingers through his dark hair, she spoke soothingly to him. "*Shh.* Don't try to talk. You're sick, Gabe, but I'm going to help you get well." Her words seemed to calm him, for his rigid body soon relaxed, and he fell into a more peaceful sleep.

Eve had never been intimate with a man, though Daniel Stedmon had done his best to seduce her. She'd often wondered if her refusal to consummate their relationship before marriage was the reason he'd dumped her at the altar and taken off for parts unknown. But then she'd heard rumors that he'd had another woman. She was glad now that she'd stuck by her guns and refused the bounder.

Eyeing the hair on Gabe's chest, Eve's heartbeat quickened. She couldn't resist reaching out to touch him, marveling at how soft the hairs felt beneath her fingers. Then she explored him more fully, caressing the firm pectoral muscles, his bulging biceps, trailing her finger up his arm to touch his lips, which were incredibly soft.

What would it be like to kiss him? she wondered, wishing she had the courage to find out.

He moaned, and she pulled back quickly, chastising herself for her unseemly behavior and renewing her ministrations to help break his fever.

* * *

Gabe awoke the following morning to find Eve sprawled across his chest, fast asleep. Her breathing was deep and even, each breath she exhaled tickling his flesh, making him more aware than ever that he wanted her in the worst way.

He thought he'd been dreaming those soft caresses last night, but he knew now they'd been all too real. Her left hand was positioned dangerously close to his groin, and he didn't dare move or she would get quite a surprise when she awakened. He was as stiff as the icicle hanging outside the bedroom window, but he sure as hell wasn't as cold.

His fever had broken during the night, but still he was burning up. Lust poured through his veins, thick and hot, heating his blood to the boiling point.

"Eve, wake up." If she didn't wake soon, there was no telling what he might do.

Her hand came in contact with his erect member, and he sucked in his breath, then she moved her head over his chest, as if trying to find a comfortable spot on the pillow she obviously thought she was lying upon. He groaned in agony.

"*Mmm*. Let me sleep a little longer, Mama. I'm having the most wonderful dream."

Biting the inside of his cheek in an effort to keep himself in check, he shook her awake. "Wake up, sleeping beauty. I'm alive. I'm not your mama. And I won't be held responsible for my actions if you don't get off me this very minute." His words were pained and harsher than he intended.

Eve opened her eyes, took in her present position, where her hand rested, and she jerked back and nearly fell off the chair she was seated upon. And would have, too, if Gabe hadn't reached out to steady her.

"Merciful heavens!" she declared, her face turning beet red. "I must have fallen asleep."

"Good morning," he said with a soft smile, not letting go of her hand, though she tried to pull out of his grasp. "I hated waking you up. You looked so peaceful, but circumstances being what they are—"

"Please! Say no more. I'm terribly embarrassed about falling asleep. You were so ill, and I stayed up half the night nursing you. I guess my eyes just drifted closed. I'm sorry. I—"

"Don't apologize, sweetheart. I appreciate all you've done. I must have caught a chill that day we were making the snowmen. I haven't felt so poorly since I was a kid. It just came upon me all of a sudden."

She nodded, trying to regain her composure. "Fevers are like that, especially this time of year."

Reaching down, he retrieved a long blond hair from his abdomen, holding it out to her, and she blushed all over again. "Glad you found me so comfortable."

"I—I know you like to tease, Gabe, but I'm just too humiliated at the moment to see humor in the present situation. I'm afraid I'm not used to spending the night in a man's bedroom, and—"

"Well, I'm glad the man you chose was me. Maybe next time I'll be awake and we can do more than sleep."

Gasping loudly, she launched herself off the chair. "How dare you say such an improper thing! I am not a loose woman."

"Never thought you were. There's nothing improper about kissing or making love, Eve. What's improper is having feelings and not doing anything about it.'' Her hair had come loose during the night and fell in soft waves around her shoulders. His fingers itched to touch it.

"I really must go. After I clean myself up, I'll fix you a nourishing bowl of oatmeal. I suggest you remain in bed another day, just to make certain the fever has abated. I don't want you having a relapse. I have better things to do than to play nursemaid to you.''

He grinned at her bossy, uptight demeanor. "Yes, ma'am. But if you don't come back up here to keep me company, I swear I'll come looking for you.'' He made to get out of bed, the sheet falling dangerously low on his hips, and Eve sucked in her breath, watching, and waiting for the outcome.

He noticed where she was staring, and his eyes darkened. "Do you think I still have a fever? Would you mind very much checking to see?''

Despite her reservations, she inched closer to the bed and held out her hand to touch his forehead. That's when Gabe latched onto her wrist and pulled her down across him, placing his lips on hers and kissing her soundly. At first, Eve tried to pull back, but when his lips began to move over hers, slowly, and with such tenderness, when the tip of his tongue searched for entry, she became pliant and opened to him.

His tongue sent shivers of desire racing through her as he explored, teased and tormented. She kissed him back with a hunger that surprised her. His lips found her eyelids, cheeks and chin, and then the pulsing point at the base of her throat.

The kiss seemed to go on forever. She never wanted it to end. Hearing a low moan, Eve realized it was her own and finally pulled back, dazed by the traitorous reaction of her own body. Her nipples were pebble hard and swollen, and she felt a dull ache between her thighs.

She wanted Gabe but knew she could never have him.

"You shouldn't have done that," she whispered, looking into the depths of his mesmerizing blue eyes to find longing that matched her own.

"Why? We both wondered what it would be like. Now we know. It was wonderful. I'm not sorry. Are you?"

She hesitated a moment before answering. "No, I'm not sorry. But I don't think it's wise to…to continue such behavior. You'll be leaving soon, and—"

"Making love is not the sin you've made it out to be, Eve. When two people care about each other, it's a wonderful experience. Didn't you find that out with Daniel?"

She took a deep breath. "Daniel and I never consummated our relationship."

His eyes widened. "Ah. That explains a lot of things."

"Like what? I don't know what you mean."

"You're a virgin. I sensed that the first moment I laid eyes on you." She stiffened, and he caressed her arm gently. "Don't go getting all huffy on me. I'm not saying virginity's a bad thing. A man puts great store by being the first. I'd like to be your first, Eve.

Think about that when you're taking your bath, touching yourself in all those intimate areas of your body, lying in your bed at night, and wondering what it would be like between us. You know it would be good. I'd make it good for you, sweetheart.''

Eve felt frustrated and close to tears. "I can't. Please don't say such things."

"You want to. I can see it in your eyes, in the soft blush of your cheeks, in the way your heart beats when I hold you in my arms and kiss you. You respond to me, Eve. And I'm telling you right now that I want you, and there's no shame in you knowing that."

"I have to go."

"But you'll be back."

"Yes," she whispered. "I'll be back."

Chapter Six

"You said you were coming back."

Startled by the sound of Gabe's voice, Eve dropped the bowl she had just removed from the china cabinet. It went crashing to the floor, splintering into pieces at her feet, not unlike her composure.

Clasping her throat, she whirled about. "You scared me half to death, Gabriel Tyler! What on earth are you doing out of bed? I told you to stay put." He was fully dressed, and for that, she was grateful. A naked Gabriel Tyler was just too much for any woman to handle, and she had no experience in such matters, at any rate. Though she knew he'd be quite willing to teach her everything she needed to know.

"I've been waiting upstairs for hours for you to come back like you said. When you didn't, I figured you were probably trying to starve me to death, so I came down to see what was the matter."

Eve's cheeks filled with color. In truth, she hadn't been able to face him again. Not after the kiss they'd shared, and all the provocative things he'd said. She was weak, and he knew how to prey on that weakness. "I got busy doing other things and forgot," she lied. "It's best you don't eat too much anyway. You're supposed to starve a fever. I'll bring up some broth in a few minutes. Why don't you—"

He shook his head, threading impatient fingers through his hair. "Oh no, you don't. You're not getting rid of me that easily. I feel fine, and I'd just as soon eat down here with you. It's not often I have such good company."

Her heart squeezed at the comment, for she knew exactly how he felt. She'd spent too many days alone, and would again, after he left. "You'll have a relapse," she tried to reason, knowing his nearness, the masculine scent of him, gave her thoughts, yearnings that no decent woman should entertain.

"I doubt it, though I might die of starvation." He rubbed his midsection. "Got anything to eat besides broth? I'm as hungry as a hibernating bear."

With a sigh of resignation, she bent over and picked up the pieces of her mother's china bowl, knowing it could never be repaired. Like her life, it was too big a mess to fix. "I've prepared a ham, green beans and scalloped potatoes for dinner. I was just setting the table when you came rushing in here, scaring me out of my wits."

He looked genuinely contrite. "Sorry. I hope that bowl wasn't a family heirloom or anything. I know women put a lot of store by such things."

Cradling the broken pieces in her apron, she moved to the trash bin and dumped them in. "It was my mother's. And yes, I cherished it very much. But it's gone and there's no sense in crying over spilled milk."

He rubbed the back of his neck. "Damn. I'm really sorry."

"Cursing will not repair the bowl, Gabe, so you may as well take a seat at the table. I'll have dinner on in a few minutes."

Noting her high color, the way she went out of her way to avoid eye contact, he knew she felt uneasy about being around him, and he was saddened by that. They'd just started getting comfortable with each other, sharing confidences and entertaining stories. He didn't want her to distance herself from him. "You're mad about the kiss, about the things I said, aren't you?"

Setting the platters and bowls of food down on the table before him, she shook her head. "I'm not mad, just concerned that I've given you the wrong idea about me. I'm not looking for a dalliance, Gabe. Perhaps it seemed like that by my…my behavior, but I'm not in the habit of kissing men I hardly know and going to bed with them." There. She'd said it. Let him think what he would. She was sure he thought her a prude, but that couldn't be helped.

"So coming back upstairs was too much of a temptation for you, huh?" He grinned when her face flushed red with embarrassment, indicating he'd hit too close to the truth she was trying to hide.

"You have great conceit, Mr. Tyler. It was your health I was concerned about, not my—I assure you that I have a great deal of willpower. You caught me at a moment of weakness this morning. I had just awoken, and—"

He held up his hand. "I get the idea. You're trying

to tell me you're not interested. I don't believe you, but I'm not going to force myself on you.''

"Well, isn't that just a very great relief," she replied, not bothering to disguise the sarcasm in her voice as she pulled out her chair and fell into it. So far this had been one heck of a horrible day, and she couldn't wait for it to end. Of course, then the dreams would start. She'd been having all sorts of strange dreams since Gabriel Tyler had moved into her house. Some of them downright lascivious. Most, actually.

"I still want you, Eve. That's not going to change. But I'm not going to do anything you don't want to do, so there's no need to tiptoe around, or avoid being in the same room with me. I was raised a gentleman. And even though I've drifted these many years, I still know how to treat a lady. And I do consider you a lady.''

Smiling tentatively, she said, "Thank you." Then her eyes widened and she reached into the pocket of her dress. "Goodness! I nearly forgot. The reason I came to your room in the first place was to give you this letter. Florinda Cooper brought it by yesterday. I think it's from your family." She handed it to him.

Noting the postmark, Gabe eased into a smile. "It's from my brother." Opening it, he scanned the missive, his smile fading. "No one's heard a word from, or about, my ex-wife, though Zach's hoping with the coming Christmas holidays that she might get in contact with her family. He's got an associate working inside the Trusslow estate, who isn't above exchanging information for money. We've had several promising tips over the years, though none that panned out.''

Though Gabe looked resigned, as if he'd had this kind of disappointing news before, Eve saw hope glittering in the depths of his eyes and felt renewed sadness for his loss. "I wish there was something I could do to help. A father should be with his son, his family, during the holidays."

Though her words were meant to comfort, they did little to assuage the emptiness inside him. "That's not in the cards for me. I've reconciled myself to that. And—" he smiled hopefully "—I'm content to spend them with you, if you'll let me."

Eve didn't take even a moment to consider. "I'm afraid that's not going to be possible, Gabe. You agreed to leave by Christmas Eve, and I expect you to honor that agreement." She was starting to fall in love with him. If he stayed and they grew closer, made love, the way she desperately wanted to...well, she wasn't sure she would ever recover from his leaving. And he would leave. She knew that, just as certain as she knew what was in her heart. The pain of his loss would be unbearable. Just thinking about it made it so.

Disappointment rode him hard. "I'm sorry you feel that way. I thought we were getting along well, enjoying each other's company."

Locking gazes with him, Eve sucked in her breath, hoping she could make him understand. "I'm a woman looking for a lifetime. I don't think you're the kind of man who wants that. I understand that there's a physical attraction between us. I won't deny it. But I refuse to make another mistake, refuse to let any man make a fool out of me again. For a woman, a few hours of pleasure usually results in a lifetime of unhappiness. I already have that, and I don't need a repeat performance.''

Everything she said left a bitter taste in his mouth, and trying to wash it down with a glass of milk just wasn't going to cut it. He couldn't deny her assumptions, because for the most part they were true. He couldn't confess that he had feelings for her, because he didn't know what those feelings were as yet. And he knew he'd be leaving and didn't want to offer false hope. She'd been left once before, and he couldn't blame her for being wary, for being afraid. But knowing all that didn't make him want her any less.

''I understand how you feel, better than most, I suspect, having been in somewhat of a similar situation myself. I'll try to behave in a more circumspect manner, and I will leave on Christmas Eve day as we agreed.''

''Thank you,'' she said, barely above a whisper, the pain in her heart a tangible thing.

''Now that we've gotten that out of the way, what do you say about sharing some of those cookies you've been baking? I smelled cinnamon and vanilla all the way up the stairs, and it was pure torture.''

Glad to have the unpleasantness behind them, Eve's smile was full of indulgence. ''You may have a few. The rest I must deliver to the church tomorrow, so they'll be there for the children's pageant rehearsal.''

''Are those kids going be able to get to the church, with the weather like it is?'' He looked skeptical. ''Doesn't seem likely.'' After crossing to the window, he pulled the curtain back and looked out. ''It's still snowing like a sonofa— Sorry.'' He smiled sheepishly.

"I have no idea, but I'm not going back on my word. I'll trudge over there, even if the snow's waist deep, and make the delivery as promised. I guess Reverend Brewster's cat can eat them, if no one else shows up.''

"Seems a waste of perfectly good cookies to me.'' He bit into a white-frosted sugar cookie and released a sigh of pure pleasure. "Mmm. These are even better than the ones my sisters used to bake. And theirs were pretty darn good, if memory serves.''

Eve liked a man who appreciated the efforts of a woman in the kitchen. It made all the hard work seem very worthwhile. She would bake anyway, because she loved it so, but it was nice having her efforts prized.

"Well, I may decide to bake more, since you like them so much. I always keep baked goods on hand for my guests.''

"Guess I'll tag along with you tomorrow then, just to make sure you make it there and back safely. The depth of the snow can be treacherous. And you're not that tall. You might sink clear into a drift and never be seen again.''

At his comment, she threw back her head and laughed, and his gut knotted tighter than a hangman's noose. "I've survived living here for almost twenty-eight years, and never once have I fallen into a snowdrift and disappeared.''

His gaze moved from the top of her head to the tip of her toes, resting several places in between. Eve felt as if she was being devoured by that hungry bear he'd spoken of earlier. ''There's always a first time for…everything, Eve. Wouldn't you agree?''

She thought it best not to answer the question.

Eve studied the sign posted on the front door of the Methodist church and breathed a sigh of relief. The pageant rehearsal was still scheduled for seven o'clock that evening. Reverend Brewster's hungry cat would not devour her winter cookies, after all.

''Thank goodness,'' she said, trying to open the heavy door with her index finger and hold the plate at the same time.

Gabe noted her difficulty and stepped forward to do the honors. ''Well, at least we didn't get soaked to our knees for nothing,'' he said. ''Though I'm not sure I like sharing your cookies with a bunch of snotty-nosed kids.''

She would have laughed at his childish reaction if it hadn't hurt so much to breathe. The frigid air burned her lungs, numbing her cheeks and hands, despite the heavy wool clothing and outer garments she wore.

Eve knew that if it had been any other time of the year besides Christmas, Reverend Brewster would have canceled the pageant. She thought it was foolish on his part not to have done so. Christmas certainly wasn't worth a child catching pneumonia, or worse. But she also knew that the town set a great store by the tradition of the pageant, the annual caroling event Mr. Purdy had tried so hard to convince her to attend, and the various decorations that were already being strung up around town.

Several of the stores and businesses they had

passed on their way to the church were decorated with wreaths and colorful ribbons. They looked quite festive and pretty, if one enjoyed that sort of thing, which she didn't. Gabe apparently did, because he'd commented on how Christmas decorations always put him in a good mood, which made hers even sourer.

"We'll just set these on a table in the back of the church," she said as they entered the darkened building, grateful no one was in attendance. Only the spill of light coming from two stained-glass windows offered any illumination. "The reverend will know where they came from."

"Guess you'll be rewarded for your good deed in the next life. Are you going to attend the pageant? It'd be fun to see the kids all decked out in their nativity costumes."

She shook her head. "No. I haven't been in years. I just bring the cookies. That's my contribution."

Clasping hold of her arm, he guided her down the snow-laden path toward her house. "Bet the children are disappointed you don't come. What could it hurt to—"

"I'm not going, and that's final!" Eve's voice was as cold as the air they breathed. "I'm not going to the pageant. I'm not going to celebrate the Christmas holiday. And I'm not going to be bullied or made to feel stupid because I choose not to."

He stiffened at her tone. "Well, hell! Don't go getting your corset strings all in a knot. I wasn't trying to—"

"I don't wear a corset," she interrupted. "They are very uncomfortable, not to mention extremely unhealthy. I don't wish to have misshapen organs."

He grinned, and his face felt as if it would crack. "Is that a fact? *Hmm.* Now that's a mighty useful bit of information." He'd already held her in his arms and knew firsthand that her soft body hadn't been encumbered by anything but what the good Lord gave her.

"You promised to behave," she reminded him, but didn't look him in the eye, for fear of what she'd see.

"So I did."

When they reached Eve's home, Gabe pushed hard on the stubborn gate, digging out some of the snow with his boot. Glancing toward the house, his brow wrinkled in confusion. "What's that on your porch? Someone must have come by and dropped off a Chris—" She glared at him. "Package. Maybe your friend Mrs. Cooper from the post office."

"I don't think so. Folks around here know better." Though her cousins weren't above sending her gifts, despite her instructions to the contrary. It could have come from them, she supposed. Last year they had sent her a lovely woolen shawl and a book of poetry. Keeping with her refusal to honor the holiday, she hadn't returned the gesture, which, to this day, she still felt guilty about.

Hurrying through the gate, Eve's scarf caught on the fence post, and Gabe helped to free it, though it was difficult, as his hands were as numb as hers. "Let's hurry inside and sit by the fire. I need to thaw out."

Her teeth started chattering. "Me, too."

Making their way up the walk was an arduous task. They had to lift each leg out of the snow and plant it, and hope they didn't fall in the process.

When they neared the house, Eve heard a mewling sound and wondered if a stray kitten had wandered onto her property, looking for a place to get warm. "Did you hear that? I think it might be a kitten."

Gabe heard the noise, too, though it didn't sound like a kitten to him. He stepped onto the porch, kneeling beside the wicker basket that had been left there. The basket was covered with several heavy wool blankets, and he lifted the edge and peered in. "What the hell?" he said, his eyes widening.

"What is it? Did someone drop off a litter of kittens? I hope—"

"It's not a kitten. You'd better come up here and take a look."

Eve hurried to the porch and Gabe lifted the blanket, allowing her to look in. She gasped, then clutched her throat. "Merciful heavens! That's not a kitten!"

Gabe picked up the basket and cradled it to his chest. "No, ma'am," he said with a delighted smile. "It sure as heck's not. It's a baby."

Chapter Seven

"It's a baby!" Eve said stupidly, following Gabe into the house and shrugging out of her winter wear as quickly as she could tear off the heavy garments. She dumped it all on the floor, instead of hanging it up, as she normally would. But this was not a normal day.

"Who on earth would leave a baby on someone's front porch?" she asked. "And why would they leave it on mine, of all places? Everyone in town knows I'm not married."

Setting the wicker basket down in front of the hearth, Gabe peeled back the blankets covering the child, hearing the confusion and fear in Eve's voice. "Maybe whoever left the child wasn't from around here. I suspect this note that's attached will explain some of the mystery." Despite everything it had gone through, the child slept the sleep of the innocent, and Gabe did his best to unpin the note without awakening him or her. He wasn't quite sure yet if they were dealing with a boy or a girl. All babies looked alike to him, especially when they were infants, and this child couldn't have been more than a month old, if that.

"Is the baby all right?" Eve asked anxiously. "Do you think it might have gotten too cold and developed frostbite or pneumonia?"

Gabe shook his head. "I don't think it was out there long enough for that to happen, and the baby had plenty of coverings to keep it warm. The mother or father was trying to protect it from harm. I'm certain of that." He held up the wrinkled notepaper. "Do you want me to read it, or will you?"

Eve held out a trembling hand. "I'll do it." She drew in a breath, then began reading aloud:

"Dear Friend, I can't care for my baby girl no more, and hope you'll take good care of her. She's a sweet baby, but she don't have a name, so you should feel free to call her whatever you want.

"Please don't come looking for me. I'll be gone by the time you read this. I'm not a bad person, just someone in trouble who needs help, so please don't you judge me too harshly. God will do that soon enough. Please find room in your heart for my baby and give her all the love I can't. Bless you!"

"It's not signed," Eve said, not surprised by that fact, handing it back to Gabe. "I guess we should notify the authorities."

"I thought Cedar Springs didn't have a sheriff."

Eve's frown deepened. No sheriff. No doctor. What on earth was happening to Cedar Springs? "We don't. Barney Piper quit two months ago. Left in the middle of the night, so no one could talk him out of it. I guess Mayor Moody would be the best person to tell about this.''

''Don't think that'll be possible,'' Gabe said. ''Burt's gone home to Denver for the Christmas holiday. Told me last time we spoke that he was heading home two weeks before Christmas to visit his parents. That'd be about now.''

''Then we'll tell the reverend.''

''Guess we could, but it's not likely he'll be able to do anything about this, with all he's got to contend with at the moment. Besides, the child was entrusted into your care, not his.''

Tiptoeing over to the basket, she stared down at the sleeping infant, and her heart felt heavy in her chest. She was a beautiful baby, all pink and rosy with soft downy hair the same blond color as her own. She was perfect, like the little porcelain doll Eve played with as a child; only this baby doll was all too real.

''I can't keep her, Gabe. We need to find someone who knows how to care for a baby. I don't have any experience with such matters.''

''I do,'' he said, making Eve's eyes widen. ''I have a son, remember? And that son was once a baby.''

''Are you suggesting that we keep this child?'' She could see by his determined expression that that was exactly what he was suggesting. The notion was impractical, not sensible at all, totally absurd.

''Just for the time being, until we can locate her parents.'' The mystery of the child's sex had at least been established. He'd always wanted a daughter to spoil outrageously.

"But the mother—I'm assuming the note was written by a woman—doesn't want the baby. And there was no mention of a father. We may never locate them," Eve tried to reason.

"I suspect the poor woman doesn't have a husband, or if she does, they can't afford to keep the child. Or maybe they were just too young, or maybe she's sick. Hell, I don't know."

"You can't go around speculating about such things. And I can't have this baby living here, especially during the Christmas holidays. It wouldn't be fair to the child." The baby awoke and started to cry. "See? There's a problem with her already."

"Why can't she stay here? You don't celebrate the holidays." Gabe bent over and picked up the crying infant. "The 'problem,' as you put it, is that she's soaked clean through and needs a dry diaper and clothing. Do you have anything we can use?"

"I—" Eve was so nervous she was shaking. A baby! She didn't know anything about babies, about how to care for them. She loved children, but she wasn't equipped to take care of them. And children needed two parents. They didn't need a spinster who...

"Eve, do you have anything we can use for diapers?"

Looking up, as if she'd just heard the question for the first time, she nodded. "Yes. I'll get some clean dish towels. And I may have something up in the attic that she can wear. My mother saved all of my baby things, thinking that someday I'd be able to use them for my own children."

"Well, I'm relieved that your mother was such a

smart woman," Gabe said to Eve's retreating back, cradling the screaming infant to his chest and uttering soothing words of comfort.

"You just hold on, little baby. Gabe's gonna get you fixed up in no time. You'll see."

A few moments later, Eve rushed back into the parlor, holding several clean linen towels and two safety pins. "Here," she said, handing them to him. "I'll go up to the attic while you change the baby. You know how to do that, right?" He certainly seemed at ease with the child.

"Are you sure you don't want to change her?"

Eve looked horrified at the prospect. "I've never in my life changed an infant. I wouldn't know where to begin, and I'm afraid that I might stick her with the pins."

Gabe was tempted to tell her that she should begin at the bottom, but didn't think she'd appreciate his humor at the moment. "It's not hard. I'll teach you. But first I guess you'd better go fetch those baby things, then we'll get you properly instructed in taking care of this baby."

"I don't want to learn to take care of this baby," she said. "It wouldn't be wise."

"You've got to quit being afraid of life, Eve. You're afraid to form attachments, to let yourself feel anything. That's no way to live. Life comes with risks. That's just the way it is."

His comment hit a bull's-eye, and Eve's face whitened. "Not for me," she blurted, disappearing up the stairs.

Staring after her, Gabe shook his head. "Damn stubborn woman! Come on, Noelle," he said, deciding the name was perfect for the sweet cherub, especially since it was getting so close to Christmas. "Let's get you comfortable, then we can think about what we're going to do about Miss Eve Barlow. She's a stubborn, opinionated woman," he said to the child who was mesmerized by his deep voice, "but I think you're gonna like her as much as I do."

Upstairs in the attic, Eve was sorting through her mother's trunks, trying to locate her old baby clothing, bottles, and such. Alma Barlow, bless her heart, never threw out anything, so Eve had a pretty good assortment of baby items by the time she was finished sorting through the various trunks and boxes.

Holding up the small pink sacque and the tiny silver rattle that used to be hers, she heaved a sigh. She'd always wanted a baby of her own, and now someone had left one on her front porch. How odd was that?

If she believed in such things as Christmas miracles, she might have thought God had lent a hand in what had happened today. Florinda was always saying that he worked in mysterious ways. But Eve was too realistic not to think that some poor unfortunate woman had unknowingly chosen her—inept, knows-nothing-about-babies Eve Barlow—to care for her infant.

"I can't care for a baby," she whispered softly. And even if she could, would she really want to subject an innocent child to her ill-fated curse? No one she loved—or professed to love, as in Daniel's case—and with whom she had shared the Christmas holidays, had survived. The infant was in jeopardy.

"We can't keep that child," she told Gabe when

she returned to the parlor a few minutes later. He was holding the now sleeping infant in his arms, walking back and forth in front of the fireplace, singing softly to her, and Eve's heart twisted at the beautiful sight. She knew he would make a wonderful father.

"*Shh.* I just got Noelle to sleep."

"Noelle? Why are you calling her Noelle? You can't name that child. It's not yours. And besides that, we can't keep her. Christmas is coming, and—" His brows raised in question. "I told you about what happens during the Christmas holidays. If I allow this baby to stay here with me, something dreadful is going to befall her." Tears filled her eyes at his look of disbelief. "I'm not being foolish. I'm not."

Crossing the room in quick strides, Gabe nestled the baby in one arm, and with the other wrapped it around Eve's shoulders. "You're not cursed, Eve. I know you think you are, because of what's happened to you in the past, but you're not. And yes, you are foolish to think that way. Nothing is going to happen to this child. Your arriving home when you did probably saved little Noelle's life."

She refused to believe him. "That was pure coincidence."

"Was it? Maybe it was a miracle. Did you ever think of that? Maybe you were destined to find this child, like the three wise men were destined to find the baby Jesus."

"Gabe, I'm sure you think you're doing the right thing by wanting to keep this child, but we both know we'd be doing a disservice to her in the long run. Our relationship with this baby, with each other, is for the short term. We'd grow attached to Noelle, and then we'd have to give her up. How wise is that?''

"Christmas is the season for miracles. I say we wait and see what happens. I'm willing to take care of the baby. I'll do her feedings and change her nappies, if you don't feel comfortable doing it. I was pretty good with Robby when he was an infant. Marilyn preferred to let the nursemaid take care of him, but I did as much diaper changing and feeding as I could. I wanted to form a deep bond. One that would never end.''

Sadness filled his eyes, and it tore at Eve's heart. She hated seeing him look so wounded, and clutched his arm. "All right. Let's keep Noelle for now and see what develops. Maybe we'll be able to locate her parents.''

He nodded in relief, kissing the baby's cheek. "I'll send a telegram to the Denver police tomorrow, notifying them of the child, the note and the fact that we're taking care of her for the time being. I doubt they'll have any objection.''

Eve heaved a deep sigh of longing and wished she, Gabe and Noelle were a real family, not just three misfits who had come together out of necessity and bad weather. Thinking that such a thing was possible was foolish, she knew. But a tiny corner of her heart still hoped that miracles really did happen.

The following two weeks passed by in a blur for Eve. She grew proficient in diapering Noelle, feeding her a bottle, and getting up in the middle of the night to change and feed her again, which, she had decided, was the biggest struggle. During those times, she usually found Gabe in the makeshift nursery ahead of her, and they ended up taking care of the baby together. Like parents. Though she tried not to think along those lines.

The entire town was abuzz about the foundling infant and had started referring to Noelle as the "miracle child."

Reverend Brewster had come by to say how pleased and proud he was that Eve had taken another lost soul into her home and heart during this holiest of seasons.

Gabe had made the rounds of shopkeepers, and had even gone door-to-door to many of the neighbors, despite the inclement weather, making inquiries to see if anyone might know to whom the child belonged. Though no one had any idea, they had given them generous donations of baby clothes, diapers and foodstuffs. It seemed everyone was in a giving mood, just as Gabe had predicted would happen during the Christmas holiday.

As promised, he had contacted the Denver authorities, but the telegram they'd received back just yesterday from the police department hadn't shed any light on the matter. It instructed Gabe and Eve to keep the child until further notice. They offered little hope that the parents would ever be found and suggested that adoption would be a strong possibility for them to consider.

Sitting in front of the fire that evening, Noelle sleeping contentedly on Gabe's stomach as he reclined on the sofa, Eve was reminded once again of how real their present situation seemed. It was as if the three of them were already a family. Gabe had made no further mention about leaving, and despite her reservations concerning next week's Christmas holiday, neither had she.

"I can't imagine why anyone would give up her child," she said for what seemed like the thousandth time. "Noelle is so precious. Her mother must be beside herself with grief and worry."

"I suspect the woman had little choice in the matter. Knowing firsthand how difficult it is to lose a child…well, I just think Noelle's mother had a damn good reason for doing what she did." He'd read the note over many times, and had finally come to the conclusion that the woman was ill, possibly even dying. He couldn't contemplate any other reason remotely strong enough for someone to have abandoned a child.

"I've grown so attached to her, I don't know what I'll do when and if they finally find her parents," she said, staring into the crackling flames. She'd thought about adoption but didn't think that would be fair to Noelle. The baby needed a loving home with two parents. Eve wanted her to have the kind of childhood she, herself, had had while growing up.

Gabe heard the pain in her voice, watched as her gaze fell on the baby, and wished that the love and yearning he saw reflected there had also been for him.

He hadn't touched her again, not physically anyway. But he'd reached out to Eve emotionally, offering support and encouragement during this difficult time.

He loved her. It was clear to him now. He thought he'd probably fallen in love with her that first day she'd slammed the door in his face. But, of course, he hadn't been wise enough to know that then.

Gabe knew he would never give up his search for Robby, but he also knew that it was time to put the past behind him and begin again. With Eve, with the baby they'd been given, and with a new chance for happiness and happily-ever-after.

His life would never be complete without Eve. He wanted to marry her, to make a family with her and Noelle. But would he be able to convince her of that? Would he be able to overcome her self-doubt, her fear of this curse she'd blown all out of proportion? Marriage wasn't something she was eager to enter into, and she'd already made that perfectly clear.

Despite all that, he had to try. "Eve, I—"

She turned to face him, her face blushed pink from the heat of the fire. "I've decided that you don't have to leave before Christmas Eve, Gabe. I…I want you to stay." For however long you want, she wanted to add but was too afraid to say the words. Gabe was content to play nursemaid and companion for the moment, but he'd never indicated anything beyond that.

Setting the baby carefully on the sofa, Gabe rose to his feet and pulled Eve to hers, wrapping his arms about her. "You don't know how happy I am to hear you say that, sweetheart," he whispered, brushing her lips. "I know I'm not supposed to kiss or touch you, but I want to hold you in my arms. Will you let me?"

Swallowing past the lump in her throat, she nodded, resting her head against his chest and listening to the steady beating of his heart.

Steady. That's what Gabe was. Steady, kind and dependable. He was all those things. And she loved him more than she had ever hoped to love anyone again.

Take a risk, he had told her. Well, she had decided to take his advice. Tonight, after they put Noelle to bed, she would go to his room and offer herself to Gabe.

It would be her gift to him. A Christmas gift, like no other she had ever given.

Chapter Eight

Dressed in the rose silk nightgown she had purchased as part of her trousseau to wear on her wedding night with Daniel, Eve stared at her reflection in the long cheval mirror, and her heart started beating triple time. With her hair down and curling riotously around her shoulders, flushed cheeks, and her nipples poking through the fabric of the thin gown, she looked like a wanton woman.

"You can do this, Eve," she told herself as she felt herself starting to weaken. "Don't chicken out." Taking several deep breaths to calm herself, she walked to the door, said a silent prayer that Gabe wasn't going to laugh out loud when he saw her, then exited her bedroom, making her way down the darkened hall toward his.

Her hand was sweating as she reached for the brass knob and turned it. She opened the door to find him shirtless and standing at the washbasin. The sight of his corded muscles and smooth skin left her breathless and more certain than ever that she was doing the right thing.

Gabe turned at the sound of the door closing, and his eyes widened in surprise. "Eve? Is something wrong? Is it Noelle?"

She shook her head and went to him. "The baby's fine and sleeping soundly."

Tossing the towel aside, he held out his hand. The erotic smile he wore said more plainly than words that he knew exactly why she had come. "You look beautiful, Eve, just like I'd imagined."

"I'm nervous. I've never done anything like this before."

"Don't be. You've made me very happy." Drawing her into his arms, he kissed her passionately. It was a kiss from the heart, deep and warm, and Eve knew in that moment that she had made the right decision. If she never had another moment of love and happiness, she would have this one to remember.

Wrapping her arms about his neck, she pressed into him, and, tentatively at first, then more aggressively, slid her tongue into his mouth. He moaned, then deepened the kiss, his hands moving down her back, her buttocks, then back up again to fondle her aching breasts. "You have such perfect breasts," he told her, guiding her toward the bed. "They fill a man's hands just right."

Her cheeks flushed at the compliment. No one had ever said such things to her before. "If you keep up with that kind of talk, you'll embarrass me."

"Why? I think you're beautiful, Eve. I want to see all of you, cherish your body, as I do your mind and heart."

His words soothed and comforted, and she didn't protest when he lifted her gown up over her head and tossed it aside. The bedside lamp burned brightly, illuminating the room and the desire and longing on his face. "You're exquisite."

She sucked in her breath, trying to stem her nervousness. "Take off your clothes. I want to see all of you, as well."

With a rakish grin, he removed his pants and underwear until he was as gloriously naked as she, then joined her on the mattress. The aging bed springs creaked as he settled himself beside her.

Eve felt brazen, for she couldn't resist touching him, exploring his muscular chest and the fine hairs matted there. "I've never seen a man naked before," she admitted shyly, her gaze falling on the thick, long member that jutted out from the dark nest of curly hairs. Her eyes grew round as saucers, and she gasped as it grew even larger. "I had no idea."

Swallowing his smile, Gabe took her hand and placed it on him. "It's not usually that big. This is what happens when a man gets excited and wants to be inside a woman."

She squeezed him gently, then pulled back when Gabe moaned. "I'm sorry. Did I hurt you?"

"Not exactly, though you are torturing me. Much more of that and this'll be over before it's started."

"Oh."

He leaned on one hand, then took the other and, with his forefinger made slow, circular motions around each of her nipples, which tightened instantly. Bending his head, he kissed each one, and she moaned. "I've wanted to do that since the first moment I laid eyes on you. I've undressed you with my eyes a thousand times."

Her nipples felt like two pieces of hard candy, and Eve sucked in her breath as he moved slowly down her body, placing kisses on the underside of her breasts, her stomach, her abdomen, then gently forcing her legs apart. Realizing his intent, she panicked. "Please, don't!"

"*Shh.* It'll be all right. I want to see all of you. Taste all of you. Trust me."

She shook her head, about to protest further, but his mouth had already found the center of her being, and the flicking motion of his tongue on her swollen bud rendered her speechless. Clutching the sheets, she writhed beneath the onslaught. With every stroke the tension built, and she felt herself winding like a corkscrew, tighter, ever tighter, until she burst free, spinning out of control and crying out in climax.

Gabe mounted her then, moving his hand between her thighs to make sure she was ready to receive him. He entered her slowly, allowing her to accommodate his size. "Are you all right?" he asked, kissing her gently.

"Yes," she whispered. "I'm more than all right. Don't stop. Whatever you do, don't stop."

"This is going to hurt a little, but I'll try to be gentle. Just try and relax. If you tense up, it'll only make it worse."

She bit her lower lip in anticipation as he eased in further, breaking through the barrier of her virginity with one hard thrust and swallowing her brief moment of pain with his mouth.

Once the initial discomfort was over, there was only pleasure. Eve reveled in the feel of Gabe deep inside her. She moved as he moved, thrusting her hips up to meet him, glorying in the way their bodies came together as one entity. She was his, now and forever.

Back and forth, back and forth, he moved, drawing her again to that pinnacle of pleasure she'd reached once before. "Oh! Oh, Gabe," she said, her breath coming more rapidly as his strokes intensified.

"Stay with me, sweetheart," he urged, lifting her buttocks and sliding into her more fully.

With one last thrust, she cried out, and Gabe released into her, reaching his climax at the same moment.

Words of love teetered on the tips of their tongues, but neither was brave enough to say the words just yet.

Eve worried that Gabe would feel trapped if he knew that she loved him.

Gabe believed Eve wouldn't want to make the commitment he wanted from her. And so they remained silent as they continued to make love long into the night and early morning hours.

The sound of a baby crying awakened them at dawn. Eve groaned in protest and rolled onto her side. Gabe pulled her to his chest, nuzzling her neck and ear.

"Mmm. Stop that," she said. "I'm sleeping."

"I think the baby's up and wants to be fed. I'll do it."

She rolled toward him and kissed his chin. "I'll go. You look exhausted."

"Can you blame me? I haven't had this much activity in years." He wiggled his brows at her. "You're a wanton woman, Eve Barlow."

She laughed, then hearing the baby's renewed cries, eased herself out of his embrace and searched for her gown, finding it at the foot of the bed. "Keep that thought. I'll be right back."

She crossed the hall and hurried into the nursery to find Noelle screaming at the top of her lungs. "Hush, baby, I'm coming. Are you hungry and wet?"

Eve peered into the crib to find that Noelle's nose was running; her face looked redder than normal. Fear griped her like a vise, and she placed her hand on the baby's forehead, crying out in alarm when she discovered how warm she felt. "Oh, no!"

"Gabe! Gabe, come quickly. Noelle has a fever." This was all her fault. The baby was sick. Tomorrow was Christmas Eve. And history was repeating itself.

He rushed into the room, naked as the day he was born and not the least bit self-conscious about it. "What's wrong?"

"Noelle's burning up."

He felt the child's cheek and forehead. "She's feverish all right. We'll have to try and bring down the fever."

"It's the curse." Eve sobbed into her hands. "I've killed her."

Gabe's voice grew stern. "Stop it, Eve! You're not helping Noelle with your hysterics, and you're certainly not helping me. Now go downstairs and fetch her bottle. We'll try to get her to eat. While you're doing that, I'll change her clothing and diapers."

Eve nodded silently and, with one last look of dismay, hurried down the stairs, crying all the while she poured milk into a pan and heated it on the stove.

"Please, God," she prayed, "don't let anything

happen to Noelle. I love her so.'' She sniffed several times, then wiped her nose on her forearm, wishing she'd had the foresight to don her robe.

Gabe looked up when she reentered the room a short time later. ''I've given Noelle a sponge bath,'' he told her. ''Her fever seems to have lessened somewhat. I think she's just got a cold. She'll probably be feeling better later on.''

''But what if she's not? What if she's worse?''

''We'll cross that bridge when we come to it, Eve. No sense borrowing trouble when there isn't any.''

They took turns tending the baby all day and into the evening. Gabe believed the child was getting better, and Eve clung to that belief like a lifeline as she prepared them something to eat for dinner.

''Is she better?'' she asked, returning to the baby's room and placing the tray of ham sandwiches and milk on the dresser. She felt too tired to eat, but she knew Gabe was hungry. His stomach had been growling in protest for hours.

He inclined his head, looking as exhausted as she felt. ''I think she'll be fine by morning,'' he whispered. ''Let's go into the other room to eat, so we don't disturb her.''

Eve followed Gabe into his bedroom. Her gaze fell on the rumpled sheets, the reddish stain, and she blushed clear down to her toes, remembering what they'd done there so recently. ''I'm sorry. I didn't think to make the bed.''

He laughed. ''Only you would think of something like that, Miss Barlow,'' he said, kissing her cheek.

She smiled ruefully. "It's the housekeeper in me, I guess."

"Tomorrow's Christmas Eve. Are you going to be all right with that?" It was her birthday, and he intended to surprise her, though he knew she'd probably throw a fit when she discovered exactly what that surprise was going to be.

"I'll be fine."

"I'm going to run a few errands in the morning, but I won't be gone long."

"But what about Noelle?"

"The baby will be fine. She'll have you to look after her."

Eve knew a moment of panic, then she breathed deeply and smiled. "We'll be fine. If she's up to it, I'll teach her how to make cookies. I know you'll be expecting them."

Gabe grinned. "You surely do know the way to a man's heart, ma'am." He winked at her. "And I wasn't talking about your cooking."

The following Christmas Eve morning, Gabe left to run his errands after breakfast, while Eve busied herself in the kitchen. He had brought Noelle's cradle down and set it before the fireplace. Her fever had disappeared, and she had eaten, played a bit with Eve's hair, which she found absolutely fascinating, and then had fallen back to sleep.

Eve was seated at the kitchen table, frosting and decorating another batch of gingerbread cookies when she heard the front door open.

"Don't come in here just yet. I don't want you to spoil your birthday surprise," Gabe called out.

Gabe had gotten her a birthday present! Eve felt warm and tingly inside. She didn't celebrate her birthday anymore, and wouldn't have even remembered it, if not for his reminder, and the annual Christmas curse.

"Don't wake Noelle," she cautioned. "I just got her to sleep a short while ago."

Consumed with curiosity when she heard a great deal of sawing, banging, doors opening and closing, and Gabe's more colorful curses, Eve tried to take her mind off whatever it was he was doing by continuing her baking. In addition to four different kinds of cookies, she had made cranberry-nut bread and eggnog.

Though she wasn't planning to do any celebrating of the holiday, she knew it wouldn't be fair to deprive Gabe of the pleasure. He wasn't the one cursed, after all. And he had made her deliriously happy, so she felt it was the least she could do. That's what she told herself, anyway.

Two hours later, Gabe came into the kitchen, looking quite pleased. "Are you ready to see your birthday present?"

She licked the frosting off her fingers, and his eyes darkened. "Well, I admit to being curious. You've made quite a racket this morning, and I've been imagining all sorts of things."

He drew her into his arms and kissed her soundly. "Mmm. You've been sampling the gingerbread cookies, I see. Not fair."

"Just one."

He looked a bit uneasy, then said, "Now promise you won't get mad or anything."

Her forehead wrinkled in confusion. "Why would

I get mad? I haven't had a birthday present in years. I'm looking forward to opening it, if you want to know the truth.'' And she was, which surprised her.

"Well, it's not that kind of gift," he said, tunneling impatient fingers through his hair. "I mean, you don't have to open it."

Her brows drew together. "I—"

"Shut your eyes," he interrupted, and she did as instructed. Clasping her hand, he drew her forward. "We're going into the parlor. I'll guide you. Now don't peek. Promise?"

She felt all of ten years old, giddy and unbelievably happy. "I promise."

When they reached the front room, Eve inhaled deeply, and the familiar fragrance of fir greeted her nostrils. She grew instantly suspicious.

"Okay, you can open them now."

Eve's jaw unhinged as she gaped at the tall, majestic fir tree standing in front of the window. It had been decorated from top to bottom with the lovely red and silver ornaments from Mr. Purdy's store, and at the top rested a shiny silver star. Popcorn and cranberry strands adorned the circumference, and several presents were scattered beneath. "How on earth did you do all this?" she asked finally, unable to believe what was right before her.

"Do you like it? You're not mad, are you?"

She hugged herself and tears of joy filled her eyes. "It's so beautiful!" Her gaze moved from the tree to Gabe. "Thank you. I love it. I—" She covered her face with her hands and started to cry in earnest.

Gabe went into panic mode. "Now, sweetie, don't cry. I can take it down, if you don't—"

"Don't you dare, Gabriel Tyler! I'm just overcome with emotion. No one's ever given me such a nice birthday gift."

"Well, it's no wonder. Poor Mr. Purdy was nervous as heck about selling me those ornaments. But I convinced him that you were ready to start letting Christmas back into your heart and soul again. When he heard the news, he let loose with a whoop, then he and his wife offered to string the popcorn and cranberry garlands, and they wrapped the gifts I purchased for you and Noelle."

"But the weather, the snow..."

"You think Saint Nicholas is going to let a little thing like snow slow him down. Not if I have anything to say about it."

He pulled her forward to sit beside him at the base of the tree. "I have something else for you, Eve. I hope you like it."

"But you've given me more than enough, Gabe, and I have nothing for you in return."

"I thought you made me cookies," he reminded her.

"Well, there's that. But I don't have a proper gift."

He grinned lasciviously. "I'm sure I can come up with something suitable for you to give me later. You might have to get naked first, but—"

She gasped. "Gabriel, not in front of the baby!"

Grinning, he reached beneath the tree to extract a small package, placing it in her hands. "This is for you, Eve. Open it now. I can't wait any longer."

With trembling hands, she untied the small package and opened it. Nestled on a bed of blue velvet was a beautiful diamond-and-ruby ring. She gasped in pure delight. "Oh, Gabe! It's absolutely breathtaking."

He took the ring from her. "This was my grandmother's wedding ring. I've been saving it for someone very special. You're that someone, Eve. Marry me. I love you and can't bear the thought of living my life without you."

She stared at the ring in disbelief, then up at him. "Are you sure? We haven't known each other long, and I wouldn't want you to feel obligated because of what happened between us the other night. I have no regrets."

Placing the ring on the finger of her left hand, he clasped her face between his hands. "I love you, Eve Barlow. And I'm going to marry you, on New Year's Day, if you'll have me. Please say you will."

She hesitated only a moment, but it seemed like a lifetime to Gabe. "Yes, I'll marry you. I love you, Gabe. I have for a very long time. I didn't say anything before, because I didn't want you to feel trapped by that love."

"Oh, sweetie. I'm content here with you and Noelle. I love you both so much. The only thing that would have made this moment even more perfect was if Robby could have been here to share it with us."

"We'll do all we can to find your son, Gabe," she promised, and squeezed his hand, knowing that was one promise she intended to keep.

Eve turned to gaze at the infant, who was wide-awake and staring up at the tree, and she smiled. "We can adopt Noelle now, Gabe. We can be a real family."

"Yes. And there'll be no more talking of curses and bad luck, right?"

"As far as I'm concerned, I'm counting you and Noelle as my own Christmas miracles. They'll be no more 'bah, humbug' around here. From this day forward there will only be 'Joy to the World.'"

Gabe winked. "That's my girl. Now, where are those cookies, woman?"

"Are you positive you're not just marrying me for my cooking abilities?"

He thought a moment. "Well, there are a few other things you do pretty well besides cook. But I don't think we should discuss those in front of Noelle."

They kissed and suddenly music filled the air.

"I hear bells ringing," Eve said.

"I knew I was a good kisser, but—"

She socked his arm and rushed to the window to look out. "It's the Purdys and the rest of the caroling group. They've come to serenade us."

Wrapping his arm about her waist, Gabe kissed her cheek. "Happy birthday and Merry Christmas, Eve. You've made this the happiest day of my life."

She heaved a sigh, feeling happy, contented and very much in love. "It's mine, too," Eve whispered, and knew in that moment that she meant it.

From this day forward, Christmas would always be a gift from God, just as Gabe and Noelle had been.

It was Christmas Eve, and she was truly blessed.

Epilogue

Christmas Eve, One year later.

Eve could hardly contain her excitement. This was going to be the best Christmas ever, and last year had been pretty fabulous.

She could hardly wait to see Gabe's face when she presented him with his present. It had taken a lot of time, money and energy, but she knew it had all been worth it. And in just a short time Gabe would know it, too.

"What time did you say the Purdys were due to arrive?" he asked, looking up from the newspaper. He had just gotten home from his job at the bank, and they were seated in the parlor in front of the fireplace. The pine logs crackled and hissed, adding a festive note to the day. "It's four o'clock, and I'm getting hungry."

"We'll wait for our guests," she said firmly. "They should be here momentarily. Why don't you go upstairs and see if Noelle has awakened from her nap. The dress she's supposed to wear is lying on the chair next to the bed.''

He set the newspaper aside and rose to his feet. "There's a glow about you today, sweetie. If I didn't know better, I'd say you were really looking forward to Christmas this year. Is there a special reason?''

She smiled secretively. "I adore Christmas. And you. Now go fetch our child and bring her down here before the Purdys arrive.'' They were having their first Christmas party, though unbeknownst to Gabe, the others weren't due to arrive until seven o'clock. They were expecting another guest first, someone much more special.

The Pinkerton Agency had wired her two weeks ago to say that Robby Tyler had been located in an orphanage in San Francisco. No one knew the whereabouts of his mother, but most suspected she had run off with some wealthy banker from the area. That seemed to be Marilyn Trusslow Tyler's style, at any rate.

The important thing was that, through the Pinkerton Agency, and her unyielding desire to reunite father and son, Eve had found Robby, had arranged for him to be brought to Cedar Springs, and he and his father would be together once more in just a short time.

Gabe was going to be so happy, Eve knew. He'd waited nine long years for this reunion, and she was anxious to see the expression on his face.

As if conjured up by her thoughts, her husband appeared just then, holding Noelle by the hand. Their daughter looked adorable in her red velvet dress. Her blond curls bobbed as she toddled forward on stockinged feet.

"Mama!" Eve's heart tightened every time she heard her daughter call her that.

They seated themselves in front of the fireplace once more. She gazed at the lovely fir tree they'd decorated with ornaments and candles, and thought of the one Gabe had surprised her with the year before.

Everything was ready for Robby Tyler's arrival.

Eve began wringing her hands nervously, then glanced at the clock on the mantel: four-fifteen. Where was Mr. Randall? The Pinkerton agent should have been here by now.

At last there was a knock on the door, and Eve's heart jumped to her throat. "I'll get it," she said, launching herself off the chair. Gabe looked at her strangely and shrugged.

"Fine by me. Noelle and I are going to share a cookie, aren't we, sweetheart?" He kissed his daughter's pudgy cheek, and she squealed.

A few minutes later, Eve stepped back into the parlor, accompanied by a young boy who looked very much like her husband. "Gabe," she called out, "there's someone I'd like you to meet."

As Eve entered the room, Gabe turned, his eyes widened and his mouth dropped open. He stared intently at the boy, then looked at Eve, who was grinning broadly. "Robby Tyler, I'd like you to meet your father."

"Robby!" Gabe's voice was so thick with emotion he could hardly speak. There was a moment of hesitation, then the young boy rushed forward, as if remembering.

"Daddy?"

Eve's eyes filled with tears as she viewed the heart-wrenching reunion. Noelle started to cry, and Eve picked her up and clutched the child to her chest.

She had one more surprise to give her husband, but she wouldn't do it now. Tonight, when they were in bed and could share a moment of privacy, she would tell him her news. She wasn't sure if Gabriel Tyler was up to hearing that he was going to be a father again.

Two surprises in one day was a lot for anyone to take, even someone as strong and caring as her husband.

"Merry Christmas, Gabe," she whispered.

MARY McBRIDE

When it comes to writing romance, historical or contemporary, Mary McBride is a natural. What else would anyone expect from someone whose parents met on a blind date on Valentine's Day, and who met her own husband—whose middle name happens to be Valentine!—on the 14th of February, as well?

She lives in St. Louis, Missouri, with her husband and two sons. Mary loves to hear from readers. You can write to her c/o P.O. Box 411202, St. Louis, MO 63141, or contact her online at McBride101@aol.com.

SEASON OF BOUNTY
Mary McBride

For my dearest *Mamacita*, Maria Concepción Myers

Chapter One

Kansas, Winter of 1871

It was the worst damned winter that anybody could recall. Snow fell down from an iron-clad sky. It fell sideways with the razor-sharp winds out of the north. Sometimes the confounded stuff seemed to fall *up* from a ground already heaped with it.

Horses grew coats as thick as buffalo pelts. Cattle moved in tight clusters, seeking warmth, foraging for anything that dared to raise its head above a drift. Dogs and cats had to be coaxed, or kicked, outside. By mid-November, kids no longer took much interest in their sleds while their parents had a tendency to stay abed long after each day's bitterly cold sunrise.

Stagecoaches spent more time in livery stables than on the snow-packed roads. Trains ran late—not by hours, but by days. When the Kansas Pacific pulled into Ellsworth on a Thursday afternoon, blowing gray smoke and cinders into a gray sky while snowflakes melted down the hot sides of the big black locomotive, there was nobody hanging around outside the depot when Will Cade got off the train.

He turned his collar up against the wind while he gave the town a quick once-over, then he headed toward the mercantile.

Odd for a man down to his last few dollars.

Not so odd for a fellow with quick hands and a willingness to transgress.

Inside the store, a small potbellied stove sent out a welcome circle of warmth, unlike the redhead behind the counter who had greeted Will with a chilly "Good afternoon" and stood watching him now with her arms crossed, her eyes narrowed to blue slits and her pretty mouth thinned to a pink, suspicious line.

The sign above the door had read Ellsworth Mercantile, Charles and Matilda Favor, Proprietors. Lucky Charles, Will thought while his gaze skimmed the merchandise that cluttered shelves and half a dozen tabletops.

"Are you looking for something in particular?" the redhead asked, sounding more like a constable than a shopkeeper.

"Just looking."

What he needed was a fancy gewgaw that he could use to barter his way into one of the local brothels, something he could trade for a night in a nice warm bed and all the pleasures that went with it. Something silk perhaps. A fetching trinket. Some little knick-knack in amber or ivory or jade. Some...

He spied the silver hairbrush on a table not too far away from where he stood. It was perfect, just made for gliding past his palm and sliding up his sleeve.

"Are you in town on business, mister?"

Pilfering. Petty theft. A little larceny, lady. He met her quizzical gaze, lost himself for a second in her light blue eyes and suffered a sudden, quite unaccustomed, pang of remorse. "I'm with the railroad," he said, lying, edging closer to the object of his desire, deciding just how he'd go about obtaining it.

He fingered a bolt of calico. "A fine selection," he murmured, moving the blue fabric, picking up the red, trading red for yellow, then calico for gingham and muslin as he slowly examined and skillfully rearranged the bolts and built a wall in front of the hairbrush to conceal his worst intentions.

You sly old devil, Will. You should have been an architect or an engineer instead of a physician.

The thought, unbidden as it was, unsettled him. And the woman only made it worse by asking, "What is it you do?"

He blinked. "I beg your pardon?"

"For the railroad." She was leaning both her elbows on the counter, pinning him with her pale blue eyes. "Just what is it you do?"

Ah. She meant now. In his present life. The one in which he was a gambler and a cheat. Not his former existence, the one in which he did no harm.

"I'm an inspector," he said.

"I see."

From her tone, it was clear she didn't believe him. He should probably hurry the hell up, he told himself. Just steal the damned hairbrush and go. He stacked one more bolt on the concealing wall and slid a hand behind it. The metal handle of the brush was cool, nearly cold, against his fingertips.

"Hard to inspect anything under all this snow," she said.

"That's true."

His educated fingers, accustomed to the marks on cards, could almost read the roses and vines inscribed on the back of the brush. It slid so easily into his palm.

"Just what is it you inspect?"

"Well…"

"Will Cade?" The voice came through the mercantile's door along with a blast of icy wind and the familiar, chilling sound of a pistol clearing leather. "Are you Will Cade?"

Will's hand, the one behind the calico embankment, held absolutely still. His breath clogged in his throat. He couldn't speak, either to acknowledge or deny. He felt his past not just catching up with him but about to roll over him like an unstoppable freight train.

It was the woman behind the counter who replied instead. "Just who do you think you are, mister, coming in my store with a gun in your hand?"

"I think I'm a bounty hunter, ma'am, that's who. The name's Luther Killebrew. And I think this fella here—" he aimed a greasy, bearded smile as well as his long black pistol at Will "—is the no-good, low-down card shark that some fine folks in Leavenworth are planning a little party for."

A necktie party, Will thought, feeling the collar of his coat suddenly chafing his skin. Damned farmers shouldn't gamble if they couldn't afford to lose.

"Do you have a picture of this Will Cade?" the woman asked. There was a note of defiance in her voice as she crossed her arms and stared at the bounty hunter.

"No, ma'am, I don't. All I have is a flier that says he's six feet tall with green eyes and sand-colored hair and a crescent scar on the back of his left hand." He turned to Will. "I was sitting behind you on the train, Cade. I was minding my own business until I spied that scar with my own two eyes, and then I figured I'd make a quick two hundred bucks by bringing you in."

Damned scar. For a minute Will was back at Chancellorsville. The wounded were screaming. Arms and legs were stacked like cord wood, waist high outside the surgical tent. His scalpel slipped, bit him hard and deep, but he couldn't quit to stitch it up. Not with a boy's life in the balance.

Thankfully he hadn't cut a tendon, but the scar he carried as a souvenir was distinctive. He might as well have had his name tattooed on the back of his left hand.

"Well, you're mistaken," the woman said suddenly, and with a certain force.

She came out from behind her counter. Sallied forth, actually, like a battleship about to engage the enemy. A tiny-waisted, slim-hipped, finely fashioned craft. A sloop, Will thought. In Kansas, of all places.

Luther Killebrew looked her over from stem to stern, then drawled, "Begging your pardon, little lady, but I'm rarely mistaken. Hardly ever. And I know a gambling weasel when I see one. Especially when he's marked."

Will, the weasel under discussion, was already making plans in light of his imminent capture. Killebrew would handcuff him, as likely as not, and then put him on the eastbound train back to Leavenworth. With any luck, the bounty hunter would be fast asleep by the time they pulled into Salina. That's when Will would pick the lock on the cuffs and slide out of his seat and...

"Well, you're mistaken now," the redhead said, a fury building in her voice and the color rising in her face. "This man is my...my..."

Don't stop now, Red. Go on.

"...my husband's cousin, come all the way from...from..."

Ohio.

"...Saint Louis for a visit. He's not Will Cade. He's not the man you're looking for, mister. And that scar you're so all-fired certain about is...is..."

A sad memento of the war.

"...is from a mangy dog named Pollifax who bit my husband, Charlie, too. Only someplace where I'm not at liberty to tell."

She was good. She was very, very good. Pollifax. That was the perfect touch. The indisputable detail. The nail that sealed the coffin. The key that would set Will Cade free.

The bounty hunter blinked and rubbed his bearded jaw. "I'm hardly ever wrong."

The woman crossed her arms and pointed her chin toward Will. "You're wrong now. The fine folks of Leavenworth won't pay you a nickel for *him*."

"It'd cost me twenty dollars just to get him there," Killebrew grumbled. Worry pinched his brow.

"And twenty more for train fare back," she added,

"once you realize what a darn fool you've been. Now leave us be."

"Goddamn it." He shoved his pistol back into its holster and shook his head. "I thank you, ma'am. I most surely do. It wouldn't do my reputation as a man hunter any good at all to turn up with some dog-bit dandy, would it?"

"Not hardly." She sniffed.

"Sorry about that," he said to Will. "I'm hardly ever wrong."

"No problem." Will's voice came back at last and his heart resumed a normal rhythm. He even managed what he hoped would pass for an easygoing grin.

"I'll just be going now," the bounty hunter said, turning toward the door.

"Goodbye," the redhead snapped.

Good riddance.

"Well," she said once the door had closed on Luther Killebrew.

"Well."

Well, well, well.

Will let the silver hairbrush slide smoothly down his sleeve and back onto the table.

A well was a hole in the ground, and Matty figured she'd best find the nearest one and throw herself in it. She'd just done something very rash, probably very foolish, and—worst of all—she hadn't consulted Charlie before she did it.

She'd been watching the handsome stranger as he sidled up to the table that held her prized silver dresser set, the one that nobody in town could afford. She'd even been admiring the man for his cunning as he smoothly maneuvered her calico bolts to provide a cover for his heinous act.

What he didn't know, of course, was that Matty had rigged out the entire store with mirrors to prevent any such pilfering, mostly from the likes of a particular pair of brothers, Samuel and Hamuel Crane, as identical in their looks as in their larcenous little hearts.

She'd been watching this green-eyed, sandy-haired stranger, thinking what a pity it was that a man with such elegant and graceful hands couldn't put them to a better use, dreading the moment when she would have to apprehend him. Then, just when she was about to reach under the counter for her pistol, Luther Killebrew had come through the door waving his.

And then she'd gone and done it. It wasn't that she had thought it all out. The plan seemed to hatch itself somehow, and it seemed so brilliant at the time. She'd save Will Cade from the bounty hunter. She'd snatch him from his fate, and then the gambler would be firmly in her debt. He'd be beholden to her. Morally bound to pay his savior back. Ethically required to make things right. To set things fair and square.

Will Cade owed her, and she needed help in the store. It just made perfect sense.

Only now, with Luther Killebrew gone, it suddenly occurred to Matty that relying on the conscience and moral fiber of a thief was as foolish as trying to rob the poor. She'd just made a terrible mistake. It served her right, too, for not consulting Charlie first.

"Well." Matty swallowed hard. She'd have to get her pistol after all, she guessed, and maybe even shoot the man. But just then, in one of her rigged-up mirrors, she could see the silver handle of the hairbrush peek from his wool sleeve, then slowly ease out onto the table. Perhaps he had a conscience after all.

"Well." The scoundrel stood there, staring at her, his face impassive as a clock. "That's a mighty deep subject, ma'am."

Matty crossed her arms, standing a few inches taller than her five foot three and trying her best to sound like a Baptist preacher instead of a going-broke store-keeper. "You owe me, Will Cade."

He nodded. "That I do, ma'am. That I do. I don't suppose you'd be willing to accept a small fortune in sheer gratitude."

She shook her head. It galled her to have to admit what she was about to say, even to a stranger. "I need help here in my store."

He didn't reply, but one of his sandy eyebrows lifted slightly, as if to say, *Go on.*

"I need someone to transport heavy merchandise from the depot. Someone to tend the higher shelves."

"You need a man," he said as his green gaze skimmed her from head to toe.

Matty stiffened, feeling color blaze across her face, wondering suddenly if the fact that Will Cade was a handsome devil had had something to do with her unpremeditated rescue of him. "You're very rude."

He laughed softly while his gaze traveled around the store. "I've been called worse. But I'm also strong enough to fetch your heavy parcels and tall enough to tend those upper shelves. I'll help you, Mrs. Favor. For a while, anyway."

"You will?" Matty had expected more resistance.

"Like you said, I owe you." He glanced toward

the curtained-off back room. "Got any place I can sleep in here?"

"There's a room upstairs," she replied before considering the consequences. She didn't want him staying here, but Lord knows she needed help. "It's cold, though."

He laughed again and his green eyes glinted. "What isn't?"

"Well," Matty said. "It's a deal, I suppose." Then she narrowed her eyes. "I hope I won't have to be counting hairbrushes every day, Will Cade."

If he was surprised by her accusation, he managed to hide it. If he felt shame, it didn't show.

"Or," she continued sternly, "be forced to telegraph the good folks in Leavenworth to tell them where to find you."

He splayed a finely shaped hand over his coat in the vicinity of his heart. The crescent scar reminded Matty of a pearly slice of moon. "You can trust me," he said.

"No," she said. "I can't. But I can use you, at least until Christmas."

"Fair enough." He cocked his head, which set that suddenly comely grin of his on a precipitous angle. "What's Mr. Favor going to say when you tell him you've gone and hired a dog-bit dandy to help out?"

Maybe I just won't tell him, Matty thought as she turned away, pretending not to hear the gambler's question. *Maybe for once in my life I'll do something on my own.*

"Follow me," she said briskly. "I'll show you the way upstairs."

Chapter Two

In the following week, a fresh foot and a half of snow accumulated in Ellsworth, an inch of which found its way through a break in the window glass in the mercantile's upstairs room. It was colder than a witch's...

Will cursed as he used the handle of his razor to break the thin veneer of ice in the china washbasin, preparatory to splashing the frigid water on his face. He spent as little time as possible up here in Matty Favor's spare and arctic room. Each evening, after she locked the front door and disappeared wherever it was that her Charlie, the lucky devil, awaited her, Will would let himself out the back door and trudge through the knee-high snow, across the railroad tracks, toward the warmth of the seedier side of the little cow town.

There, once he'd thawed out sufficiently, he'd play poker until he won just enough for his evening meal and a few shots of rye. It never took him long to accumulate the necessary couple bucks. He didn't even have to cheat.

After that, rather than battle with frostbite in his

lodging over the mercantile, he'd spend the next few hours in the parlor of the sporting house with Mrs. Runyon and her little crew of hard-luck whores—Rosemary, Flo and Ilsebein. Business was slow, and the women seemed grateful for his company.

If his scheme with the stolen hairbrush had worked out, Will expected that by now he'd be a rather permanent guest there, most likely in Mrs. Runyon's own bed. The madam made it pretty clear from the outset that she fancied him. She was generous with her cigars and plum brandy, although she didn't seem to be quite sure whether she was investing in a stud or a gelding.

In all honesty, Will wasn't all that sure of his status anymore, either. What kind of fool slept alone in a bleak and freezing room above a store when he could just as well have eased between a warm and willing woman's sheets? It didn't make much sense.

Why, he asked himself for the hundredth time while he watched his breath take shape in a frigid puff, was he doing this? And for the hundredth time the answer was the same.

Matty.

Flame-haired, blue-eyed Matty.

Married Matty.

Mrs. Charles Favor.

He had yet to see the husband.

She'd done more than merely rescue Will from Luther Killebrew. Matty Favor had made him feel necessary in a way he hadn't been ever since he'd come home from the war. Helping her every day in her woebegone store had helped him forget, if only for a while, that he wasn't a good man anymore. Her presence in his dreams this past week had kept his demons at bay.

Whether those demons were chasing him or vice versa, Will couldn't exactly say. Six years ago, he'd come home from the war, back to the beautiful, misty mountains of North Carolina where he'd left his beautiful, misty bride, Caroline. He'd been ready to hang out his shingle and practice the peacetime medicine for which he'd been trained, and he'd been more than eager to begin the family he'd dreamed of for so long.

So much for dreams. Six years ago the mountains had greeted him in all their misty glory, but his beautiful bride was gone. So was his brother, Matthew—the one who'd stayed home "to keep an eye on things" while his older brother went off to war.

"Run off," his father had said. "The shameless harlot and that no-good, thankless boy. Forget about them, Will. Wherever they've gone, it's halfway to perdition."

But the demons wouldn't let him forget. The demons replaced his dreams, and Will set out on the road to perdition to find them.

While he shaved, he contemplated his face in the shard of mirrored glass above the washbasin. Sometimes he barely recognized himself. The past six years had added twelve to his visage, making him appear forty-three instead of his actual thirty-three. He had the look of a gambler now—wary and closed—instead of the open and sympathetic expression of a physician. No wonder Matty didn't trust him.

Matty.

Just the thought of her made his lips quirk in an uncharacteristic smile and his heart buck in his chest.

To say that she needed help in her store was putting it mildly. The shelves were poorly constructed and of inferior lumber, most of them groaning under too much dusty merchandise. Her odd assortment of tables displayed an equally odd mix of goods that nobody in a struggling Kansas cow town needed even if they could afford elaborate brass inkwells and silver dresser sets and delicately painted silk fans.

In addition to what he'd already transported for her, there was still half a ton of unmarked goods stacked in wooden crates at the depot, waiting to be signed for and hauled down the street to be inventoried and placed on the overloaded shelves.

That was assuming she actually inventoried anything. Her penmanship was abysmal, so the fact that she failed to make the proper entries in her account books didn't really matter. You couldn't have read them if she did.

Her business wasn't exactly brisk, either, although it did pick up once word got out about Will, the new man, the dog-bit dandy, working there. The women who came into the store, though, seemed to spend more time flirting with him than they did buying things.

Hard as he tried, he couldn't figure Matty Favor out. She didn't flirt with him exactly. One minute he'd catch her looking at him as if he were a piece of lemon meringue pie or a Christmas gift tucked beneath a tree. The next minute her blue eyes would go all frosty and she'd cluck her tongue and tell him to dust someplace or to rearrange a shelf.

Will finished shaving, then dried his face and went downstairs to stoke up the fire in the potbellied stove, telling himself not to be too eager to see Mrs. Charles Favor coming through the door at seven-thirty, as she always did, with snowflakes on her eyelashes and winter roses on her cheeks.

As always, she'd say a crisp good-morning while she whisked off her dark blue cloak. She'd hang it on the hook behind the door, and then stride behind the counter with the cash box she carried home every night. After a while, and when she thought he wasn't looking, she'd bend down surreptitiously to check the second little cash box she kept hidden under a floor-board.

Will kept wanting to tell her that if he meant to steal her blind, he'd have done so long before this. God knows he'd considered it that first frigid night upstairs, but then he'd started looking forward to seeing her the next morning and the next one after that. She was a married woman, though, so mostly what he told himself was that he was merely enjoying the view while paying off his debt to her, not to mention avoiding being on the run for the next few months, looking over his shoulder for the likes of Luther Killebrew.

"I could reinforce those shelves behind the counter today," he told her when she finally settled herself on the stool behind the high wooden counter.

"That would be fine," she said. "I consulted with Charlie last night, and he agreed it needs to be done despite the fact that the price of lumber is so high right now."

"Cheaper in the long run, I'd guess. Better than having a gross of those tins and bottles coming down on your pretty head."

He liked to make her blush, to watch her light blue eyes widen and the color creep up from her prim collar to blaze across her face. It reminded him of his wife when he was courting her a million years ago. In that other life. The one before the war. The one that didn't exist anymore, except for when it haunted his dreams.

"You're running short on black cotton thread, I noticed. Might want to order extra next time. And you might want to consider a new supplier. You're paying way too much with that outfit in Chicago."

"Mmm," she murmured while she counted yesterday's receipts. "I'll have to consult with Charlie about that."

Charlie again, goddamn it. "Maybe I'll see if I can borrow that horse and sled again this afternoon to haul the rest of those crates up from the depot." Will waited a second before he added sourly, "Unless, of course, *Charlie* has made some other plans that I'm not privy to."

"Not to my knowledge." She was counting pennies now, her concentration aided by the rosy tip of her tongue peeking out from a corner of her lovely mouth. Will could feel his temperature rise a degree or two at the sight.

"I guess you didn't *consult* him about that," he said more irritably than he'd intended.

What did they do? he wondered. Lie in bed all night talking about the price of lumber? Did Charlie ever kiss her during all these consultations? Did he sample that sweet pink tongue? Did he twine her long red hair around…?

"It's time to open up," she said, ignoring his comment, and his presence as well, while she turned to glance out the mercantile's front window. "I see Lottie Crane's already back for whatever it was she forgot yesterday."

Will unlatched the door, knowing all too well why buxom Lottie Crane was back for the sixth straight day. The woman probably hadn't rubbed up against Charlie Favor's cousin from Saint Louis quite enough the day before or thrown him ample winks. Lord, how he wished Matty were similarly inclined.

"It's surely cold out this morning," the Crane woman said when she stepped inside. Her plump cheeks were ruddy from the cold and her snub nose was running, but even so she managed to gaze at Will with a good deal of warmth while she peeled off her gloves, and then thrust her pudgy hands in his direction. "Why, just feel my hands, Will. They're like two blocks of ice."

That they were, and graceless and chapped to boot. Will let them go as quickly and politely as he could.

"Did you forget something, Lottie?" Matty asked from her perch behind the counter.

"Silly me," she said. "I meant to get a couple licorice whips for my boys."

Matty frowned at the empty jar near her elbow. "Looks like we're all out."

"There's more in back," Will said immediately. "I saw 'em yesterday. I'll go and get 'em."

He fairly sprinted through the curtains into the back room. Then, in no rush to find the licorice and return, he lowered himself onto a crate, lit a cigar, leaned back and listened to the women bantering out front. The Crane woman had a voice like a consumptive

crow in a corn patch. But Matty! She was more like
a meadowlark in springtime. You didn't even have to
see her face to know she was beautiful. Her voice
alone conveyed it.

The crow was going on at some length about her
twins, Samuel and Hamuel, and wondering aloud if
Matty couldn't order a musical instrument or two just
in case one of the dear, sweet boys turned out to be
musically inclined.

The meadowlark, quite predictably, replied that she
would consider it. No doubt after she consulted with
Charlie.

Will sat up and dashed his half-smoked cigar on
the floor, then ground it with the heel of his boot. He
was developing a real dislike for Charlie.

"I'll just go see what's keeping Will back there,"
Matty said, having heard more than enough about the
terrible twins' untapped intelligence, hidden talents
and untried musical skills.

Licorice, my Aunt Fanny's backside. Lottie Crane
was here again to ogle Will Cade. In the week the
gambler had been here, Matty had seen more women
in the mercantile than she'd seen in church in a week
of Sundays. She didn't even know there were so many
females here in town. The silly, simpering things.

"Be courteous to all of our customers, Matty, no
matter the money they spend," Charlie always said.
"Even the ones who only buy half a spool of thread
or ask for just a single needle out of a paper case.
You never know when somebody's rich old Aunt So-
phronia or Uncle Spud might pass away and leave

them a fortune they'll be happy to spend in our store.''

It wasn't easy being courteous. She didn't appreciate the women fingering her chinaware and drooling all over her dry goods even if she did appreciate their business. Matty was half tempted to tell them her new assistant wasn't Charlie's cousin at all, but a black-hearted gambler and no-good cheat, just to see how fast they'd run the other way.

But, of course, she wasn't going to spill those particular beans. Will Cade was good for business, even if she didn't trust him half as far as she could throw him. Not that she wanted to throw him. He was, she grudgingly admitted, a pure pleasure to look at. It was something she did far more often than she should have, too.

Still, she'd have to be a dead woman not to appreciate the width of his shoulders and the suggestion of hard muscle beneath the fine white linen of his shirts. His eyes were a wonderful green with just a hint of gray in them, like the tender underside of leaves. His mouth was finely sculpted, and when he smiled—which wasn't often—his teeth shone a brilliant white against his skin.

And then there was his hair. Matty had never been to a beach, but she could imagine that Will's light brown hair might sift through her fingers like warm sand.

All week she'd been telling herself she obviously wasn't dead and that it was perfectly all right to look as long as she didn't touch, and now she told herself the same thing again, just as she pushed through the curtains that closed off the back room, and charged straight into the gambler's arms.

"Whoa, now," he said in that soft and silky Southern-spun accent of his.

For a minute, Matty couldn't quite catch her breath. She just stood there, her senses suddenly drenched in shaving soap and bay rum, her nose buried in the pure male scent of wool lapels where wisps of cigar smoke and hints of rye whiskey lingered. She was dizzy with it. Good Lord, she was nearly drunk. She raised a hand in order to steady herself, only to encounter a warm and solid wall of chest and the hard beating of the heart behind it.

How could something so wrong, she wondered, feel so absolutely right?

A moment later—or was it an eternity?—she lifted her chin, knowing even as she did that she was inviting his kiss. She couldn't help it.

"Ah, Matty," he whispered as his head dipped and his lips softly brushed against hers. "Matty, how I've wanted…"

His mouth closed over hers, stealing away what little breath she had left and kindling desires deep inside her that Matty thought were long put aside, if not entirely dead. Heat swept through her at the touch of his tongue on hers and the feel of his fine hands on her back, on her rib cage, on her breasts.

But then, as quickly as she realized her body was on fire, guilt rushed in to douse the flames.

"Stop it," she hissed, pulling back from the kiss she still craved. Then, before she even knew she'd moved, her hand came up to slap the gambler hard across his cheek.

To Matty's surprise, Will Cade didn't even flinch, but took the blow as if it were his due. He stepped back, rubbing his face, regarding her with a certain wariness.

"Next time, Matty," he said, "I'd appreciate it if you'd just *tell* me no instead of showing me. I know what the word means, I assure you."

"There isn't going to be any next time."

She felt a flush of hot and shameful color rise to her face, knowing the kiss wouldn't have happened at all if not for her silent assent, her unspoken invitation, her outright brazen behavior.

Will shook his head and murmured softly, "I wouldn't bet on that, darlin'."

"I wouldn't bet on it, either," she said, trying her best to sound as chilly and forbidding as the weather outside. "I'm not a gambler."

The smallest of smiles flickered at the corners of his perfectly carved mouth and the green in his eyes glistened. "Are you so certain about that, Mrs. Favor?"

She stiffened and scowled as if the remnants of his kiss had turned sour upon her lips. "I'm very certain, Mr. Cade. Now, if you'll excuse me, I need to find that licorice."

Chapter Three

That night in the Gilded Steer, while Will squinted at his cards through a haze of cigar smoke, he came to the conclusion that—like Matty—he wasn't really a gambler, either. At least not when it came to women. If he had been, by God, he wouldn't have stopped kissing her this morning.

He couldn't remember the last time a kiss had engaged his spirit as well as his body. Probably it was when he'd kissed Caroline goodbye before he went off to the war. He'd been with scores of women since then, and a few had set his body on fire, though none had rekindled his soul. Now, after all those long and spiritless years, that soul seemed to be stirring again.

Why did it have to happen with this particular woman? God knows he'd seen prettier women, and shapelier, too. He wondered if any of them would have had the courage or wits to step between him and a bounty hunter, conjuring up a dog named Pollifax to save him.

Why married Matty when the world was full of females who were unattached? Why did his conscience have to come alive and keep reminding him that she belonged to someone else? Why bother wanting what he couldn't have?

"You gonna play those cards you're holdin', Cade, or just sit there and stare at 'em?"

Will snapped out of his lovelorn trance, laid his pretty full house of queens and deuces on the table, and then raked in enough flimsy bills and change to pay for a few well-deserved shots of rye and his evening meal.

"I guess that'll do it for tonight, gents," he said as affably as any winner could, stubbing out his cigar, and then pocketing the cash and pushing back his chair.

Across the table, young Ben Hagadorn was quick to protest when Will stood up. "Aw, stick around a while, Will. Come on. Please. Just a few more quick hands. Give me half a chance to win back some of my money."

That wouldn't happen if he sat back down this minute and played straight through till next July, Will thought. The Hagadorn kid was the worst damned card player he'd ever seen. You could read his every hand in the expressions on his face. He was wont to roll his eyes and moan "Aw, spit" when he failed to draw a third card to a pair, and the kid grinned like a lit pumpkin on a windowsill whenever a flush panned out or he filled an inside straight.

"Yeah. Stick around, Will." Grizzled Vernon Foy aimed a stream of tobacco juice at a nearby spittoon, then laughed and said, "Young Ben here can't get into any more trouble with his intended than he already is."

Ben Hagadorn rolled his eyes and moaned. "Aw, spit. I'll be lucky if I'm married before I'm ninety-five years old at the rate I'm going. That durned silver dresser set at Favors' is so far out of my reach, it might as well be on the moon."

"Sally wants that bad, don't she?" Vernon said, shaking his head. "Wants it more'n you, young feller."

Will's curiosity was piqued at the mention of Matty's store and her prized dresser set. "What's this all about?" he asked.

Ben gave another hearty moan. "My girl, Sally, promised that she'd marry me as soon as I buy her that fancy silver set from the Favors' mercantile. I guess you know which one I mean, Will, seeing as how you work there."

Will knew exactly the one Ben meant in light of his aborted attempt to pilfer it the week before. The damned, frivolous, outrageously expensive thing had been sitting there for a year or more, gathering dust and tarnishing while it tied up assets that Matty could ill afford. When he'd asked her why she'd ordered it in the first place when nobody in town could afford it, she got all huffy and thin lipped.

"It's really none of your business, but if you must know, I bought it because Charlie told me to," she said. "Charlie knows exactly what he's doing. He has a long-range plan. I won't discuss it further."

Will didn't know about any long-range plans, but he knew if Matty sold the silly dresser set, there would be cash to invest in the much-needed new shelves, and maybe even enough left over to hire somebody to assist her in the store after he was gone.

By helping young Ben, he could help Matty in the bargain.

Helping. That was something he didn't ordinarily do. He'd made it his business these past few years to stay out of other people's way while he drifted from town to town. He rarely even knew the names of the men whose pockets he picked clean at cards, much less the ups and down of their love lives.

"It's a handsome piece of merchandise," he said. "It'll make a fine wedding present, Ben."

The young man rolled his eyes and gave a snort. "Sure. When my Sally's ninety-three years old. Lord Almighty, I hope she'll still have hair enough to brush by then."

"And a face that won't crack that fancy silver mirror," Vernon Foy added with a laugh.

Will pulled out his pocket watch and stared at it thoughtfully. "It's not as late as I thought. I've got time for a few more hands, I guess."

He sat back down, wondering just how a card shark went about cheating on another man's behalf. He supposed he'd learn as he went along.

"I'll deal," he said, flexing his fingers and reaching for the deck.

It was snowing the next morning as Matty trudged along the wagon tracks from her little house to the mercantile, muttering while she tried to keep her skirts above her ankles, slanting evil looks at the elegant new sign her competitor, Henry Diehl, had put up a month ago across the street. The red and gold letters, a foot high or more, fairly shouted that The

Emporium was a finer enterprise than the humble mercantile across the street.

It probably was, she thought with some disgust, gazing up at her own sign, which was definitely showing its age, not to mention the assorted ravages of Kansas weather. The sign's white background had yellowed considerably and the black lettering was starting to flake. Maybe when the weather cleared, she'd have Will paint her a new one with those finely fashioned, graceful hands of his. Maybe...

Maybe she ought to quit dreaming. When the weather cleared, Will Cade would clear out of here so fast it would make heads spin and feminine hearts grow heavy from one end of town to the other. Besides, she couldn't even afford the lumber or a pint of the paint or varnish it would take to fashion a fancy new sign. She couldn't afford much of anything at all with Charlie forever advising her to stash the profits away.

Matty sighed as she unlocked the front door. It was still dark inside the mercantile and the air held a pronounced chill. Will hadn't lit the lanterns yet or stoked a fire in the stove. In fact, Will was nowhere to be seen.

A sudden pain, sharp as a needle, pricked her heart. Was he gone? So soon? Before Christmas?

Without even taking off her cloak, Matty made a beeline for the counter and the cash box hidden there beneath the floorboards. She didn't even bother with the file she normally used to pry up the loose board, and broke a fingernail in her haste. But the metal box was still there, thank God, and still heavy with its sacred, untouchable stash of double eagles—all six hundred and eighty dollars of them—that she'd methodically put away week after week, year after year.

So, miracle of miracles, Will Cade hadn't stolen her blind before he'd gone away!

Matty slipped the cash box back into its cranny, covered it again and then sat there on the floor a minute, with her head bowed and her hands folded in her lap, feeling relieved and disappointed and foolish all at once. Her secret little fortune was secure, but what good was it when her store was falling down around her ears? What good was saving for some future rainy day when freezing rain was coming down right this very minute? What good was having feelings for a man who cared only for playing cards and moving on?

She might have sat there feeling sorry for herself all morning if it hadn't been for a knock on the door. Now who in the world was that before she'd even opened up? Matty sighed as she rose and went to the door. If it was silly lovelorn Lottie again, looking for Will, there was going to be so much disappointment in the air, it would probably be visible—like a huge black cloud hovering over both of them right here inside the store.

It wasn't Lottie, though. As soon as Matty opened the door, Ben Hagadorn bounded through it and nearly bowled her over as he headed toward the table where her prized dresser set was displayed. He picked up the hairbrush, held it over his heart, and said, ''I'll take it, Mrs. Favor. No need to wrap it.''

Matty blinked. She knew that Sally Garrison was yearning for the silver set, and that Ben had an equal, if not greater, yearning for the coquettish little blonde. But did he have the wherewithal to purchase it?

"I don't take credit, Ben," she said firmly, but still as kindly as she could.

"You don't have to, Mrs. Favor." He pulled off a glove, plunged a hand into his coat pocket and came up with a sheaf of bills, proudly waving them in Matty's direction. "I've got it all right here. The whole darned seventy-five bucks." He waved the bills harder while he grinned. "What a night! I was playing cards at the Gilded Steer and I couldn't lose. I just plain couldn't lose."

The mention of gambling sent Matty's mood plummeting again so that even the imminent prospect of recouping her investment in the dresser set didn't cheer her.

"How lucky for you," she said without much enthusiasm.

"Oh, I don't know about luck," he said while he gathered up the brush and comb and hand mirror. "I thought so at first, but after a while, I noticed there was a lot of winking and whispering going on around the table, and then it dawned on me that I was only winning when Will Cade was dealing the cards. It took a while, but when I'd finally won my seventy-five bucks about an hour ago, the fellas all yawned and laughed and wished me well and told me I'd be better off staying home with Sally from now on."

The young man looked about the store. "Is Will here? I'd sure like to thank him."

"No, he…"

"I'm here."

Will's Southern breeze of a voice preceded him down the stairs.

"And you can thank me by keeping out of places like the Gilded Steer in the future. Stay home with your Sally, young Ben. Play cribbage with your children and confine your wagering to matchsticks."

While Ben Hagadorn laughed and said he had every intention of doing just that, Matty simply stared at Will.

He was here!

He hadn't slunk off in the wee hours of the morning after all. She felt horrible for her earlier accusatory thoughts, but ashamed as she was, Matty couldn't prevent a silly smile from moving across her lips, no more than she could keep her heart from leaping up into her throat or her stomach from dropping somewhere in the vicinity of her knees.

Will Cade was still here, looking handsome as the devil even if he did appear not to have slept more than a single wink the night before. His sandy hair strayed across his forehead above those deep green eyes that were now prominently etched with red. A day's growth of beard shadowed his cheeks and jaw. The wrinkles in his gray wool suit hadn't quite hung out overnight.

Oh, but he was beautiful, Matty thought. Not that beauty, male or female, in any way compensated for lack of character, she quickly reminded herself.

"Morning, Matty," the gambler said softly, his gaze meeting hers now. There was something quizzical in his expression, as if he sensed her surprise at seeing him, as if her distrust wounded him somehow.

"Good morning," she replied stiffly, doing her best

to coax her heart and stomach back to their rightful places. "Ben tells me there was quite a card game last night. Or should I say this morning? I hope it won't interfere with your work today." She glanced meaningfully toward the unlit stove, and added "It's chilly in here."

"That it is," he said, a hint of sarcasm in his voice and a glint in his green eyes. "And more than any firewood's going to fix. Young Ben, if I were you, I'd hand my ill-gotten gains over right quick and take off with that fancy dresser set before Mrs. Favor decides not to sell it to you after all. She doesn't much approve of gambling." He aimed a knowing look at Matty. "Or gamblers."

"Yes, sir."

Ben Hagadorn practically vaulted over the tables between him and Matty, then slapped his sheaf of bills onto the countertop. "Here you go, ma'am. Seventy-five bucks. It's all here. Every red-hot cent. No need to count it."

He jammed the brush and comb and mirror into his coat pockets, then raced for the door before Matty even had time to pick up his money, much less begin to count it. But when she did gather up all the creased and crumpled bills, she couldn't help but notice a little tremor in her hands. Thirty of these seventy-five dollars was pure, unadulterated, long-awaited profit.

It occurred to her then that with the very same wad of greenbacks, young Ben had bought himself not only a dresser set but a bride, too, and Matty was about to buy herself a brand new sign, all thanks to Will Cade's dealing off the bottom of the deck.

She looked across the room where he was bent down, blowing into the stove to start the kindling.

"You're a devious creature, Will Cade." A little sigh broke from her lips. "That was nice, what you did for Ben and his Sally."

He turned his head in her direction. An odd smile played across his lips before he spoke. "Now that you've turned a healthy profit, do you want me to get the lumber for those new shelves today? The *good* lumber?"

"Yes. Let's get it. And paint and varnish for a new sign, too. A bigger sign than Henry Diehl's." She laughed. "I'm thinking of changing the name of the store, too, to something a bit more enterprising than plain old mercantile."

He stood upright, brushing soot off his hands. "Sounds good to me." Then he cocked his head. "Have you consulted Charlie about this?"

Matty blinked and sucked in a breath. No, she hadn't! And she hadn't planned to either because she knew that Charlie would tell her to salt the profit away for that confounded rainy day he was so fearful of. She wanted to decide this on her own.

The last time she'd made a decision without consulting Charlie, though, was when she'd rescued Will from the clutches of Luther Killebrew, and despite the fact that the man was still here today, there was no guarantee that he wouldn't be gone tomorrow. Or this afternoon. Along with her seventy-five dollars.

I'll just go and get that lumber and paint now, he'd say, and then he'd never return.

Maybe his letting Ben win in the card game wasn't charity for the lovelorn after all. Maybe it was a new and improved scheme for bilking the town without actually appearing to do so. The local gamblers would spend their ill-gotten gains in the mercantile, then Will would collect his loot from one convenient location, and no one would be the wiser or likely to send a bounty hunter after him.

Maybe behind that warm smile of his, Will Cade was laughing his head off at her.

Maybe she was the world's biggest fool. She was sure that's what Charlie would tell her if she dared consult him about Will.

"Never mind the sign," she said, primly folding the bills Ben Hagadorn had given her and sliding them into her pocket. Later, when Will wasn't looking, she'd stash them in her secret hiding place. "And never mind that lumber for the shelves, either. I like things just the way they are right now. And Charlie does, too."

Chapter Four

It was a good thing Mrs. Charles Favor didn't play poker for a living, Will thought, because every emotion she entertained promptly played across her pretty features like a banner headline on a newspaper. So far this morning she had been surprised, pleased, affectionate, excited, optimistic, cautious, then finally suspicious and downright distrustful. He didn't think he'd ever seen a woman's weather change the way hers did, or been so disappointed when a mood altered from warm spring to icy winter.

The sale of the dresser set that he'd hoped would delight her had only succeeded in making Matty glum. She had crammed Ben Hagadorn's seventy-five dollars into her hidden cash box as soon as she thought Will wasn't looking, and she didn't want to hear a single word he had to say about the wisdom and the long-term benefits of reinvesting profits in her store. She was a smart woman, for God's sake, but somehow her damned Charlie, in all his wisdom, had thoroughly convinced her that a dollar moldering in a cash box was worth far more than a dollar spent on any improvements.

Will briefly considered asking Matty for a little time off from work and going to consult in private with the great Charlie himself, then decided against the plan for fear his own face would betray his feelings for the man's wife, whatever the hell those feelings were.

So, since he wasn't going to be confronting Charlie Favor right away or purchasing any new lumber, and since Matty wasn't talking about profits or improvements or anything else, Will busied himself with reinforcing the old sagging shelves. It would be a major miracle if one of them didn't come crashing down on somebody's head before the year was out.

He was nailing a crosspiece under a shelf loaded with patent medicines, wondering why people insisted on paying outrageous prices for remedies they could just as easily have obtained in a shot of bar whiskey at their local saloon, when Lottie Crane came into the mercantile accompanied this time by her infamous sons.

The twins were bundled up against the cold, but Will could still make out their carrot-colored curls, the thousands of freckles that splattered both their faces, and the mischievous glint in all four of their eyes. They were ten or eleven, judging from their height, and weighed a combined hundred and sixty pounds of undiluted energy and pure trouble.

"Good morning, Matty," Lottie said before gazing fondly upward in the direction of the shelves. "Oh, hello, Will. My, don't you look tall on that ladder?"

Behind her counter, Matty's sweet mouth flattened

in a sour grimace and her forehead crimped with worry. "You'll keep those two boys on a very short leash, won't you, Lottie?"

"Well, of course, I will, Matty." She had each boy by the coat collar as she spoke. "For goodness' sake, you don't think for a minute that I..."

Contrary to their mother's promise, the twins jerked out of her grasp. Samuel went left, beckoned no doubt by the candy jars on the counter, while Hamuel veered right in the general direction of the hammers, saws and other implements of destruction. Or maybe it was the other way around, with Samuel going right and Hamuel left. From his perch on high, Will couldn't tell the difference.

"You act like the little gentlemen you are, boys," Lottie called somewhere in between them.

"Oh, Lord," Matty moaned.

Hearing that dire pronouncement, Will decided the time was right for him to descend the shaky ladder and make himself scarce in the storeroom for the duration.

But he'd barely parted the curtains that led to the back room when there was a resounding, almost sickening crash behind him.

"He's bleeding!" Lottie shrieked. "My poor child! Lord have mercy. He's cracked his head wide-open."

Matty shoved aside the toppled ladder that had narrowly missed cracking open her own head. Her first instinct was to shake her fist and scream *I told you so!*, but her better, more charitable reaction was to rush to the fallen hellion who lay sprawled and bloody amid dented tins and shards of broken bottles.

The floor was so slick with cough syrups and patent medicines she nearly took a tumble herself.

"There, there, Samuel," she cooed softly as she pushed her skirts aside and knelt down beside the boy.

"It's Hamuel," Lottie wailed. "My poor baby!"

Whichever twin it was, his face was practically unidentifiable for all of the blood that covered it. Matty was afraid that the child might indeed have cracked his skull. She reached out in an attempt to brush the boy's hair back from his forehead at the same moment that someone nudged her aside.

"Here. Move aside, Matty. Let me take a look," Will said calmly, squatting down beside her.

Then, while Matty watched, the gambler's exquisite hands performed a thorough but gentle inspection of Hamuel's person, pausing occasionally, at an elbow or a rib or a knee, to quietly inquire, "Does that hurt, son?"

"Nothing's broken," Will said at last.

"Are you sure?" Matty whispered behind her hand so Hamuel didn't overhear. "That's an awful lot of blood."

"There always is from facial and scalp wounds. The vessels are close to the surface."

Lottie, who'd been weeping inconsolably while she hovered above them, repeated Matty's question. "Are you sure, Will? Are you positive his poor little noggin is intact? Are you sure he didn't crack his head wide-open?"

"You look like you've been scalped, Ham," his brother said. "We oughta take him to the doc, Ma."

"That's a good idea," Will said. "A couple of

stitches will close those lacerations, and the boy will be just fine.''

"Doc Sedge is out of town,'' Matty said. ''He went to Kansas City for some medical convocation. Last week as I recall. He won't be back till after Thanksgiving.''

"Oh my God!'' Lottie wailed and wrung her hands. ''Whatever will we do?''

Matty looked at Will in the hope he'd have a suggestion. Up until this moment he'd been calm and competent in the face of this emergency, but now he appeared decidedly uncomfortable, if not downright nervous. A sheen of perspiration glistened on his forehead and above his upper lip. ''Is there anything you can do?'' she asked him.

"No.'' His lips tightened while his gaze slid away.

Hearing that, Lottie's hysterics increased tenfold. Both twins began to cry, and the blood on poor Hamuel's face started running pink, diluted by his tears.

Matty sighed. ''Well, I'm pretty good with a needle and thread. My last quilt managed to take first prize at the Ellsworth County Fair.'' She looked down at the bloody little boy and, none to her surprise, began to feel her courage waver. ''Of course, I've never stitched anything that was breathing.''

"I'll do it.''

Will sounded angry and confident all in the same breath, just before he started barking orders.

"Matty, get me a packet of new needles, the finest ones you've got, and some white silk thread. I don't want cotton. Samuel, you run outside and bring me half a dozen hard-packed snowballs. Lottie, you go sit someplace and stay out of my way, you hear?''

* * *

Will didn't pay his usual call on Mrs. Runyon and her bevy of soiled doves that night. Not that he hadn't seriously considered the benefits of a deep and sated sleep in the madam's big warm bed, but after a few honest hands of poker at the Gilded Steer, he had enough change to buy a bottle of rye, which he carried past the brothel and back to his frigid accommodations at the mercantile.

The cold and the grim dark of the attic suited his mood. He gathered all of Matty's soft quilts around him, leaned his head against a rafter and lifted the bottle to his lips, again and again.

It was his hope…no, it was his fondest and most deep desire, his heartfelt yearning, to drink and keep drinking until he had obliterated the memory of the events of that morning.

The crash of the boy's fall. The sickening smell of the spilled medications. The blood. The tears. The hand-wringing helplessness of those who couldn't help, who didn't know how to stop the bleeding, stitch the cuts or ease the pain. He knew how, but he'd sworn he'd never practice medicine again in any form or fashion, and he'd kept that vow with an almost religious fervor in the past few years.

He'd forced himself to walk away from epidemics that roared through little towns like wildfire. He'd turned his back on the victims of more than a few shootouts and barroom brawls, a burning hotel and even a train wreck or two.

If anybody shouted "Is there a doctor in the house?", Will had schooled himself to keep his face impassive and his hands folded in his lap. He had tempered those natural instincts of his to render aid and comfort, and had recreated himself as a by-stander, a do-nothing, the kind of man who turned a blind eye to distress.

His demons had finally banished his better angels, assuming he'd ever had any.

Will tipped the bottle again, trying to drown the vision that haunted him. It was worse today. So much worse. He could see it all too clearly.

He could see his runaway bride, his beautiful Caroline, as she lay on a bloodstained bed, abandoned and near death, struggling to give birth to his brother's child. It had taken Will nearly a year to track her down, and when he finally had, it was too late. It was too late to love her or to hate her, though he tried. Too late to save her or the child, though he had tried to do that, too.

Hadn't he? He rolled the cold glass of the bottle across his forehead, but it failed to ease the throbbing there.

Hadn't he brought all of his skill and expertise to bear in those last moments? Hadn't he done everything in his power to bring both Caroline and the baby through?

Or had he held back somehow? Had he killed her by withholding his skill and expertise?

Sometimes in his dreams, when he was back in that foul, infested room, he made no attempt to turn the baby from its dangerous breeched position. Instead, he would stand by Caroline's bed, gazing down at her suffering, breathing in and out, silently ticking off the seconds until she was dead.

Sometimes, in the darker dreams, he'd take a scal-

pel from his black bag but, rather than making a help-
ful incision, his hand would move to slice her throat.

Sometimes he'd simply sigh and walk away, closing the door on his wife's weak, depleted moans.

Sometimes—most of the time—he wasn't sure
what it was he'd actually done all those years ago.
His dreams and his demons seemed more real to him
now than the actual events. All he knew for certain
was that he'd buried Caroline along with her child,
and that he'd tucked his black medical bag, along
with all his goodness and his soul, into a corner of
the coffin before he'd left in deadly pursuit of his
brother.

This morning brought it all back with a bloodred
vengeance, and his attempt to wash the memories
away with rye was futile. The liquor was only making
his head pound and his stomach churn.

Setting aside the bottle, Will drew the quilts more
closely around himself and tried to think about Matty
instead, to let her sunset-colored hair and sky-blue
eyes drive all other thoughts from his brain. That
wasn't hard to do, but it only succeeded in making
him feel worse. He was no better than his brother,
Matthew, coveting another man's wife.

No. That wasn't true. He wasn't like Matthew at
all. He had no intention of acting upon those feelings.
They were dreams. Pure fantasies. Warm thoughts to
keep the cold away. Flickering images to light the
darkness in his soul.

So it was all right, he told himself, to imagine
threading his fingers through all that rich red hair,
kissing her delicate eyelids, skimming his knuckles
along the pale skin of her neck, feeling the beat of

her heart beneath his hands. And since it was pure fantasy, it was permissible to slip the buttons on her woolen dress, one by one by one, and to slide the fabric over her shoulders to expose the soft and fragrant flesh hidden beneath the sturdy gabardine.

His hands would find the sweet and succulent weight of her breasts, and his mouth would follow, savoring every taste and texture. Matty would sigh, an exquisite sound that would come from deep inside her, harmonizing with his own irrepressible groans of pleasure.

She would bow her head and her warm red hair would spill over him, closing like a velvet curtain, making it impossible to hear or to see anything but her. There would be nothing in the world but Matty, and he would enter her—slowly, gently—as if he were going through a door to a better life.

Will almost laughed out loud.

"You've had too much to drink," he muttered into the surrounding dark even as he was reaching for the bottle again. "That's a hell of a lot to ask from the act of love, don't you think?"

Somewhere deep in his besotted brain, he silently agreed. Then, at the same moment, he heard the crunch of footsteps in the snow outside and wondered what fool was out at such an hour. A second after that, a key jiggled in the lock downstairs, the front door creaked open, and Matty called softly, "Will?"

Will's heart surged. He lurched up, but then immediately hunched back down. Why was she here at this hour of the night? What did she want? How could he possibly trust himself to be within arm's reach of her right now, half-drunk and wholly in her thrall?

"Will?"

He didn't answer, but lay still with one eye slightly open to watch the yellow lantern light wash across the stairwell as she climbed, and with one ear cocked to listen to the oncoming swish of her skirts, the soft tread of her shoes and the thundering beat of his pulse.

At the top of the stairs she paused and shivered. "Lord, it's cold up here."

Not anymore, he thought.

"Will? Are you awake?"

He held so still he was sure he'd stopped breathing. But for the pounding of his heart, he might have imagined himself dead. What the devil did she want? No. He didn't want to know. It was enough to know what *he* wanted and what he couldn't have.

"Will?" she whispered a little more insistently.

She stood there for what seemed an eternity before she sighed and muttered a soft little curse, then turned and started back down the stairs.

The chill air in the attic was still replete with her sweet fragrance. The rafters were still vibrating from her presence.

So was Will.

Chapter Five

Matty awoke the next day still thanking her lucky stars and all the planets that Will Cade was such a solid sleeper. She'd gone back to the mercantile the night before with a plate of oatmeal cookies meant to cheer him and to erase his glum mood, the one he'd been in ever since Hamuel's accident.

At least that was what she'd told Charlie when she consulted with him at dinnertime about her unhappy assistant at the store. Taking him the cookies was a simple, kindly gesture, she had pointed out. It seemed the considerate thing for an employer to do. She was worried about Will Cade in a neighborly sort of way.

That's what she'd told Charlie. It wasn't exactly a lie. But it wasn't so easy for Matty to convince herself of those purely charitable intentions. She'd told herself that visiting the store so late at night had nothing to do with any feelings she had for the gambler. Yet, once she was there, waiting for Will to awake in that cold attic, listening to him breathe and seeing his handsome face just touched by lamplight, all of her nice and neighborly sentiments gave way to a longing so fierce it nearly brought her to her knees.

If he'd awakened...if he'd spoken her name...if he'd held out his elegant hand in her direction...

She thanked her lucky stars again while she ate breakfast, dipping an oatmeal cookie into her coffee, chewing slowly in order to postpone her walk to the mercantile, so afraid that Will would be able to read the traces of that longing on her face.

It wasn't right, what she was feeling for him, but she didn't seem to be able to stifle her emotions or slow down her heartbeat or cool her blood. At least not as long as they kept brushing shoulders in the mercantile day after day.

She couldn't very well consult with Charlie about this. It was one thing to ask for advice about friendly oatmeal cookies for an employee, but imagine asking her husband what to do about a gambler who'd come to town and set her heart aflame! Matty wondered just what his advice would be if she *did* ask.

Fire him.

It came to her in a flash. It wasn't Charlie's voice this time, but her own, somewhere in the back of her brain.

Get rid of him.

Well, of course. She was a fool for not thinking of it before this. Why keep suffering such temptation and guilt when all she had to do was say goodbye? Why wait for Will to disappoint her or even break her heart by slipping out of town, when she could take control by demanding that he leave immediately?

Fire him.

That was exactly what she intended to do.

"You've more than paid your debt to me," she'd say, even before she took off her cloak this morning. "Thank you for helping out these past two weeks, Will, but I won't be needing you anymore."

She'd pull off a glove and then she'd shake his hand in a businesslike way, all firm and final. She'd ignore the smooth length of his fingers and the fine shape of his nails and the warmth of his palm against hers. If necessary, she'd remind herself that his were the sly hands of a gambler rather than the competent ones that had stitched up Hamuel's head or the hands that had given her such pleasure in her unfaithful dreams.

"Best not shake hands," she muttered. "Don't touch him. Just tell him to go."

Matty came through the door of the mercantile like a flame-haired bat out of hell. At least that was what she looked like to Will, who was just finishing up the new shelves in place of the ones that young Hamuel had brought down the day before. It was the least he could do, he figured, before he told her he was leaving town. Leaving before something happened that the two of them would forever regret.

"Good morning, Will," she said, sounding like a schoolmarm and clutching her cloak around herself as if she were still out in the cold. "After a great deal of thought, I…"

Her words drifted off as she stared at the shelves, a fine example of carpentry if Will did say so himself. Matty, however, seemed more horrified than impressed. By now he was so familiar with, and so in love with, every expression that passed across her lovely face, he didn't have to be a mind reader to know what his pretty, parsimonious darling would say next. From the look of her, one foot was already on the doorstep of the poorhouse.

"What in blazes do you think you're doing, Will?" She let go of her cloak to stab a finger toward the shelves. "Take those down right now. This very minute. You know damn well I can't afford that finished lumber."

He wanted to wrap his arms around her, hold her close to his heart and tell her that she'd never be poor, not as long as he had breath in his lungs and an ace up his sleeve. Instead, he told her the truth.

"I'm leaving, Matty. Today. Just consider those shelves the final installment on my debt of gratitude."

"What do you mean?"

"I mean I traded my gold watch to old man Davidson for this lumber. You don't owe him a penny for it, and don't let him try to tell you any different."

"No. Not that." She waved her hand like a teacher erasing a cuss word from a blackboard, a woman trying to erase words she didn't want to hear from the air in front of her face. "What do you mean, you're leaving?"

Will forced the most engaging smile he could. "It's time to move on to greener pastures, Matty. Or maybe I should say greener pockets. You haven't forgotten I'm a gambler, have you?"

"No. Of course, I haven't forgotten," she snapped. "How could I forget?"

Annoyance flared in her eyes for a second, but then her expression changed to one Will had never seen before and her blue eyes brimmed with tears even as she began to laugh. Or cry. He couldn't tell exactly what she was doing.

"And here I was going to fire you this morning," she managed to say. "Only now I won't have that satisfaction."

"Fire me!"

Unable to speak now for the chuckles or sobs or whatever the hell they were, she just nodded her head.

Fire him! Why the devil would she do that? What had he done but help her here in this den of disorganization, this mercantile mess? Fire him! He'd been invited to leave gaming parlors, sometimes politely and sometimes not so politely. He'd even been escorted to the city limits once. That was back in Joplin, Missouri, as he recalled. But nobody had ever fired him.

Didn't she hear him say he'd traded his goddamn watch for the lumber her precious Charlie was too cheap to buy? Couldn't she see he'd do anything for her, including walk away?

"Why the devil were you going to fire me?" he shouted.

Matty was wiping away tears now and dabbing a hankie at her wet nose. "It really doesn't matter now, does it? You're leaving." She glared at him, the moisture in her eyes nearly boiling. "I knew you wouldn't last till Christmas."

"You knew that, did you?" Will kicked a board out of his way, then crossed the room in a few long strides and grabbed her by the shoulders. But all of a sudden, just touching her drained the anger from him. Instead of shouting at her, he whispered roughly, "Matty, don't you know I'd stay here for a thousand

Christmasses if you were free? Don't you know I'd
stay forever if you didn't belong to another man.''

She made a tiny gulping sound as her wet gaze
flicked up to meet his. She knew! She felt the same
way Will did. God help him, he could see it shining
there, like a treasure of diamonds in her eyes.

His heart slowed ponderously. Had Caroline looked
at Matthew this way? he wondered. For a painful moment, Will almost sympathized with his brother and
very nearly forgave him. Perhaps to deny these feelings was a sin far worse than any other. Surely being
in hell for loving Matty would be the closest to
heaven he'd ever get. He had one foot in brimstone
already, but he'd be damned if he'd take this beautiful
woman with him.

He traced a finger down her soft, moist cheek while
he slid a hand beneath her hair and curved it around
her neck. Her pulse leaped beneath his thumb like a
spark that could so easily set him on fire if he allowed
it.

"One kiss, Matty, my love," he whispered. "Just
one. For goodbye.''

Hello or goodbye, right or wrong, sweetest of
blessings or blackest of sins, Matty might have let
Will Cade kiss her forever if the front door hadn't
opened just then and Lottie Crane's cheerfully rau-
cous voice hadn't boomed out, "Good morning, all!''

Will breathed a soft curse against her lips before
he pulled away and then stepped back from her so
fast that Matty felt a rush of cold air slice between
them, one that seemed to penetrate all the way to her

hammering heart. The fact that he felt compelled to protect her reputation made it hurt all the more.

"Morning," Will said, sounding almost like his affable self again as he returned to his shelves. "What can I do for you, Mrs. Crane? How's young Hamuel today?"

If Lottie had witnessed their illicit kiss, she wasn't letting on. She gazed at Will as soulfully as always when she answered, "My sweet boy's doing just fine, thanks to you, Will. And don't you dare ask what you can do for me. Why, I sat up half last night wondering what I could do for you to show my gratitude."

For her part, Matty didn't know whether she felt furious or grateful, or whether this silly woman had just robbed her of heaven or rescued her from perdition. Both, she supposed.

She took off her cloak, shook it and gave a little sniff. "Well, if you're going to do something for Will, you'd best do it fast, Lottie, because he's leaving today."

The woman's face went pale except for her plump pink cheeks. Her little brown eyes rounded in distress. "Today! Oh, no! You can't do that, Will. You just can't! Tomorrow's Thanksgiving Day! I've come to invite you to dinner."

Brushing past Lottie, Matty slung her cloak on the hook on the front door. Thanksgiving! She'd completely forgotten about the holiday, but why should that surprise her? What on earth did she have to be thankful for? Will's imminent departure? Freedom from sweet temptation? The aching heart she undeniably deserved? A kiss goodbye? Right now, with the taste of Will's kiss still on her lips, she felt churlishly ungrateful.

On the other side of the counter, the gambler was making polite, deferential noises about why he couldn't accept Lottie's very kind and generous invitation, but Lottie was having none of it.

"Oh, but you must come," she insisted. "I'm cooking two turkeys, a ham, a huge roast of beef and three kinds of pie. There's enough food for a cavalry troop. Matty, you must come, too. I won't take no for an answer."

"Yeah, and don't forget good old Charlie," Will said, the affability gone from his tone and the honey in his voice suddenly turned to vinegar. "Hell, if anybody in this town appreciates a free meal, I'm sure it's Charlie Favor."

Lottie stood there looking confused all of a sudden, as if Will had just been speaking in Chinese. Matty wished he had been speaking in some foreign language or that Lottie had gone instantly deaf.

"Charlie Favor?" the woman exclaimed. "Did I hear you right, Will? Did you say Charlie Favor?" She turned toward Matty then, shook her head, and said, "Oh, Lord, you're not still going on about *him*, are you?"

"Never mind that," Matty snapped. "I'll come to dinner. What time? Five? Six? Just tell me when."

"Whoa now." Will came around the counter. "Wait just a minute here. Still going on about him? What do you mean, Lottie?"

Lottie was still looking at Matty with an expression that wavered between veiled disgust and undisguised pity while she shook her head slowly back and forth.

"I had no idea," she said. "I thought...well, I thought you were better, Matty. Truly I did. Everybody in town thought so."

Matty knew that look although she hadn't witnessed it in a long time. Oh, how she knew that look. *Poor Matty. Poor, daft Matty.* And she knew that "poor thing" tone of voice, too. As always, it made her see bloodred.

"I don't care what you or anybody else thought, Lottie Crane," she snapped. "And you can just stop looking at me that way. Right now. If you're here to make a purchase, do it. Otherwise—" Matty stabbed a finger in the direction of the door "—get out. Go on. And don't come back, either. Do you hear me? You or those two ungovernable young savages of yours."

Lottie's jaw, which had gone rather slack during Matty's tirade, snapped shut, but not for nearly long enough. The woman opened her mouth to draw in a shocked and aggrieved breath, and then she let it out in a torrent of words punctuated by flashing eyes, jabbing fingers and flecks of spittle.

"I wouldn't come back here if you were selling everything for a penny! Not even if you were *paying* customers to take your ratty merchandise away! And as for you...you ought to be carted off to an asylum, Matty Favor, and locked away till the end of your days. It's downright crazy, talking to a ghost the way you do and making believe he's alive! Why, it's just not natural! *Consulting* a corpse! The very idea!"

Lottie's face had gone a frightening purple, forcing her to drag in a deep gulp of air before she could continue. "If you ask me, I bet there never was any

Charlie Favor, dead or alive. The man never existed anywhere but in your addled head. I think you made him up when you came to town just so nobody would take you for what you really are. A dried-up old spinster.''

Matty felt her own face flaming all the way up to the roots of her hair. Her hands were fisted at her sides, and it was all she could do not to pull out Lottie's tongue and tie it around the woman's neck.

''Get out of my store,'' she told her.

Lottie sniffed, lifted her meaty chin and narrowed her eyes. ''I guess I know why you're so eager to be alone here. I guess I know what's on your mind. If I was a dried-up old prune of a spinster, I'd want to keep Will all to myself, too. I saw you kissing him, by the way. You should be ashamed of yourself, Matty.'' She snorted now. ''Why, whatever would your precious Charlie say?''

Matty was shaking. ''Get out!'' she shrieked. ''Get out and don't you dare come back. Ever.''

''With pleasure.''

The floorboards quaked as the big woman stomped toward the door, and when Matty slammed it behind her, the penny candy rattled inside the glass jars on the counter.

She stood there a moment, watching her cloak sway on the back of the door through a hot sheen of tears. She wasn't crazy. She wasn't! Dried up, maybe, and getting lonelier and very likely loonier by the year, but she wasn't a spinster and she…

Somewhere behind her she heard the soft clearing of a throat. Will! Matty had completely forgotten he was here to bear witness to her anger and humiliation.

She whirled around, ready to lash out at him, too. No doubt he'd gotten a real kick out of the spectacle she'd just made of herself. This was better than the circus! Will Cade—damn his handsome hide—was probably trying not to laugh his head off.

The look on his face was pretty much what Matty had expected. His head was cocked to one side, and there was a glitter of amusement in his green eyes while the corners of his mouth were toying with a grin. It made her furious and sad all at once, although it was the fury that got the better of her.

"Well, go on if you're going," she said, swiping with both hands at the hot tears she couldn't hold back any longer. "Go on like you planned. Get out of here."

Damn the man. He didn't move a muscle, but just kept smiling at her that way.

"I said get out," she shrieked.

"Tell me about Charlie," he said, his voice as slow as molasses and sweeter than a Southern breeze.

"There's nothing to tell." Matty whisked past him to take up her customary place behind the counter, feeling safer there somehow with three feet of wood between them. Safer, perhaps, but no less angry. "You heard what Lottie said. I'm a crazy person. A crazy, dried-up, prune of woman who should be locked up somewhere. She's probably right. Anyway, it's none of your business. You're leaving, remember? Goodbye, Will."

Still, he didn't move, but stood there grinning as if he were half crazy, too.

"I believe I'll stick around a while, Matty," he said. "If that's all right with you."

Chapter Six

That it wasn't all right with Matty didn't come as a total surprise to Will. Lottie Crane hadn't left her victim with much more than a few ounces of dignity and a shred or two of pride this morning, but the little redhead summoned up every one of those to lift a big glass jar of horehound candy and throw it halfway across the mercantile, just missing him by inches.

"Get out!" she screamed, following up the horehound jar with containers of lemon drops and peppermint sticks.

It was when she hurled her metal cash box at him that Will truly appreciated her distress. Standing in a sea of candy and coins and broken glass, he finally forced himself to wipe the grin from his face. It wasn't an easy task, considering his elation.

There was no Charlie Favor! Matty wasn't married after all. She was free! Dear God, Will had almost leaped over the counter and kissed Lottie Crane's red, ferocious face this morning when the woman had bellowed the astonishing news. Will couldn't help but think that if Lottie had come into the mercantile just half an hour later, he would already have left town, never to learn that no one stood between him and the woman he so desired.

Well, except for Matty herself.

"Get out," she screamed again, looking around for something else to hurl in his direction. "I mean it, Will."

He didn't think she was crazy. Will would have bet his life on that. He'd seen demented people, mostly in the war, and Matty just didn't fit in that same sad and misunderstood category. The crazy people he had encountered were either wildly agitated for no apparent reason, or they were motionless and mute as stones.

Matty was agitated, no doubt about that, but she seemed to have her reasons. So, if she wasn't crazy, what exactly was she, he wondered, other than beautiful and all of a sudden decidedly and deliciously unattached?

On the other hand, it struck Will as quite possible, even highly probable, that *he* might be the crazy one for deciding to linger here in Ellsworth rather than move on in search of his wife-stealing brother. His longtime pursuit of revenge, it seemed, had taken a sudden back seat to the pursuit of other, less bloodthirsty, but equally strong emotions.

He wanted her. Here. Now. He wanted her more than he'd ever wanted a woman before. He wanted to turn the lock on the mercantile's front door, sling Matty over his shoulder, carry her up the stairs to the bleak little attic, and then make love to her the way he'd dreamed of time and again. Sane. Crazy. It didn't matter now that he knew she was free. Whether he was worthy of her wasn't something he even wanted to consider at the moment while his body was nearly shaking with need. In an effort to control himself, he bent to begin extracting nickels and dimes from the broken glass and candies on the floor.

"Don't touch my money," Matty said fiercely. She was beside him now, flourishing a broom. "Stop it, Will. I mean it. I want you out of here right now. I don't need your help anymore. I don't need anybody's help."

To emphasize her point, she swatted him with the straw bristles. "And I especially don't need you smirking at me."

"That wasn't a smirk, Matty," he said, dropping a handful of coins into the cash box while trying to deflect the relentless broom. "That was a smile of anticipation."

"Just what is it you're anticipating?" She gave a less than dignified snort. "That I'll start foaming at the mouth like any decent crazy woman should?"

"Not exactly."

Will dropped a few more coins into the cash box, then stood, deliberately towering over Matty as he took the broom from her hands and let it fall to the floor. Then, before she could protest, he pulled her into his arms.

"I was anticipating something more like this."

Will lowered his head and kissed Matty the way he'd been longing to do ever since laying eyes on her. A while ago he had kissed her goodbye, believing he'd never see her again. Now he was saying hello with a kiss meant just as much to ignite her as to claim her.

He sampled the sweet warmth of her tongue and tested the soft give of her lips with his teeth, and the more he tasted her, the more he wanted her, the more urgent was his need to have her completely.

Matty's response was nearly as fierce as his. If she was crazy, then Will thanked God for her dementia. Her tongue met his almost feverishly while her body pressed against him, closer and closer, until he was forced to widen his stance in order to stay on his feet.

Then it was Matty who moaned in protest when he finally broke the kiss.

"I wanted you the moment I laid eyes on you, Matty," he whispered, taking her lovely, flushed face in both his hands. "I thought it was impossible. I was going to leave town before I made sinners of us both. But now..."

He smiled as he kissed her shining eyes and the sweet shape of her nose. He skimmed his lips across her soft cheeks and teased the corners of her eager mouth again. "Now there's no Charlie. Now you're free, my love. There's nobody, nothing keeping us apart. Let me stay, Matty. Let me love you. Everything's different now."

"No, it isn't," she said, biting her lips and blinking back the tears that were gathering again in her eyes. "You don't understand, Will. Nothing's changed. Nothing's different. I shouldn't have kissed you that way. I'm sorry."

"I don't understand," he said. "What are you saying?"

"It's Charlie."

"Charlie!" He rolled his eyes toward the ceiling, wanting to shake her in his frustration. "What the hell does he have to do with us? I thought the man was dead."

"He *is* dead, but that doesn't make any difference."

Will clenched his teeth, seeking the patience he didn't feel at the moment and making a conscious, even hard-won, effort not to exclaim "Are you crazy?"

Matty stood before him looking as earnest as she was lovely while she searched for the proper words. He sensed that whatever she was about to tell him, she meant with all her heart, perhaps with all her soul as well.

"Why doesn't it make a difference?" he finally asked, taking her trembling hands in his. "Tell me."

Despite the tears in her eyes, her voice was unwavering when she replied. "Because dead or alive, Charlie Favor's the only dependable thing in my life. Because he's a good man and I trust him completely." She shook her head sadly, then added, "Most of all, I trust him to stay. I don't care if he is a ghost or a figment inside my head. I won't betray him. I won't. Because long after you've moved on, Will Cade, my Charlie will still be here with me."

"Matty, I..." Will started to argue, then realized there was nothing he could say. He wasn't a good man anymore, but he had a shred or two of decency left, and as much as he wanted Matty, he couldn't lie to her and promise that he'd stay.

Matty closed the store at three o'clock that afternoon. With Thanksgiving almost here, business had slowed to a trickle. What good was staying open, she finally decided, when she probably didn't carry what any last-minute customer needed anyway? Most of her penny candy was in the trash bin along with the broken jars, and she'd sold her last vanilla beans and cinnamon sticks a little after noon.

On her walk home she tried not to think about Will. She tried not to picture him sweeping up the broken glass and candy and the last of the wood shavings from his newly installed shelves, or the way he had looked a while later when he came downstairs with his carpetbag in his hand and said he knew she'd understand why he couldn't keep on working so close beside her in the store every day.

Just because she understood didn't mean she wasn't disappointed, though.

"I guess you'll be leaving town," she'd said to him, barely able to look at him or to suppress an acidic *see—I told you so* trill.

"I guess I will," he'd answered somberly. "Sooner or later. I'll be at the hotel if you need me, Matty."

"I won't," she'd told him, but now the temptation to turn in her tracks and race to the hotel nearly overpowered her.

She imagined herself striding across the lobby, running up the staircase and down a hallway, then knocking on Will's door while her heart beat wildly in her throat and she searched for words to tell him it didn't matter about Charlie. Not anymore.

Charlie was dead. He didn't warm her with kisses or make her feel blissfully alive. How could he? Had she fit in his arms as perfectly as she did in Will's? Had his body felt so solid against hers? Had he ever even existed in the flesh? Sometimes—Lord forgive her—unless she consulted his photograph, she couldn't even remember what her young husband looked like.

I'll be at the hotel if you need me, Matty.

If she needed him!

She imagined herself standing breathless and nearly giddy before Will's door. She'd knock just once, and he would open it, stand there a moment looking handsome and unsurprised, with one of those cocksure grins on his lips as if he'd been waiting for her, as if he'd known she would come, the way a gambler knows a particular card will turn up to complete a winning hand. He'd open his arms to her and then he'd whisper like a Southern breeze and then…

"And then he'd leave," she muttered, glaring at the hotel door and trudging past it on her way home. What good was it to court happiness, knowing all the while she'd lose it? What good was coming fully alive, realizing she'd feel dead again so soon? Why gamble when all she'd do was lose?

She wished Will Cade had never come to town, or that she'd never spared him from the bounty hunter. She nearly wished, when she'd stood marveling at those graceful hands of his while they tried to steal her dresser set, that she'd shot him dead.

Once home, Matty didn't even bother taking off her cloak, but walked straight to the bedroom where she lit the lamp on the nightstand and then opened the drawer where she kept the framed tintype of Charlie. She kept it tucked away because it made her unbearably sad to look at it. Hearing his voice was one thing, but seeing his dear face day after day would have broken her heart.

She sat for the longest time, studying Charlie's straw blond hair, his pale and innocent eyes, the delicate line of his jaw and the almost fragile set of his shoulders beneath the rough blue wool of his uniform.

He was just a boy! He looked nearly young enough to be her son. A gangly boy who might amble through the door of the mercantile with a quarter from chores burning a hole in his pocket, calling her "ma'am" while he tried to decide between peppermints and lemon drops, slingshots and peashooters.

Matty looked up and studied her own face in the mirror above the dresser. Had she ever been that young? How long had that line been digging deeper and deeper between her eyes? How long since those eyes had lost the shine of high hopes and bright dreams of the future? Where was the girl who belonged to the boy in the tintype?

It seemed a thousand years ago, the day before Charlie was set to be mustered into the army, when they'd stolen away to say their secret, sacred vows before a justice of the peace in the next county, and then hurried home to spend their wedding night in the hayloft of the Favors' barn.

Matty's only memory of their lovemaking was the awkwardness of getting in and out of clothes. If there was pain, she'd quite forgotten after all these years. If there was passion, she'd forgotten that as well. Their coupling had more to do with their youthful dreams than their young bodies, anyway, and they spent the night whispering about going West, and the little store that would grow to be a big emporium and then, at last, an enterprise.

"We'll move up from penny candy and pickles and

soda crackers," Charlie had crowed, "to the finest silks and laces and the fanciest silver dresser sets that anyone could ever want. You'll see, Matty. Just you wait and see."

She didn't have long to wait, as it turned out, to see her husband's name on the list of soldiers who had fallen at Pea Ridge. She'd wanted to die, too, until she heard his voice so clearly.

You can do it, Matty. Go on with what we planned. It'll be easy. You won't ever be alone. I'll be there all the time, right beside you. I'll tell you what to do.

Now, nine years later and hundreds of miles west of that honeymoon hayloft, she wanted to tell him it wasn't as easy as they'd dreamed.

She wanted to tell him, if he didn't already know somehow, that despite all the consulting, the store was no closer to an enterprise than it was the day she'd proudly climbed a ladder and nailed the freshly painted sign above the door.

Buy that inexpensive lumber with the knotholes, Matty. No sense in wasting capital on shelving nobody ever sees.

That silver dresser set's a crackerjack investment.

Double up on flyswatters, honey. You can always count on flies.

A penny saved is a penny earned, Matty.

She wanted to tell him that his cheap shelves were wearing out from holding all the merchandise she ordered but couldn't sell, and the back room was full of flyswatters when what it should have held were affordable linens and basting brushes and pie tins.

She wanted to tell him that all the money she was saving for some distant rainy day wasn't doing her or the mercantile a bit of good right now. She wanted to scream that the metal box she kept hidden under the floorboards may have been full, but what good was that when her heart felt so poor and empty?

She ached to tell him about Will. A living, breathing, warm-blooded man. A man, all flesh and blood and beautiful hands! Not a seventeen-year-old boy who really didn't know her anymore. Who really didn't know much of anything at all when it came to running the store.

She gazed at his pale, boyish face again, tracing a finger across the sweet, clean-shaven image. The sadness she usually felt when she looked at him wouldn't come.

"I've tried so hard, Charlie, and so long to make our dream come true. I couldn't have done any of it without you. But, Charlie, I'm alive. I've learned a thing or two. And I'm not afraid anymore to be alone. Maybe..." She sighed. "Maybe it's time I stopped consulting and started thinking for myself."

Matty held her breath, half expecting the face in the photograph to frown in disapproval, listening for a distant clap of thunder, anticipating a stern reprimand from the voice inside her head.

But nothing happened. Charlie's face remained just as sweet and placid as always. The heavens didn't shake with thunder, and the voice inside her head was silent.

As silent as the dead.

Chapter Seven

Just because it was Thanksgiving didn't mean Will could find much to be grateful for. With families gathered together to celebrate their blessings all across town, the saloons and gambling halls had closed their doors for lack of customers. The sporting houses had followed suit. Mrs. Runyon invited Will to share turkey and all the trimmings with her girls, but Will declined, not being in the mood for female company unless it was Matty's. But she, of course, had made it quite clear she preferred the company of corpses to living, breathing men.

If the trains had been running, Will would have gotten out of town early Thanksgiving morning, but the Kansas Pacific was on holiday, too, so he stayed put in his room in the hotel with a glum meal that consisted of a dry ham sandwich, a few hard-boiled eggs and several bottles of warm beer.

While he ate, he considered his plight. Wallowing in self-pity had never really been his style, but the irony of his current predicament hadn't escaped him. Here he was, his life completely sidetracked by a faithless wife, longing for a woman who insisted on being faithful to a dead husband. God damn her. And God bless her, too. He was forced to admire Matty for that fierce loyalty even if it meant he was thoroughly miserable because of it.

He couldn't help but think that if his Caroline had possessed even a scant portion of such loyalty, he'd be back in North Carolina now. He'd be home, a staunch and respected pillar of the community, a good and happy man. He'd be Dr. William Cade, as he was meant to be, presiding this holiday at the head of a high-glossed cherry-wood table in a fine, candlelit dining room, smiling at his lovely wife and laughing out loud while he ostentatiously carved the big Thanksgiving bird, showing off Papa's renowned surgical skills to a captivated audience of hungry little green-eyed towheads.

There were little boys in crisp linen shirts and off-kilter silk cravats, squirming like young pups in their chairs. There were little girls sitting primly with blond curls as thick as sausages and green hair ribbons to match their sparkling eyes. He could feel their feet straying mischievously underneath the tabletop. He could hear their impish laughter and the cherubic murmurings of their prayers as they joined in saying grace.

For a moment he could see and hear it all so clearly. He held his breath, the better to preserve the vision of what might have been. It was the life denied him in the happy home he never had. He was seeing the children who were never meant to be.

Then, suddenly, the picture before him wasn't quite so clear. The woman who smiled serenely at the foot of the table seemed less and less like Caroline, more and more like…who? Was it Matty he was seeing all of a sudden? he wondered. And did the children gathered about the table all have her flaming hair and her sky-blue eyes? Was he looking at Caroline and a past that never happened, or was he seeing Matty and a future that might yet be?

So real was the vision, in spite of its shifting cast of characters, that Will was forced to blink in order to bring back the sight of his actual surroundings. It surprised him for a second to see the hotel room with its serviceable walnut furniture and printed list of rules tacked to the back of the door, to see the half-eaten sandwich in his hand and the bottle of beer on the bedside table. It surprised him even more that he was looking at these objects through a hot sheen of tears.

Ah, God. A good man might have been impelled to get down on his knees and pray for deliverance from past sorrows, to implore the Almighty to bestow only his most bountiful blessings in the future.

A good man would know how to earn Matty Favor's trust, if not her undying love.

Will Cade wished with all his heart and all his soul that he could be the good man that he used to be. But, expert gambler that he was now, he knew it wasn't in the cards.

During the next two weeks, Will made valiant and repeated attempts to leave town. But short of buying a pair of snowshoes and hiking east, it simply wasn't going to happen. Apparently leaving wasn't in the cards for him, either. If he'd been a superstitious man, he might have believed the Fates were conspiring against him along with the weather.

On the morning after Thanksgiving, the first time he tried to leave Ellsworth, a blizzard was mounting when he trudged past Matty's store on his way to the train depot. He could hardly see two feet in front of him, but he couldn't miss the huge paper banner pasted inside the mercantile's window. Big Christmas Sale it proclaimed in huge red letters.

Retracing his boot prints on Main Street, after being told the train had derailed in a snowbank twenty miles east, Will noticed that a second sign had gone up at the mercantile. Free Fly Swatter With Every Purchase. He couldn't help but smile. Good for her, he thought. That dunderheaded ghost she depended on was finally giving her some good advice. Matty might make a go of the business yet. If nothing else, her sacred cash box would be filling faster than ever before.

He longed to go inside if only to congratulate her for coming to her senses commercially, maybe even getting one of those flyswatters as a souvenir, when someone called his name. Will turned to see a man running toward him through the snow.

''Thank God you're still here, Cade. Lottie Crane says come quick. Her Samuel's run his sled into a tree.''

''I can't...''

''Come on. Hurry. Follow me.''

Will followed, cursing all the way.

In spite of the bad weather, Matty's business was so brisk that she was almost out of flyswatters. Even

Henry Diehl with his fancy sign on the emporium across the street couldn't compete with her now that she was pasting a new enticement on her window every morning.

She was giving away needles with the purchase of cotton thread. Throwing in one foot of ribbon for every four she sold. Measuring with the new *long* yardstick she'd made up from a scrap of Will's good lumber so that her customers got forty inches of fabric for the price of thirty-six. Wrapping gifts for free.

For the first time in her life she was making her own decisions, using her own experience in the store as a guide instead of relying on the advice of an inexperienced seventeen-year-old boy whose dreams had outpaced his practical knowledge.

Every morning she'd stand at her window pasting up a new sign at the same moment Will came by, carrying his carpetbag on his way to the depot. After a couple of days, she started calling out to him.

"Leaving town?"

"Trying," he'd call back.

Then she'd stand there, paste drying on her fingertips, her heart hardly daring to beat and almost afraid to breathe, until she saw him walking back.

"No train today?" she'd ask, trying not to grin.

"Tomorrow," he'd say. "For certain."

Matty blessed the terrible weather but wondered how long it could last. She would have consulted with Charlie about it, but he wasn't exactly an authority on weather, either, and besides he wasn't speaking to her anymore. When all was said and done, she guessed the farmer's almanac was probably more reliable than any man.

* * *

Two weeks before Christmas the skies over Ellsworth turned a brilliant blue and the sun beamed down as if it were making up for a month's worth of lost heat. When the whistle of the Kansas Pacific sounded in the distance, Matty stepped outside the mercantile into the bright sunshine to watch Will slog through the slush on Main Street one last time.

"Leaving?" she asked, shading her eyes from the brilliance of sun on melting snow.

"Trying," he said as he always did.

Matty stood there half an hour, until the whistle blew again and a cloud of steam rose over the depot to proclaim that the train was underway with Will Cade on it.

"Sorry you missed your train, Will," the stationmaster said, levering up from the bench where he'd been lying, the color at last coming back into his craggy face and his pulse rate diminishing. "I ain't had one of those spells in years. It just came over me all of a sudden. Out of the blue. If it hadn't been for you, I don't know what would've happened. I might've bit my tongue off."

Will heard the departing blast of the steam whistle a mile or so down the track, doubting that he could still run fast enough to catch up, wondering if he could "borrow" a horse from the livery and then, once he was on the train, hope the animal would find its way back to town so horse theft wouldn't be added to his crimes.

By God, he'd almost made it. He'd had one foot on the parlor car's metal step just as the old man had pitched off his stool with a seizure, and everybody simply stood around, not knowing what to do except to call for Will.

"There'll be another train tomorrow," the station-master said. "I'm mighty grateful, Will. I'll let you on for half the fare."

"Thanks," Will said. "See you tomorrow."

He ambled back through town, thinking the good people of Ellsworth could almost set their watches now by his comings and goings and comings back again. When he passed the mercantile, Matty came flying out the door. She looked as if she'd been crying tears of joy and relief, no doubt, at his presumed departure.

"Leaving?" she asked as she leaned over the hitching rail.

"Trying." He slowed his pace. "Tomorrow for certain."

"Maybe you'd like to come to my place for a farewell supper tonight?"

Will stopped. He studied her pretty face. She looked sincere enough. "With you and Charlie?"

"Just me."

Well, I'll be damned. "What time?"

"I'll close up here about five. Why not come by then and walk me home?"

"I could do that," he said, trying to keep his heart from breaking through his ribs, doing his best not to let his mouth slide all over his face in a smile of the grandest proportions. "I'll even bring a bottle of wine."

"That won't be..." The frown that started to instinctively possess her features suddenly smoothed out. "That would be real nice, Will."

Well, I'll be damned.

Will's boots barely touched the ground as he headed out toward the Gilded Steer for a quick game of cards and the money to offer Mrs. Runyon in exchange for one of her dusty bottles of French Bordeaux.

At ten minutes before five that afternoon, Matty closed the lid on her cash box and stashed it back beneath the floor. Just because she'd invited Will to dinner at some risk to her heart didn't mean she was ready to risk her life savings, after all.

At five she was looking out the window, eager to see the gambler's tall and graceful form coming toward her down the street. Maybe there was something to be said for gambling, she thought, feeling her heart race and her insides tie themselves into extravagant bows. Maybe he'd stay, but even if he didn't, she vowed she'd never regret taking a chance for once in her life.

At quarter after five, the lovely bows in her stomach tightened into knots and taking chances lost a good deal of its appeal. She glared at her fine new shelves, wishing she had the cash instead.

Finally, at five-thirty, when she was about to lock up—the store, her heart, everything—a man walked into the mercantile.

"I'm sorry. We're closed," Matty told him.

"Miz Favor?"

"Yes. That's right. Come back tomorrow."

"I brought you a message from Will Cade, ma'am.

He says to tell you he's sorry but he won't be able to join you for dinner tonight.''

"Where is he?" Matty demanded. "Has he finally left town? Or is he so deep in a streak of good luck at the Gilded Steer that he couldn't be bothered to come tell me himself?"

"No, ma'am." The man shrugged. "Although he did have a pretty good streak earlier this afternoon. Then he went to…well, I don't know if I should say, ma'am."

"Where?"

"Well, he went to Mrs. Runyon's. He said he was going to get himself a real fine bottle of wine. And that's where he is."

"He's at the sporting house." Her voice was almost toneless while she wavered between howling with disappointment or shrieking with anger at the insult.

"Yes, ma'am." The man reached into the depths of his coat and came up with a dark green bottle, which he held out to Matty. "This is for you. Compliments of Will. He says go on and drink it if you want to. He says you can send him messages at Mrs. Runyon's, if you like. He'll be there two weeks."

"Two weeks? In a sporting house?"

"Yep. Quarantine. Seems those poor girls have all come down with chicken pox. Shame, ain't it? And right before Christmas, too."

Chapter Eight

Will lifted the quarantine a day early so that Mrs. Runyon, along with poor Rosemary, Flo and Ilsebein could attend the Christmas service at the First Methodist Church on the one day it was fairly certain that peace on earth and goodwill to men would extend to hapless working girls, and perhaps even to physicians who had long ago lost their way.

The church was crowded so he sat in back with the madam and her whores, leaning into the aisle every once in a while to catch a glimpse of Matty up in the front row, sitting practically under the preacher's nose while the man went on at length about forgiveness and salvation, two subjects Will had had plenty of time to consider these past two weeks.

Maybe it wasn't in him to forgive his brother…yet…but he'd decided to stop looking for him. If there was any salvation to be had, it would be here in Ellsworth, carving out a life with Matty once he'd convinced her that he wasn't going to leave. If it took him the next fifty or sixty Christmases to accomplish that, then so be it.

Maybe he wasn't a good man, but by God he was a patient man, and he could wait as long as it took for all that stubborn loyalty of hers to shake loose from Charlie Favor and attach itself to him. She didn't trust him yet, but one of these days she would.

He was leaning out over the side of the pew, looking past the formidable bulk of Lottie Crane and contemplating the pretty wisps of red hair that peeked from Matty's bonnet, when another latecomer let in a blast of cold air from the church's double doors. Instead of settling unobtrusively in the back, however, the man sauntered down the center aisle all the way to the pulpit.

"Pardon me, Preacher," he said as he scraped his hat off to reveal long, greasy locks that looked vaguely familiar to Will. "This shouldn't take long. I'm looking for somebody."

Then the man drew his pistol, cocking it as he spun around to face the congregation. "Nobody move," Luther Killebrew said. "I'm looking for a no-good, cheating card shark by the name of Will Cade."

While Will debated the pros and cons of vanishing into thin air, the bounty hunter's gaze moved from face to face until it lit on Matty's. "How do, ma'am," he said. "Remember me? You pulled a fast one on me a month ago, but I've got me a picture now." He waved a piece of paper in her direction. "And the citizens of Leavenworth have upped the bounty considerably to a thousand bucks."

A murmur riffled through the crowd as hats tilted and heads bent together. On Will's left, Mrs. Runyon whispered, "Here, honey. Take this." The madam slid a little nickel-plated derringer from her reticule and pushed it into his hand.

Up by the pulpit, Luther Killebrew was grinning through his greasy beard and aiming his gun directly at Matty. "Now where's that dog-bit dandy?"

Will stood up before Matty had a chance to answer. "I'm right here." He dropped the little one-shot back in Mrs. Runyon's lap. A few months ago he might have used it to hold the bounty hunter off, but now he was unwilling to risk any harm to the church-goers. It was bad enough that his problems had spoiled their Christmas service. It was worse that his tribulations had sullied Matty's life. By God, she'd been right not to trust him.

"I won't give you any trouble, Killebrew," he said, holding out his wrists. "Just put the cuffs on and let's go."

The bounty hunter strode toward him. "I'm glad you're a man who knows when he's licked, Cade." He clamped one metal circle around Will's proffered wrist.

Matty sat in the front pew, trying to get herself to move, but her whole body had gone numb. She couldn't breathe. She couldn't even think.

She hadn't even known that Will was here in the church until she'd heard his rich, warm voice telling Luther Killebrew that he was giving up without a fight. And now, after longing to see him for two in-terminable weeks, she couldn't move. She couldn't speak.

Once she'd used her wits to rescue Will from the bounty hunter, but now—now when her whole life seemed to hang in the balance along with his—her brain simply wouldn't function. She couldn't even pray. And then, as if by instinct, she murmured, "Charlie, what'll I do?"

And then the oddest thing happened.

"How much are those people paying you to bring Will in?" Mrs. Runyon's voice rose above the general commotion. "How much? A thousand dollars?"

"That's right," Luther Killebrew growled in reply.

"We can do better than that," the madam said. "I've got fifty dollars here. That's a decent start. And it's hardly enough for what Will did to help my girls while they were all so sick. What do you say, folks? I know you all don't think so much of me, but are you going to just stand there and let this varmint take a good man like Will Cade away?"

Whispers rippled through the congregation, and nobody seemed to know just what to do until Lottie Crane stood up directly behind Matty.

"If it hadn't been for Will, both my precious boys might have bled to death. I'll pledge a hundred. Fifty for each of my boys."

Nearby, old Tom Sturgis, the stationmaster, stood. "He's a good man, Will is. He got down off the train to help me when I was having a fit. Here's a double eagle for the pot."

Up in his pulpit, the preacher cleared his throat. "Shall we pass the collection plate?"

"I'll pass it," Ben Hagadorn piped up. "And I'll put in a silver dresser set I never would've had if it hadn't been for Will. My Sally'll marry me anyway, won't you, Sally, darlin'?"

"Well, of course I will, you silly thing," said Sally.
"All you had to do was ask."

One by one, people stood to offer their fives or tens
or twenties, accompanying each donation with a story
about something Will had done for them and what a
good man he was. Ben Hagadorn worked his way
through the crowd and then brought the collection
plate up front. You could have heard a pin drop while
the preacher counted it.

"Four hundred and forty-five dollars," he announced.

"That's not enough," Luther Killebrew shouted.
"Come on, Cade. Let's go."

Oh, Charlie, what'll I do?

"Just give me a minute to say goodbye to somebody," Will said, searching over the heads and shoulders of the crowd for Matty.

He'd watched her while young Ben passed the collection plate, and hadn't been at all surprised that, true
to her skinflint nature, she hadn't reached into her
handbag to come up with a contribution the way the
others had. To say he was touched by their generosity
didn't even begin to describe his feelings. He was
truly humbled. Their testimonials almost made him
believe he was the man he once had been. He only
wished that Matty believed it.

"Has anyone seen Matty Favor?" he called out.

"Matty? She left by the side door a couple of
minutes ago," somebody said.

"Come on, Cade." Luther Killebrew grasped
Will's arm. "Let's go."

The bounty hunter spun him around, and there was

Matty standing in the church door, pink roses on her cheeks and her cash box in her hands.

"There's six hundred eighty dollars and fifty cents in here, Mr. Killebrew." She shook the metal box, and Will almost thought he was hearing sleigh bells instead of the clattering of coins. "If I've got my math right," she said, "that means we're offering you over eleven hundred dollars to get on the next train out of town—alone—and never come back to Ellsworth again."

"Well..." Luther Killebrew scratched his jaw.

"It's a good deal," Matty told him, putting the cash box in his hands. Then she lowered her voice to a whisper. "I'd take it if I were you. And quick, too. Before somebody decides it would be a lot cheaper to put an ounce of lead into your heart."

"You've got a point, little lady." He stowed the box under his arm while he unlocked Will's handcuffs. "Merry Christmas, Cade. Guess I'll just have to tell the fine folks of Leavenworth that the bad hombre they're looking for is dead."

It was snowing again as Will drew Matty's arm through his outside the church. With all the cheers and hurrahs and "for he's a jolly good fellow" they'd hardly had a chance to speak.

"You're a gambler, after all, Matty Favor," he said softly, matching his steps to hers.

"I guess I am, at that." She laughed. "Come home and have Christmas dinner with me, Will."

"I'd like that, Matty. And next Christmas, too. And the ones after that, if you'll have me."

She smiled and hugged his arm affectionately, but

Will wasn't sure if she recognized it as a proposal of marriage. Later, he thought, he'd get down on his knees and ask her properly.

They'd only walked a few feet farther when she stopped to look up at him. There was a challenge in her eyes, but there was the glow of love, too. "You're staying, then?"

Will wanted to laugh. "I'm trying."

"Are you asking me to marry you, Will?"

"Yes, Matty, I am." Taking her face between his hands, he bent to kiss each corner of her pretty mouth. "Take all the time you need to answer, darlin'. Do you need to consult with anybody first?"

He'd asked that in jest, but Will found he was holding his breath as he waited for her reply. Then, when she said she did have to consult with somebody, he felt his heart sink inside his chest and his happy countenance turn upside down.

"Oh, Will! What's wrong?"

"Charlie," he said. "I thought...I hoped..."

"I'm not consulting with Charlie. Anyway, he's not talking to me anymore. I haven't heard a peep in weeks."

"Well, if you're not consulting with Charlie, then who...?"

"The preacher." Matty grasped his hand and pulled him back toward the church.

LIZ IRELAND

is the author of both contemporary and historical romances. She became fascinated by the pioneers who settled on the prairie by reading such great women writers as Laura Ingalls Wilder and Willa Cather. A native of Texas and a recent immigrant to the wilds of Portland, Oregon, Liz lives with her husband, two cats and two dogs.

COWBOY SCROOGE
Liz Ireland

Chapter One

Texas, December 1885

By the time the train began its slow, noisy entrance into Otis, Texas, Ivy Ryan had absolutely and completely changed her mind about marrying a total stranger.

"And I'm not going to feel guilty about it, either," she said resolutely to herself.

Sure, back when she was moldering in the Boston women's jail, desperate for any scrap of newspaper she could lay her hands on to read, Josiah Murphy's advertisement for a wife had seemed heaven-sent, the answer to all her problems. Marry a self-described handsome businessman? In a state where no one, least of all her husband-to-be, knew she was a jailbird? Oh, yes—a dandy idea!

Now it seemed more like madness. Her change of heart had nothing whatsoever to do with the fact that she didn't love Josiah. Love was a fairy tale. The one time Ivy had kidded herself that she was in love, her handsome prince, Zack Hamilton, had turned out to be a pickpocket whose exploits landed *her* in jail. But when she'd accepted Josiah's proposal, not to mention the train fare west, she hadn't anticipated how isolated the world out here would be. How foreign. Details she hadn't worried about from two thousand miles away scared the daylights out of her now—Indians…rattlesnakes…a husband she'd never clapped eyes on.

After all, if she had misrepresented herself to Josiah Murphy, he'd probably done the same. Handsome, he'd said? Businessman? In a godforsaken place like this? He was probably a toothless old geezer living in a shack! Why else couldn't he find another woman within two thousand miles to marry him?

So that was that. She'd changed her mind. Josiah Murphy would have to lump it and find himself another bride. Also, because she didn't have a penny to her name, he would have to pony up more money for train fare to get her back to somewhere civilized. Somewhere big. Populated. Snakeless.

When the train finally lumbered to an ear-splitting stop in front of a lean-to that served as Otis's depot, Ivy stepped off and gripped her carpetbag uneasily. "What the…?"

A crowd had gathered. In fact, it would appear that the town's entire population—all twenty of them—had turned out to meet the train. Was a train's arrival all these poor souls had for entertainment? Weather-beaten faces stared at her in anticipation, as if they expected her to break into a song and dance.

"Ivy Ryan?"

A squat, ruddy-faced man broke through the crowd and bustled up to her, smiling tentatively. Good heavens, it was worse than she'd feared! He had teeth, all right—brown ones—but he barely reached her height, and when he removed his hat he revealed a head as bald as an egg. She felt no qualms whatsoever about jilting him now. But she had to be nice to him, at least till she got her mittens around that train fare she needed.

She gritted her teeth and held out her hand. "Mr. Murphy?"

"Uh...no." The man's smile faded. "My name is Nulty. Mayor Douglas Nulty."

"Oh." Ivy bit her lip. She hoped she wasn't going to have to stand around jawing with this chowderhead forever. For one thing, it was high noon and the sun was beating down on her back. The wind was a little chilly, but she was dressed for winter in Boston—not whatever this was. You'd never guess Christmas was just a little over three weeks away.

The train pulled away, rumbling and screeching, making Ivy nervous. Would there be another train through here soon? It didn't matter which way it was going; she was going to be on it. She wanted to start a new life, but one glance around this dust trap was all it took for her to know she didn't want to begin it here. She stood on tiptoe to try to see over the heads of the crowd. Where the heck was Josiah?

The mayor blocked her view and stammered nervously, "I'm afraid I have some rather bad news for you, Miss Ryan. You see, your husband...that is, your *intended*, is..." The man wiped his brow with a yellowed handkerchief, then kept on going and wiped his whole bald head.

Drunk, Ivy finished silently. How typical! Her own

father had always gotten drunk on his wedding days.
Josiah was probably passed out on the nearest bar
stool. Irritation coursed through her as she tapped her
foot impatiently. "Yeah?"

"Well he's..." Nulty gulped. "Dead."

Surprise bolted through her. "Dead!"

The mayor nodded gravely. "Killed. There was an
argument involving money...and liquor, I'm
afraid...and..."

Ivy watched the man's lips moving, but she
couldn't say she actually heard what he was saying.
Josiah Murphy was dead! For a moment, her legs
went rubbery with relief—if he was dead, he certainly
couldn't pressure her to marry him—but just as
quickly, panic overcame over her.

Merciful saints! Josiah was dead...and she was
stuck. In Otis, Texas. Without a cent!

Her whole body felt numb, and she barely noticed
as the mayor, still droning on, shoved something at
her. "After his untimely demise, we found this ring
in Josiah's pocket," he stumbled on. "We, the people
of Otis, thought you should have it as a token of re-
membrance."

The band that had been placed into her limp hand
sparkled in the sunlight, resurrecting her spirits and
her wits. Goodness' sakes, it even had a diamond chip
in it! She felt almost dizzy as she rocked from despair
back to hope. The ring might not hock for much, but
it was something. Enough to get her out of Otis, at
least. Tears of relief welled in her eyes, and she
gushed with gratitude. "You don't know what this
means to me!"

"You have our deepest sympathies, my dear."

Ivy wiped her tears away and tried to remember…the mayor said Josiah had been killed over a money matter. If he could bring an entire town out to meet his would-be widow, maybe Josiah *did* have money. She'd never known strangers to show such kindness to someone unless that someone had money.

She straightened, resolving to play her hand for all it was worth. When she spoke, she injected an emotional quaver into her voice. "Thank you so much, Mayor Nutly."

"Nulty."

"Oh yes." She looked demurely over those assembled. "Thank you all so much. I'll never forget the kindness of the good people of Otis. Naturally, I'm heartbroken. Shocked. But I want you to know I'll cherish Josiah's memory." She sniffed for effect. "And of course, if there's any little thing I can do, any matter regarding my beloved's estate…that is, if he left anything behind…" She glanced back at Nulty. "You understand?"

The mayor grinned. "Indeed I do, Miss Ryan. And I must say, he *did* leave something else for you."

Ivy's heart beat like a rabbit's. She'd heard of good luck, but this was too much! The mayor took her hand and the crowd parted for them, as if she were a queen and they were her subjects. *What did Josiah leave me?* she wondered greedily. A house? She'd always dreamed of having a house! No more landlords barking for their money every week, no sharing facilities with filthy neighbors, no…

"Here you are, Miss Ryan," the mayor announced with a flourish. "Josiah Murphy's legacy."

Ivy came to an abrupt halt and spun on her heel,

confused. She didn't see anything. They were just standing on the edge of the dusty street, such as it was. "What is this, a gag?"

Mayor Nulty repeated his grand gesture so that this time Ivy focused on three towheaded children standing beside them. She hadn't taken any more notice of them than she would have three scrawny cats skulking in an alley. "Joe Junior, Sophie, Linus—meet your new mama!"

The children directed unblinking glares at her.

Ivy's mouth dropped open in horror. She was paralyzed, speechless, stunned. She'd never seen such filthy ragamuffins. They were different ages—the oldest around ten, the girl seven or eight, and the littlest boy perhaps four—yet they were undoubtedly of the same undesirable tribe. All had limp, colorless hair, sun-reddened skin, and cornflower-blue eyes. They were also scrawny thin, with knobby knees and elbows poking out of the holes in the patched and re-patched soiled rags they wore. They resembled human weeds more than actual children. And the mayor was saying *she* was now their mother?

"Oh, no! No sir!" She took a step back and began shaking her head, flapping her hands and stuttering out every form of negative she could think to utter. She wasn't about to be trapped into this! "These kids are not my responsibility!"

Though she was practically shouting, the mayor seemed not to hear. "Joe Junior, ain't you gonna say hello to your new mama?"

"Stop calling me that!" Ivy exclaimed. "I'm not their mama! Josiah never even told me he had kids!"

Nulty just chuckled. "But surely you like children, Miss Ryan."

She put her hands on her hips. "Wrong again, Nutly. I took care of my sister and three little brothers and don't intend on minding a stranger's whelps now. Not a chance!"

The mayor was beginning to appear more desperate. "Sophie, Linus—don't you have a greeting for Miss Ryan?"

The little girl followed her older brother's lead and squinted in proud, mute hostility at Ivy. But the littlest, on whose face mucus and dirt had combined to form an elaborate mask, swaggered right up to Ivy. After a moment's intense thought, he reached back his leg then let fly at Ivy with a swift kick to her shin.

Ivy jumped back, yowling in pain. "Ouch! You little bugger!" The boy darted out of her reach.

"There now!" the mayor exclaimed approvingly. "You're getting acquainted already."

"Acquainted, my granny! That little kid comes near me again, I'll whale the tar out of him."

"I can tell you have a real way with children." Nulty turned back to the crowd. "It's all settled, folks. The Murphy brats—er, children—will trouble us no more."

A heartfelt cheer went up among the citizens of Otis. Ivy could just imagine what kind of *trouble* he was talking about. Towheaded scamps is what these kids were! When the townspeople began to retreat, she stumbled after them. "Listen, you!" she called to the mayor. "You can't do this! These kids aren't mine!"

He waved a pudgy hand dismissively. "They aren't ours, either, Miss Ryan."

"But they must have some other relatives!"

He shook his head. "None. At least, the children don't seem to know if they do or not. They don't talk, you see."

Marvelous! "But—"

"He *was* your intended, wasn't he?"

"I'd changed my mind, damn it!"

"But he spoke most eagerly of your arrival."

"I'll bet!" The man had obviously spent his last dime trying to import some sucker of a woman to look after his three little angels. She shook her head then looked down at the ring in her hand. "Here, take this back! I don't want the man's ring *or* his kids!"

The mayor drew back as if the ring were poison. "You can't put the children out on the street. Don't you have a heart?"

He was a fine one to talk about heart! "Heart!" She practically spat the word. As far as she could tell, *heart* was what caused most of women's problems. Wasn't losing her heart to that pickpocket Zack Hamilton what had landed her in women's prison? "What's heart good for? I don't have *money,* Mr. Nulty, and I don't want any kids. I wasn't even planning on staying here in Otis!"

The mayor raised his brows in surprise. "Oh, we don't want you to stay here—good gracious, no! We expect you to take the children and leave."

She sighed in frustration. "Haven't you been listening? I have no intention of keeping Josiah Murphy's brood. And even if I did, I wouldn't have the money to leave here. I don't have *any* money. Not a red cent!"

"Frankly, Miss Ryan, that isn't our problem."

"It will be your problem if me and these kids are stuck begging on your streets from now till doomsday!"

Nulty's brows knit together and he convened an impromptu conference with several of his townspeople. When he turned back around, he beamed broadly at her with his stumpy teeth. Ivy assumed this meant more bad news.

"The good people of Otis have agreed to take up a collection for your behalf. Be at my office tomorrow morning."

Ivy stamped her foot in frustration. The man had her between the devil and the deep, and he knew it. If she took this money, she would be accepting responsibility for these kids. But if she didn't take it, what was she going to do?

As if seeking advice, she looked at the Murphy children, but three pairs of pale blue eyes squinted back at her impassively. It was almost as if they didn't care whether anyone helped them or not. They were steeled for disappointment. Expecting it.

As much as she wanted to turn and run, money or no money, and head for the hills, she just didn't have the...

Heart. Damn! Maybe she was crazy, but something in those dirty little mugs of theirs tugged at her at just the wrong moment, clinching her fate.

Not as if she had any choice in the matter. She needed that Otis collection as much as they did. She

and the three Murphy orphans were joined like two
cars on an ill-fated train.

"Where's your office?" she asked the mayor resentfully.

Nulty pointed to one of the weathered gray buildings that lined the single street of Otis. "There." The
building's sign read Dentist & Undertaker.

She crossed her arms as gloom settled over her.
How appropriate! She might need an undertaker herself after a day with these kids.

By sundown Ivy knew without a doubt why Josiah
Murphy couldn't find a woman within two thousand
miles to marry him. She was exhausted. All day she'd
been running. Running from the barber whose window Joe Junior had broken. Chasing after Linus, who
scampered off every time her back was turned. Evad-
ing the merchant from whom Sophie had swiped an
apple. Frankly Ivy had been shocked at the girl's resourcefulness. Other than her theft, Sophie's main oc-
cupation was to stand stock-still and squint angrily at
her new keeper until Ivy wanted to scream.

So far not one of them had spoken to her. She
would have doubted they could talk at all except
she'd heard them whispering among themselves when
they thought she wasn't paying attention.

A mere seven hours after she'd arrived in Otis, Ivy
wanted nothing more than to remain collapsed in the
unraveling cane-back chair and bemoan the day she'd
ever left Boston. Josiah's landlord had informed Ivy
that Josiah had died thirty dollars in arrears, a debt
the landlord was willing to forgive as long as Ivy
promised to vacate the premises the next day. She was

ready to vacate the man's rat-infested fire trap that very instant, except she wouldn't have money till tomorrow. And once she had some money, she didn't know where she was going. And even if she did know where to go, she couldn't go anywhere till she found Joe Junior, who had vanished sometime around dusk. Just vanished!

She looked down wearily at the remaining two snuggled on the bare mattress like two puppies and wondered whether these could be the same children who'd run her ragged all day. She'd thought Linus, with his ability to dart off and squeeze himself into impossibly small hidey-holes like a cockroach, would never run out of steam. And it was a relief to be spared Sophie's glare, which seemed to pierce right through Ivy, exposing her flaws. Of which there were many.

Oh, Ivy admitted it. She'd never been the best daughter, sister or friend. Too busy looking for an angle for herself. Growing up in mostly two room flats with four siblings tended to make her dream of escape. And when she finally had gotten out and was making a little money for herself as a maid, she'd met up with Zack Hamilton. The cocky young fellow had promised her the moon, then plunged her back down to reality in a great big hurry. Jail was about as realistic as Ivy cared to get.

The irony was, sitting in a cold cell with five other women, she'd actually missed that two-room flat with the folks at home. She missed her family now, too, especially little sister, Carol. Though only two years younger than Ivy, and shouldering responsibility beyond her years, Carol had always had a laugh ready when things seemed the most bleak, a song on her lips when the day was at its dreariest. Months ago, Ivy had hoped to make good in her job so she could buy Carol a few nice things. Maybe a new dress for Christmas.

So much for that cockeyed dream.

She pushed herself reluctantly out of her chair to embark on her hunt for Joe Junior. Some leftover instinct from her years at home made her scan the room with an eye to the children's safety. The meager fire she'd managed to build had burned itself out long ago, and Sophie and Linus wouldn't awaken anytime soon. There were no locks on the doors, yet she doubted there was a criminal wandering around Otis with an eye to kidnapping Linus or Sophie.

If there was, good luck to him.

When she crept out of the shack, she wrapped her coat tightly around her against the chilly wind. What a place this was! Land as flat as a pancake, where the sun beat down warm during a December day then turned into a cold blast after dusk. She couldn't help harkening back to Boston, which was at least predictably miserable all winter long. Maybe now there was fresh snow on the ground and air pungent with the comforting, homey smell of chimney fires. Soon men would be stacking up spindly cedar trees on street corners for people to transform into Christmas trees. Otis definitely lacked a festive, holiday air.

Then again, Otis lacked everything.

She walked along toward town, peering into corners of houses for signs of Joe Junior. She poked her head into the one barroom in town, but didn't see him there. She investigated the town from one end to the other—not much of a task—and wound up at the lean-to by the train tracks. Where the heck could Joe Junior have got himself off to?

She heard a cough and whirled in the direction of the sound, startled. Sophie, her blue eyes as big as saucers, stared at her steadily from about five feet away.

Had she been following her all this time? Ivy was about to tell the girl to go home when suddenly Sophie spoke to her for the first time.

"You're leaving us, aren't you."

The words, though spoken in a child's voice, were uttered in a tone of stark desolation and finality—the resignation of a child used to a hard life that was just about to turn a little bit harder.

Ivy knew it well. One day about six years ago, she'd awakened to find her second stepmother gone. Not that there was any love lost between that old bag and herself, but at least the old bag had been someone older, someone who could help them. Without her stepmother, most of the responsibility for the family had fallen onto Ivy's shoulders, then Carol's.

Ivy closed her eyes, willing herself to stop thinking of her family, to stop the band that seemed to be squeezing around her chest. But when she opened them again, Sophie was still staring at her implacably. And that band squeezed a little tighter.

If she'd been smart, Ivy would have left Otis straight away, Mayor Nulty and his child-sluffing scheme be damned. Or maybe tomorrow, when the mayor handed her the town's collection, she would have hotfooted it for the nearest town big enough to have an orphanage and dumped her charges on anyone who would take them. A part of her would have liked to think she was at least that good at looking out for herself. Because she honestly didn't see what chance she would have at starting a new life if she had to tote these three kids around with her all the time.

But the fact was, she hadn't thought of running. And now, looking into Sophie's big blue eyes, owl-wide in the moonlight, there was a lump in her throat as big as a brick. The same lump she'd felt when she'd said goodbye to Carol for the last time. It took her so by surprise, she almost choked on it.

"I'm not going to leave you in the lurch." Once spoken, the words became a solemn vow. She didn't know how she would manage it, but she would find these kids a home.

Sophie tilted her head skeptically. "Then why're you waitin' for the train?"

"I wasn't waiting for it. I was looking for Joe Junior."

"He sure idn't gonna be on it. 'Sides, it doesn't even come till tomorrow."

The kid could talk well enough once she got started. "Well, where is he?" Ivy asked. "Not that I miss his companionship, mind you, but I did tell the mayor of this cockamamy town I'd look after him."

The girl shrugged. "He likes horses. Maybe he's at the livery stable."

"I looked there."

Sophie nodded. "Then I bet he's gone to find a prairie dog."

"A *what?*"

"Prairie dog."

Ivy only had the vaguest notion of such a creature. "Has Joe Junior taken it into his head to have a prairie dog for a pet?" she asked, a little perturbed. She didn't intend to go traveling with three kids *and* their pet!

Sophie shook her head, clearly perplexed. "Not for a pet. For breakfast."

Nausea burned in Ivy's throat. Rodents for breakfast! Had she really come to this? *Dear lord, what was she going to do?*

She might have even spoken that last thought aloud. In fact, she might have wailed the plea skyward, entreating any deity within shouting distance for guidance.

But guidance, this time, came in the thin form of Sophie Murphy. The little girl shuffled her bare feet for a moment in indecision before again looking Ivy solemnly in the eye. "I ain't supposed to tell you this. I swore to Joe Junior I wouldn't, even took a solemn oath."

"Tell me what?" Ivy said, a little incuriously. She was still too distracted by the prospect of dining on roast prairie dog, and she didn't hold out much hope that Sophie's revelation would be a bombshell.

But it was. In fact, it was a bolt out of the blue.

"Me, Joe Junior and Linus?" Sophie said. "Well, we got an uncle."

Ivy almost thought her knees would crumple beneath her. "Hallelujah!"

Sophie shook her head. "He's a real bad man…evil…you probably won't want to meet him."

Wrong again. Ivy didn't care if the man was Attila the Hun. She was just itching to meet this uncle of theirs!

Chapter Two

Justin Murphy idled at the notions counter at Tomlin's Mercantile, gazing curiously at a cheery array of ribbons and bows in holiday colors—red and green and shiny gold. It was as close to a Christmas display as he was likely to get this year, or any other year. His ranch, the Bar M, didn't exactly go berserk with Christmas cheer. At most, folks finished up their chores a little early and relaxed awhile. John Tall Tree usually cooked up something special, if only so the old Indian could righteously take Justin to task for depending on a "heathen" to honor the white people's traditions.

But Justin dreaded the holiday. No matter how he mentally readied himself, December twenty-fifth always made him feel torn to pieces. For a whole day he was reminded of being a child, of the parents he'd lost too young, and the big brother he'd lost too late. What was the use in remembering those things? Those recollections had nothing to do with the life he'd made for himself. He was a bachelor with no family. He had a ranch to run, workers to pay and, in good times, a profit to be made. Looking back, he'd learned, was a waste of time.

He glanced up and caught Hank Tomlin beaming a full-denture grin at him. "Thinkin' of buying yourself some pretty hair ribbons, Justin?"

Justin sprang away from the display. He shrugged his shoulders, annoyed at having been caught, then cleared his throat. "Don't know why you waste shelf space on things like that, Hank."

Hank chuckled. "Haven't you heard? It's Christmas."

Justin harrumphed. "Sure, for one day. How the heck are you going to sell all this stuff?"

The storekeeper drew on his pipe. "Oh, the ladies like to deck themselves out for that one day, Justin. 'Sides, they can use ribbons to decorate trees, maybe a package or two. You know...do things up right."

"Waste of time and money," Justin muttered reflexively. Though actually it was the sentimentality of it that made him uncomfortable. Women always did act whimsical and sentimental, but in his experience they could be the most brutally self-serving people in the world.

"Lookee here now," Hank drawled as a customer approached outside. "This little lady'll likely be wanting to buy something in the holiday spirit."

As he looked through the window, Justin wasn't so sure. He couldn't see much of the woman but her dark cloak and funny flat blue hat—a ridiculously impractical thing—but the three children with her had a lean, hungry aspect about them, and it wasn't a hunger for hair ribbons. The bell above the door jangled as the woman blew through backward, swatting the children back and shouting at them not to follow her in. "Just wait out here!" she yelled at them in a clipped tone. Her voice was pleasantly husky, and she sounded as if she were from the North. "Stay put!"

When the door was safely shut, she whirled on her heel and looked quickly from Justin to Hank, who, she could tell by his apron and his position behind the counter, was in charge.

Justin was just as happy to be able to stare at her unobserved. He wasn't a sucker for a pretty face. God knows, he'd learned the hard way to subsume that weakness. But this woman's face was exceptional, and every particle of him seemed to snap to attention and take notice. Beneath her funny blue hat, she had curly dark hair and eyes a startling shade of green. Green the color of new spring leaves. Aside from cheeks flushed with color from either the brisk wind outside or her battle through the doorway—Justin suspected both—her skin was pale and soft looking, highlighting the dusting of freckles on her nose and the lush redness of her cupid's bow lips.

She had the face of an angel, but her expression was something else. Her eyes held a flurry of exhaustion, exasperation, with maybe a dash of expectancy tossed into the mix. She might appear soft and pretty, but something in her bearing suggested steeliness, too. Small wonder. The dust coating her clothes bespoke at least a week of travel, but the three kids with their dirty noses pressed against the glass bespoke a lifetime of affliction.

She marched up to the store keeper and planted her hands on her hips. Justin took advantage of the gesture to admire the way her hands nipped her dusty coat in at her waist, accenting her curvaceousness. "I'm trying to find somebody around here," she announced. "Can you help?"

Hank smiled, taking his time answering. "Well, now, let me see. I guess I know most folks around here."

She let out a husky laugh. "I'll bet! This town's even less than the last nothing place I was at!"

"Where was that?"

"Otis!"

The name caused a frown to pull at Justin's lips.

"You havin' some kind of trouble?" Hank asked her.

"Trouble!" The woman rolled her pretty green eyes toward the brim of her hat and blew at a curly lock of hair that had fallen across her forehead. "Mister, I've had nothin' but. Only I didn't really know the meaning of the word till I hooked up with these little hellions outside." She flicked a glance back to the window, where the three towheaded children had disappeared. A look of dread crossed her face. "Damn! Now it'll take me hours to round those scamps back up again!"

"You said there's somebody you're lookin' for?" Hank asked.

She dragged her distracted gaze away from the window and back to the storekeeper. "I'm supposed to see someone here. Only I'd have thought the man would have the manners to meet the coach we drove in on!"

"Just who is this person you're lookin' for?" Hank asked.

"Name's Justin Murphy. You know him?"

Justin strangled a gasp of surprise. This woman was looking for *him?* What in heaven's name for?

"Know him?" Hank's long face lit up with mischief and he pointedly avoided looking Justin's way. "Sure I know him! But what do you want with him?"

"*Plenty!* Where can I find the rascal?"

"Well, he's got a ranch around here," Hank declared circumspectly.

"Fine thing when a man doesn't even meet the stagecoach after you send him a telegram!"

Justin looked at Hank in surprise. Hank, eyes wide, lifted a finger, remembering. Then he turned back into a pigeonhole-lined hutch and withdrew a thin piece of paper, which he handed across the counter. "Forgot to mention it, Justin. You got a telegram."

The woman pivoted toward Justin. *"You?"*

He nodded uncomfortably. "Guilty." He tilted his head, studying her face more closely. "Should I know you?"

She crossed her arms, looking him up and down like a buyer at auction inspecting an animal for fitness. "I can't believe it!"

"Believe what?"

"That *you're* Uncle Justin! I'd have never guessed from *their* description." She jabbed a thumb toward the empty window. "I was expecting Old Scratch himself to meet us in Wishbone!"

He frowned. No one had ever called him *Uncle* Justin. Maybe because as far as he was concerned, he had no brother. And as for his brother's children...

A coldness spread through Justin's chest, and he very determinedly did not look out the store's front window again. In fact, for a moment he stood clutching the telegram and staring into the woman's green eyes as if he could will her away.

"I don't understand why you're here," he said.

The pert woman blinked up at him. "Maybe you should read that telegram."

He unfolded the missive slowly, without relish.

Regret to inform you of your brother's death. Left three orphans. Arriving on stage Thursday. Please meet. Ivy Ryan.

Justin crumpled the message. So. Josiah was gone. He'd stopped thinking about his older brother years and years ago. But somehow, knowing he was dead was a lot more desolate than just thinking of him that way.

He forced himself to meet the woman's gaze again. "I'm sorry, Miss Ryan. You've made a mistake."

He began to walk away, forgetting whatever it was that had brought him into Hank's to begin with. He just knew he needed to get away from this woman.

She stopped him with a hand to his arm, and her touch was as searing as if she'd poked him with an iron. "Wait just a second, Mr. Murphy. Me and you's got business!"

"I doubt that," he said, jerking his arm away.

"You're not Josiah Murphy's brother?"

"I was."

She planted her hands on her hips and fired an angry look at him—a look that telegraphed Ivy Ryan was down to the last thread of her patience. "Look, I got three children out there who—"

"Who are none of my concern."

"That's what everybody says about them!"

"I've never laid eyes on them." Except that one glance through the window. Now that he remembered, he was astounded. Those pitiful, scrawny waifs were Josiah and Mary's children?

"Then isn't it high time you did?" Ivy fired back.

Justin felt every muscle in his body tense. Finding out that Josiah had died had been confusing enough. Having this stranger flying at him with accusations of being derelict in his avuncular duties was almost more than he could absorb. He'd barely been aware he was an uncle. Josiah had written something about children when he'd informed Justin of Mary's death, four years ago.

His hands clenched into fists. "What do you want, lady? Money?"

Her lips twisted sourly. "I brought you your niece and nephews, that's all. Out of the goodness of my heart. I thought you'd want to take responsibility."

"Why should I? Aren't there orphanages?"

She gasped. "You *are* the devil!"

"If Josiah wanted to have children, he should have provided for them."

"But he didn't."

Justin let out an irritated sigh. Just like Josiah! It was hard to believe that he could still feel the same old anger toward his brother when his brother was no longer even alive. Just like Josiah to rile him even from the grave. "That's the kind of fool he was, all right."

"Children shouldn't have to suffer because their parents are fools, Mr. Murphy."

"So what was your relationship to Josiah? Was he a neighbor of yours?"

"No, he was…well, I guess you could say he was my fiancé."

If she'd taken one of the heavy shovels that were hanging from nails off the wall and slugged it into his gut, he couldn't have found himself more flabbergasted. Furry old Josiah…engaged to this beautiful creature? The iniquities of the world never failed to shock him. First oily, irresponsible Josiah had up and sweet-talked the most beautiful woman in Wishbone into marrying him, and then, by some miracle, he'd convinced *this* woman to take Mary's place.

He felt sick. Not only that, he felt angry. At Ivy Ryan. She might be pretty, but she obviously didn't have a lick of sense. "If you were Josiah's sweetheart, you obviously know these kids of his better than I do."

"Pull your brake, mister," she shot back at him. "I said he was my fiancé, I didn't say anything about sweetheart."

"Well, if you—"

"I came to Texas to marry the man, but I'd never clapped eyes on him. I was gonna be what you call a mail-order bride. Only it turns out all I was was a mail-order chump. The good folks of Otis took advantage of my arrival to unburden themselves of Josiah's three kids. Gave me money, in fact, to take them off their hands. Now I've used up that money bringing them to you."

"I'm sorry you wasted your cash, then, because I don't want them."

He started to walk past her again, but this time her

hand grabbed his arm in a viselike grip. "Want them or not, they're yours."

"I have no use for children. I have a ranch to run."

"Doesn't being their uncle mean anything to you? They're your flesh and blood!"

Justin flinched at the stern rebuke in her voice. When he could pull his gaze away from her fiery green gaze, he saw Hank scowling at him disapprovingly.

Maybe some people would condemn him for being callous in the matter of his three young relations, but he and his brother hadn't been close for years. Hadn't even been on speaking terms since the day Josiah had waltzed out of his life with Mary, Justin's bride-to-be. From that day forward, Justin had felt like a man who'd had the brightest light of his life, the very heart of him, snuffed out. By the two people he loved best.

"Don't condemn what you can't understand, Miss Ryan."

The woman went rigid with indignation. "But you can't just toss them out on the street! It's almost Christmas!"

He shot her a sharp look. "What's that got to do with anything?"

She folded her arms and scowled at him. "You're supposed to think of things like family at Christmas, Mr. Murphy. You're supposed to care about your fellow human beings...unless you're like that character, that what's-his-name in my old storybook, that Mr. Scrooge! I've got an old copy of the book in my bag in case you want to read what nearly happened to *him!*"

Justin knew that story. *A Christmas Carol.* He

clamped his mouth shut, because for a moment he actually feared the words *bah, humbug!* would spill from his lips. Who did this woman think she was? What right did she have to stomp in here and berate him publicly?

While he fumed, she inspected him from head to toe, her withering gaze taking in his weathered but clean clothing, his sturdy boots, the hat he'd bought just last month. "You're obviously a man of some means. Would it break you to help out three children? At least give them a square meal?"

Justin glanced away guiltily and caught Hank gaping at him with a hound-dog stare. He narrowed his eyes at the storekeeper, who, at the silent rebuke, scurried over to the coffee barrel as if to hide the fact that he'd been eavesdropping on every single syllable that had been uttered.

"All right," Justin relented on an angry breath.

Ivy appeared to deflate with relief. "Oh, thank you!"

"Meet my man outside this store in an hour," he instructed her. "He'll drive you to the ranch in the wagon."

"Me?" Her voice was practically a squeak.

"Yes, of course."

"But *I* can't...I mean, I expected to leave them with you." She rushed on, only a little hesitantly, "In fact, I thought that because I'd brought them all this way...you might be inclined to pay me for my troubles."

All of the sudden, Justin saw why Ivy Ryan might have made a good match for his brother—she apparently wasn't above seizing any opportunity. And he remembered anew just why it was he had sworn off women. They were dangerous. Their sweet looks masked deceptive hearts!

But he understood Ivy Ryan now. And he saw her more clearly, too. Those beautiful green eyes glittered harshly at him, without any trace of warmth. She was as lean and hungry-looking as the children had been. Her funny hat, even, when he gave it a second glance, was a cheap-looking thing. She had a worn, wary look about her.

"We can talk about a reward, and whether you deserve one, once you've delivered the children to my ranch."

"But I hadn't intended on going one step past Wishbone, Mr. Murphy. I've been traveling for days and I—"

"Then it won't hurt for you to travel some more," he barked back at her. "That is, *if* you're interested in whether I'll pay you for your troubles."

Her mouth popped shut and her chin jutted out stubbornly. She looked angry, resentful, tired and cornered. Finally she cast her eyes down at Hank's well-swept floor. "All right, I'll escort them to your ranch."

"Good. And Miss Ryan?" When she glanced up at him, Justin sent her a warning look. "Don't make those children any promises. I only intend to keep them till I figure out a better solution."

Chapter Three

A cowboy named Wink Carpenter drove them to Justin's ranch, the Bar M. The three children were buried under a small mountain of blankets in back, huddled between flour sacks and the coffee, peering out at the landscape, which didn't seem all that different from the land they'd traveled through on the stage. Ivy sat up front, tensing against the bitter wind. This was not where she wanted to be.

"Not like I had any choice in the matter," she muttered to herself in consolation. She needed money—story of her life—and her only hope of getting any at this point was begging a little from Justin Murphy. Just for now, she had to do his bidding. Wishbone hadn't looked like a town brimming with employment opportunities for women, except those of an immoral nature. She'd left Boston to escape a blight on her reputation, not create brand-new ones.

What a fool she'd been! When she'd received the money from the citizens of Otis, she'd unwisely sent precious dollars home to Carol along with a rather sentimental Christmas letter, then spent the rest of the money getting her and the children to Wishbone. She'd been so cocksure that Justin Murphy would pay her for her trouble!

Live and learn, they always said. Why did she always seem to learn life's lessons too late for it to do her any damn good?

"Mean, stingy ogre!" she grumbled, thinking of Justin Murphy. He was exactly what the children said he was. Though, of course, the children, only knowing their uncle by reputation, couldn't have warned her how handsome he would be. That had thrown her. His appearance—tall, with dark hair, and brown eyes that were as dark and liquid as warm coffee—had taken her aback. Then he'd opened his mouth and out had come his callous words.

"The old grouch!"

"Ma'am?"

At the sound of the deep voice, Ivy looked over at the burly cowboy Wink, who was perhaps thirty, with long side whiskers on his pudgy face. He'd barely spoken three words at her as he'd helped her up on the wagon and seemed bemused more than anything else by his unexpected passengers.

"Yes?"

"Um, I don't know if you was aware, ma'am, but you was talking to yourself."

"Oh!" Ivy felt her cheeks redden. Talking aloud to herself was a bad habit she had picked up while in jail, where she much preferred talking to herself than to the other unfortunates around her, some of whom had looked as if they would have gladly cut her throat if she'd said boo to them. But of course she'd never admit this to Wink Carpenter. Or anyone.

She had come to Texas to escape Boston and start anew, but in no time she had made hash out of her plans. The thought depressed her. Damn Josiah Murphy! she thought forlornly, not for the first time. Couldn't the useless man have stayed alive long enough to get her back on a train?

Of course, Josiah hadn't had any money. Unlike his skunk of a brother, who had it but didn't appear to enjoy parting with it.

Behind her, there was a commotion as the children, packed in the wagon like dry goods, fidgeted. She heard a slap, then a cry go up from Linus. She couldn't wait to deposit those kids on Murphy's ranch, though she wondered what kind of life the kids would have there.

"Are there any women on the Bar M?" she asked Wink.

The cowboy's face fell slack. "Lordy, no! Mr. Murphy's a bachelor, and likely to remain so."

Ivy frowned at that rather odd but certainly emphatic answer. A bachelor Justin might be, but why would his employee be so certain that would remain the case? Justin owned his own ranch and was obviously prosperous. Clean. His clothes well turned out. And as for the man's appearance…well, the less she thought about that, the better. In her limited experience, handsome gents just gave women trouble. And that's exactly what Justin Murphy had dished out to her, wasn't it? More trouble.

"The troll!" she couldn't help muttering under her breath.

Joe Junior had said that Josiah had hated Justin and had spoken his name like a curse. Justin had done something horrible to their mother, because whenever his name had been spoken in her presence, she'd wept bitterly. Joe Junior had further asserted that Uncle Justin must have swindled their father out of all his money, or maybe even killed someone. He was a bad man, and they were traitors to their parents' memories by merely asking for his help.

During Joe Junior's tirades, Sophie had remained silent. Apparently her reverence for her parent's memories had given way to necessity. Ivy had only managed to lure them onto the stage out of Otis by assuring them that there would plenty to eat at their uncle's. Finally even Joe Junior had put his stomach before his pride.

She could well understand why. She was feeling famished now herself. She hadn't had a square meal in days and days. The thought that she would have to rely on Justin Murphy to feed her was irksome, though.

What could he have done to those kids' mother? Something terrible, she bet, to cause so much animosity between two brothers.

Or maybe Justin was just a foul woman-hater. "If Mr. Murphy is unmarried," she piped up to Wink, "who takes care of his home? Who cooks?"

"That would be John. He takes care of the house." He cast a dubious glance at Ivy. "He probably won't take none to you hornin' in on his territory, neither."

"I won't be staying long enough to trouble anyone," she assured Wink. The last thing she needed now was to start making enemies. "I'm just delivering Mr. Murphy's children to the ranch."

Wink shook his head but said nothing until a group

of buildings came into view in the distance sometime later.

"That there's the Bar M," he announced.

Despite the fact that she hadn't wanted to go there, Ivy perked up curiously. She'd been a city girl from the day she was born—nature was a lucky, infrequent stroll through a park to her—and she was curious. The ranch was vast, she discovered, and consisted of several buildings. The main house was a rambling structure made of wide wood beams and stone, and there was a smaller bunkhouse attached to it. But the barn behind the main house seemed larger than any she had seen, the real showplace. Its white painted boards stood out against the horizon like a beacon. Running alongside the buildings was a line of trees, tall and impressively stark in their present naked state.

And all around the buildings was land dotted with grazing cattle and horses. She saw pigs—huge ones—milling about the side of the barn, and in the dusty yard in front of the house, chickens idly pecked the ground. She felt her stomach do a flip of anticipation as she looked at the houses, the property. One man owned all of this? It was inconceivable!

She glanced back at the children, who had tossed off their blankets to get a clear view of their new home. When the wagon stopped, the worried yet intensely curious looks on their young faces probably mirrored her own expression.

"You better get yourself inside and see to feedin' them young 'uns," Wink told her. "They look about ready to start chewing on the buckboards."

Ivy laughed, especially when her own stomach growled greedily. Food—maybe a whole plate of it!

She never imagined the day when just a simple meal would seem like an unbelievable luxury.

She herded the children, who for once were surprisingly obedient, following where Wink's gesture had directed them. She knocked tentatively at the back door, not sure whether to barge right in. In the next moment, the heavy door was jerked open and she stood chest high to a tall, unsmiling, gray-haired Indian!

Shocked at having at least one half of her nightmare about the West standing not one foot away from her, his black glittering eyes glaring down at her, Ivy barely managed to gulp down a reflexive screech.

"You have brought children here," the Indian said.

Ivy wasn't sure whether it was a statement of fact or an accusation or a question. She nodded mutely, then swallowed again, trying to find her voice. It came out as a squeak. "Wink sent us."

She might as well have said *Open sesame*. The tall, imposing figure stood aside, allowing them entrance. Ivy scooted by quickly, but the children didn't seem to see anything strange about having a hulking old Indian manning a kitchen. All they seemed to care about were the delectable smells emanating from the warm house. Without being told, they settled expectantly at the long narrow table that dominated the room.

The meal the Indian had fixed for them was better than anything Ivy had prepared for. Within moments, thick steaks were piled on a platter in the middle of the table, along with potatoes dripping with butter. In addition, a heaping bowl of beans cooked in onions was placed before them, along with cornmeal muffins and honey. The children's wide blue eyes looked almost as if they would pop at the sight of so much food, so easily obtained.

All four of them attacked the meal as if they hadn't eaten for weeks…and, in the case of the children, they probably hadn't. All Ivy had offered them so far today had been some jerky she'd bought at the store in Otis. Now they ate until they couldn't stuff in another forkful. Ivy had never tasted food so wonderful.

"Delicious!" Finished, Ivy leaned back and slumped in a decidedly unladylike fashion.

The cook, who had stood mutely watching them gorge, now regarded them with an expression of pleasure and disdain. "White people enjoy eating like this."

Ivy shifted uncomfortably, feeling as if she had been vaguely insulted. John looked at them almost as if they were…savages.

"You must go talk to Mr. Murphy now," he told her. "He asked it."

She frowned, looking at the children. The moment of reckoning had arrived. She needed to prepare them to meet their dreaded uncle. "Is there a place where the children can wash their faces and hands?"

Linus, especially, needed work. Grease from his steak dripped through the dirt coating his chin, and his hands looked sticky with honey.

John eyed her steadily. "Not the children. Just you."

Ivy felt doubly uneasy now. Didn't Justin at least want to meet the children? Or was he going to tell her, now that she was sated and sluggish from her heavy meal, that she could take his nephews and niece and be on her way?

She glanced at them again and felt a prick of foreboding. The meal had been a rare moment of calm for the three of them, but now they showed signs of the fuel beginning to stoke their natural tempers. Joe Junior was kicking Sophie under the table. Linus was bouncing absently and peeking at the back door with interest. There was no telling the amount of mischief he could get into on this vast ranch.

Maybe she wouldn't have to find out, however. Maybe Justin would be calmer now and realize that he owed it to her to give her the money she needed to make a new start. After all, what else *could* he do?

"Very well," she said, bucking herself up.

Joe Junior scraped his chair back. "Be careful!" he said. "Remember he's a bad man."

"Very baaad!" Linus seconded.

Sophie looked worried for completely different reasons. "What are we supposed to do while you're gone? What if you don't come back?"

Ivy stared at them, dumbfounded. They were worried about *her?* About what they would do without *her?* She shook her head, then looked numbly up at John.

"I will take care of them," he said.

She shook her head. "You don't know—Joe Junior can disappear in an instant and Linus gets into everything and—"

"There will be no problems," the cook said. "They will do as I say."

Sophie giggled, then was quieted by a glare from the Indian.

''They will do as I say because I have a great big apple pie to give them if they sit quietly at this table.''

The three, who had been stirring restlessly, suddenly went still all at once.

The old Indian smiled smugly and then led a stunned Ivy out of the kitchen. From the kitchen they passed a large open sitting room with an iron stove smack in the center of it. There were plenty of simple wood chairs lining one wall and a small desk at the other end of the room. But other than a large braided rug on the floor, the room was completely without adornment. It was also without Justin.

The Indian cook escorted her down a dark hallway lined with closed doors on either side. Then he stopped, rapped sharply on one and left her standing there.

''Come in!''

Outside the door Ivy patted her hair and straightened her dusty clothing. Her pulse sped, but she couldn't say whether it was in anticipation of seeing Justin again, or the idea that she might be on the verge of getting some money to be on her way. In fact, if she played her cards right, she might be in San Francisco by Christmas!

She entered the room quickly, before she lost her nerve and wound up standing out in the hallway all day long. She was shocked to find herself in a bedroom. She'd assumed this would be a kind of study or library. Justin was standing in front of a high bureau with a shaving mirror atop it, his face covered with lather. More shocking still, he wasn't fully dressed; just pants over his gray undershirt.

Embarrassed, she began stammering apologies and backing out the door.

"No, stay," he barked at her. "I need to talk to you."

"Oh. Well, I'm sure it could wait until you're…"

"I don't like to put things off."

She couldn't help staring at his chest. Ogling it, actually. Back in the store in Wishbone, she'd noticed right away that Justin was a handsome man. She just hadn't known *how* handsome. His chest was broad, and muscles bulged beneath the thin woolen material of his undershirt. He seemed to be built like a statue of a man rather than real flesh and blood.

She felt her heart flutter uneasily in her chest, then upbraided herself for being so foolish. A handsome face had gotten the better of her once before. "I'd better come back later," she said.

"Miss Ryan!" His voice came out in a bellow of displeasure. "Hours ago you were telling me I was derelict in my duty to my young relatives, and now you seem to want to avoid the issue altogether."

She couldn't say that it wasn't the issue but his masculinity that she wanted to avoid. Justin had a strange effect on her. He made her skin feel flushed, made her want to cross him. Which was probably as wise as crossing a rattlesnake!

"You'll be happy to know that I've changed my mind about my niece and nephews," he said. "You win. They can stay."

Relief rushed through her. A happy ending. The children had a home. She'd rarely done good in her life, and the satisfaction she felt sat strangely in her. "I'm glad!"

"I thought you would be." She detected a hint of mockery in his expression. "Aren't you curious about what I've decided about you?"

Her chin jerked up, and suddenly she was all ears. Her heart beat double time. If he'd suddenly turned generous toward the children, maybe he was going to be generous with her, too. "Well, yes, I suppose so," she replied, not wanting to sound too eager for her reward. "But of course I'm most happy that you have decided to reunite with your niece and nephews."

His lips twisted up. "Naturally! You're all heart."

She frowned and tilted a glance at him. Crossing her arms, she said, "All right, what is it you've decided?"

He turned back to the mirror and dragged the razor carefully down his cheek. When he had cleared a pathway of skin and rinsed the blade in the bowl in front of him, he smiled and announced, "My taking in the children depends on taking you as well."

Justin looked in the mirror to catch Ivy's reaction, expecting fireworks. He wasn't disappointed.

The little woman blinked her green eyes at him in surprise. *"What?"* Her voice arced up an octave.

"I want you as part of the bargain," he said.

Her cheeks bloomed red. "I've never been so insulted!"

He chuckled and turned back to the mirror, wiping his face clean with a towel as he kept an eye on her. He'd never known a woman to get prettier when she was in a fit of anger, but Ivy was. Her whole body was stiff and her head was shaking so that her riot of curls fairly jangled around her face. "You mean to tell me that you were plenty willing to marry a man sight unseen, but you're offended at a proposition that you take care of three children you already know?''

She tilted her head skeptically. ''Take care of children? That's all?''

''Yes, of course.''

''Oh!'' If possible, her face turned redder than before. ''I didn't know…I mean, I thought…''

He laughed inwardly at her embarrassment. But the idea of her thinking he wanted to bed her…that wasn't so risible. In fact, it was too damn close to the truth for his comfort. He didn't want anything to do with her or any woman, but the fact was, he'd never been around children and he didn't have a burning interest to start now. He might take responsibility for these orphans of Josiah's; that didn't mean he wanted to take an active interest in their lives.

''All I ask is that they don't get in the way,'' he said. *So that I don't have to look into those blue eyes of theirs,* he could have added.

She lifted her head. ''But I'm not, I mean I can't—''

He cut her off. ''I don't want them bothering my men at work.'' *I don't want them reminding me of the woman who betrayed me….*

''But I'm going to San Francisco!'' she blurted out.

He frowned. ''What would you do there?''

''Start a new life,'' she answered. ''Is that a crime?''

''That depends on how you intend to come by the money to get there.''

''But I thought you…'' Her voice trailed off, but her meaning was clear. She thought that on further reflection he would joyfully embrace his new responsibilities and be so grateful to her that he would ship her wherever she wanted to go.

Unfortunately, he couldn't do that. Though he didn't particularly want her here, he needed her. "I'll give you a dollar a week, plus board. That should allow you to raise enough money...eventually."

Within moments she was quivering mad again. "Eventually is an understatement. It would take me years to earn enough to get anywhere! I'd practically be your indentured servant!"

"I wouldn't turn the offer down so quickly, Miss Ryan. Jobs here are scarce."

He could see acknowledgment of that fact in her expression during the heated silence that followed. He had her cornered, just as she had cornered him at the store.

"I'm a bachelor," he explained. "I have a ranch to run. I don't have time to raise children."

She sputtered incoherently for a few moments. "But I am not a nanny!"

"What are you?"

She blinked. "What do you mean?"

"I mean, what do you do?"

"Well...nothing, at the moment. I was a maid."

"Then you *could* be a children's nanny. You certainly proved yourself a worthy advocate for the children this afternoon."

"Sure, but—"

He grinned and turned to her, crossing his arms. "But what?" When she hesitated, eyeing him resentfully, he finished for her, "But that was just because you were so eager to get rid of them? To get a little reward money?''

She glared at him some more, then stubbed her toe angrily against the puncheon floor. ''I didn't come out here to take care of children!''

''No, you came out here to marry a chiseler, as I understand it.''

''At a dollar a week you're a fine one to talk about chiselers!'' she shot back.

He couldn't help it. He laughed aloud. Ivy Ryan was a piece of work, and he wasn't sure he actually wanted to have her around. A woman like her could wreak havoc on a ranch full of cowpokes. But what he'd told her was true. He needed someone to look after the children, and Wishbone wasn't full of other candidates for the job. She was in a better bargaining position than he was though, thank heavens, she didn't know it.

What winding path of misfortune had brought a woman like Ivy Ryan to Wishbone? Poor she might be, but she was pretty enough that she should have been able to marry well back at home. Unless something bad had happened to her. He didn't want to think too hard about what that bad thing could be, but it must have been considerable to make her willing to marry a man like Josiah sight unseen.

Which probably meant that she was more trouble than he had reckoned on. He looked into Ivy's face, which was torn with misery, and felt a little like a cat teasing a mouse. ''Do you want the job or don't you?''

For a split second she agonized. Then she relented. ''Yes, damn it!''

He nodded. "Good." Then he opened his bureau, pulled out a clean shirt and began to dress.

Ivy stood awkwardly behind him. After a few moments, he heard her clear her throat.

"Well?" he asked.

She blinked in surprise and blushed again. "Don't you have any instructions?"

He nodded. "Just keep those children out of my sight."

"That's not as easy as it sounds," she huffed.

"I didn't think it would be, or I wouldn't have hired you."

She glowered at him, obviously still wishing that he *hadn't* hired her. "And nothing else?"

"Oh, yes…"

She raised her brows.

"You might try to watch your language, Miss Ryan. From hearing you, anyone would think you'd lived around ruffians."

Her cheeks burned red, and she threw a final glare at him. "Fiend!" she spat, just before turning and slamming the door behind her.

Chapter Four

It was easy for Justin to command her to keep the children out of mischief. Actually following up on that order was another matter entirely.

Though to be truthful, no one minded the children's high jinks like Justin did. Wink was patient to the point of saintliness with them. The other two hands, Arnie and Sam, even appeared flattered by the attention and admiration the children gave them. Arnie, an old-timer who seemed to have been through everything from the Mexican War to the first big cattle drive, was a born musician and loved their repeated requests for songs. And wiry Sam, who at nineteen seemed barely more than a boy himself, watched the children with interest, as if looking for something of his own family he'd left behind somewhere. None of the three men had much time to spare, but they spoke to the children and were kind to them even though Ivy tried to keep them out of the way.

But inevitably, there were problems. Linus started the trouble. Ivy should have known when she saw his sticky fingers, during their first meal, that the boy was enamored of the sweet honey. The next afternoon Linus managed to find and overturn a whole jar of the stuff so that for days, even after both John Tall Tree and Ivy had vigorously scrubbed and scrubbed, everyone's boots stuck to the floor and left dirty honey-mud tracks all over the house.

Ivy wasn't certain whether Justin's order to keep the children out of sight extended to mealtimes, but she couldn't ask John Tall Tree to fix another meal just for the benefit of the children and herself. She could tell Sophie's steady stare during dinner unnerved the men, especially Justin. But it served him right, the uncivil beast! He'd only acknowledged the children once, with a curt nod. And he could hardly complain about Sophie, who in the presence of grown-ups was solemn and silent, just as Justin had requested.

Unfortunately, the same could not be said of Joe Junior. Immediately, despite Ivy's warnings, he was all over the ranch, especially anywhere there were horses. In the barn. In the corral. Underfoot. Getting in trouble. You'd think that the huge ranch would be big enough to swallow one boy and his shenanigans, but no. Not Joe Junior. Every time he was dealt a reprimand, he just seemed to hang back for a while and cook up something worse to do next.

He stole Justin's favorite mare one day to take for a pleasure ride. Then he interfered while Sam and Wink were corralling heifers, sending cattle running for the farthest reaches of the ranch; it took hours to get them back in.

Justin pulled Ivy aside after that episode. Yanked

her aside, really. "I know you said you were no nanny, but you didn't tell me that you couldn't control the children *at all*."

She laughed. "You don't know what your life would be like if there were no curbs on them *at all*."

He sighed raggedly and let her go. "What did you do before coming here? Don't you have any idea of order?"

Oh, didn't she! A flash of her crowded, putrid-smelling jail cell came to her, of days regulated by ruthless matrons. The memory made her cold right down to the marrow of her bones. But jail, the shame of it all, wasn't an experience she could talk about, especially not to a man who was employing her to take care of his children. Even if the pay was only a lousy dollar a week.

"If you wanted references, Mr. Murphy, you should've said so right off."

He stared at her long and hard, so intently that she finally averted her eyes. "Just make sure Joe Junior keeps out of trouble," he said.

But how? How could you keep an eleven-year-old boy from running wild on a ranch? When she told him to stay close to the house, he created havoc for John Tall Tree, and the last thing in the world Ivy wanted was an angry Indian on her hands.

John had already been kinder to Linus than she ever would have believed, especially after the honey episode. But the old Indian seemed fond of having a child about the kitchen to taste batter and dough, and to lecture on the proper way to dress and wash his hands and speak, "in the white man's way." And wouldn't you know, Linus behaved for John Tall Tree as he never would for her!

One day she'd been in the house reading the children *A Christmas Carol* aloud, becoming lost in the story that so reminded her of the Ebenezer Scrooge in her own life, when she glanced up and realized the children had slipped away. With Arnie's help she traced them to the barn, where Sophie and Linus were pitching hay at each other and Joe Junior was climbing monkey-style across the rafters. She could just imagine Sophie poking one of Linus's eyes out with that pitchfork, or Joe Junior falling from the ceiling and breaking every bone in his body. Why, they could all get themselves killed!

Cursing the day she had ever even heard of Texas, she braved the rickety ladder up to the hayloft and retrieved the pitchfork. "Get down from here this instant!" she scolded Sophie and Linus, then leveled a gaze at their brother, who was hanging upside down about twenty feet away. "Joe Junior, you climb down from there, too!"

To emphasize her demand, she planted the pitchfork tines down into the hay, causing a high, shrill shriek to go up. Looking down, she saw she'd inadvertently stabbed a fat lazy rat in the tail. She shrieked right back at him, jumping away, then, losing her footing, found herself falling bustle-first back on the hay. Not just the injured rat but also one of his companions streaked across the bottom of her skirts, and she flailed wildly in the hay for a moment, yelling curses she hadn't heard since leaving jail. She was frantic. Sophie and Linus were doubled over with laughter and blocking the ladder, so in her hurry to escape the angry rats, Ivy dove for the edge of the hayloft, flipped over the side with an acrobatic skill she never dreamed she possessed and dropped into the stall below.

A stall, she discovered to her dismay, which had yet to be cleaned.

The milk cow, Katy, gave her a blank stare as Ivy pulled herself out of the muck and stood on wobbly feet, flapping her hands and twisting to inspect the damage to her dress. She groaned at the stain all over her seat. And the stench! She wanted to weep. She couldn't wait for the day when she got back to the city, where she never had to deal with cow flop and barns and inadvertently stabbing rats with farm implements!

At least it had just been rats, not snakes, she thought in consolation. She limped out of the barn as fast as she could, trying to ignore the delighted giggles she left in her wake. So much for maintaining discipline! Thank heavens, she had no adult witnesses.

But, of course, who should she run smack into as she fled the scene of her embarrassment but Justin himself? She walked right into his chest. Reflexively he pushed her away from him, dark eyes wide and his nose twitching in revulsion as her ripe smell struck him a split second after her body had.

"What the he—"

Ivy was too cross and miserable to put up with questions. "I've been watching after *your* niece and nephews, trying to keep them from breaking their necks!'' she shot back before he could get his question out. ''And if you're going to criticize *me*, maybe you should start setting some traps in that barn of yours.''

His brows rose. ''Traps?''

''For rats!''

''I let the barn cats worry about them.''

''Well, what about snakes?''

He frowned. ''Did you see one?''

''No,'' she huffed, ''but I'm sure that'll be next!''

He shook his head. ''If we sat around trapping snakes here we wouldn't have time for anything else in the spring time. Right now it's too cold for snakes.''

The wild beating of her heart settled down some. ''Too cold?''

''We'll start seeing them again around February.''

''Fine! I'll be gone by then.'' She hoped. Oh, Lord, how she hoped.

''I wanted to talk to you about something, Ivy,'' he told her.

She let out an exasperated breath. No doubt she was in for more criticism, and right now she wasn't in the mood for it. ''First, let me tell you a thing or two, Justin Murphy. You might have grievances against those kids—heaven knows they're no angels!—but this place isn't exactly the best setup for them, either.''

He looked surprised that she had the nerve to lecture him. ''Oh, it's not?''

''How's a boy supposed to react to the temptation of having a whole barn full of horses? Of course, he'll have to sneak a ride at least once. Would you consider him a red-blooded healthy boy if he didn't?''

"I don't know," Justin replied. "I'd be grateful, I know that. Also, I'd be grateful if Linus wouldn't shred my best, newest shirts to make himself a rope to lasso the chickens with."

She put her hands on her hips. As if the man didn't have a shirt or two to spare! "Your problem is you know nothing about children. You can't blame them for being a little...rambunctious. They just got here, and frankly *you* haven't been much of a help."

He straightened. "I've opened my home to them, haven't I?"

But what about your heart? she was tempted to ask. She, who had laughed at the very notion of heart just days before. Of course back then she had yet to come up against Justin Murphy, a man with no apparent heart at all. She'd never met a man with less family feeling! It made her boiling mad to think that here was a man with his family handed him on a silver platter, with no financial worry about three more mouths to feed, and the holidays coming up—the very time for family—and all he could do was grump and grumble and find fault!

"Sure, you've given them a roof over their heads, and you can bet they're grateful. But you, you old curmudgeon, you just act like a mean old crank and don't even speak to them."

"What am I supposed to say? 'Thank you for terrorizing my livestock and shredding my wardrobe and nearly burning down my barn'?''

"Wink said that *anyone* could have knocked over that lamp!"

He let out a sigh of irritation. "Wink is a soft touch."

"Just have a civil conversation with them," she pleaded. "All you've done is grunt and glare."

"I noticed *you* weren't so happy with them when you stomped out of that barn," he pointed out.

"But *I'm* not their uncle! Why should you hate them so? You should have every reason to love them."

His cheeks were mottled red. "Careful, Ivy, you don't know what you're talking about."

"Don't you think they consider it odd that you'd board them and feed them and not have the slightest curiosity about them? Haven't you wanted to talk to them about their father, your own brother?"

"No!"

"Don't you think they *need* to talk to you, then?" Maybe she was speaking too frankly, but she didn't care. Justin wasn't doing her any favors. She had nothing to lose. "They've just lost their last parent. Don't you have a human heart beating under one of those precious shirts of yours, or are you really just a penny-pinching ogre who doesn't care if he goes through life like some reptile, cold as a snake and completely unloved!"

He flinched, and for a moment, to her shock, the expression in his dark gaze seemed vulnerable. Then his eyes narrowed on her. Pierced her like two daggers.

Perhaps she had gone the teeniest bit overboard,

but once she'd started, a week of bottled-up indignation had simply blown out of her like smoke from a stack. Now she was caught in Justin's blazing glare, and she swallowed anxiously. Anger throbbed in his temple. Even though they were standing in the middle of the barnyard for all the world to see, he looked as if he might reach over and throttle her.

It seemed an eternity before he spoke, his voice a bare rasp. "By the by, that matter I wanted to speak to you about…"

She lifted her chin and steadied herself as if preparing to absorb a blow. His criticism was bound to be merciless now. "Yes?"

"I wanted to *thank you*, Ivy," he gritted out, "and furthermore to inform you that I had intended to pay you an extra four dollars a week which, after some consideration, I had decided would be more fair."

As she listened to the speech, the blood drained out of her face. He wanted to thank her? To…

And *she'd* called the man a reptile!

She swallowed. "Oh." The word was barely audible.

His lips twisted cynically. "I suppose you're going to apologize now."

She would have, if she'd been able to find her voice. But she knew from his sneer that pleading forgiveness would be the worst possible mistake. He would just accuse her of saying the words because she wanted the money. So she shook her head, hoping to look contrite, even if she couldn't say so. She didn't have to ask if he *still* intended to raise her pay.

"You'd better get back to the house and clean up

now.'' The dismissal was as icy, as reptilian, as she'd accused him of being.

She didn't point that out, however. She just went, and gladly. She'd never felt so small, or so smelly.

The next week was a struggle. Ivy wanted to apologize to Justin, but of course she couldn't. Every time she passed him coming and going through the house, at meals, around the barn, she tried but failed to meet those dark eyes of his, to at least convey silently that she was sorry she had spoken so frankly and insulted him.

Actually, the word that most often came to mind when she remembered that rare moment of vulnerability she'd caught in his expression was *hurt his feelings*. But how could she have injured the feelings of a man who seemingly had no emotions?

She spent more time puzzling over this question than she cared to admit. The man had cut off his own brother. He'd committed, according to the children, some unspeakable insult against their mother. And he certainly hadn't been killing his nephews and niece with kindness. How could she have hurt his feelings by telling him the simple truth? The man *was* a reptile!

Only she'd never seen a reptile look so wounded.

She decided that the only way she would be able to make it up to him was to try to get the children to behave, and she did a fair job of it, if she did say so herself. There were no major incidents for five days running. She began to expect that Justin might pull her aside again, to thank her and tell her all was forgiven. Maybe he'd decide to raise her pay again after all. At five dollars a week she would be on her way in no time!

Then, at the beginning of dinner on a Friday night, Wink asked where Joe Junior was. Ivy frowned at the empty chair across from her. She couldn't remember the last time she'd seen him. Neither, apparently, could anybody else.

"Seems to me he took the mule and went riding sometime around noon," Arnie said.

Noon? That was seven hours ago!

"I haven't seen Beulah all day, neither," Sam said. "I's lookin' for her this afternoon to haul brush."

Good heavens. It seemed everyone had missed Beulah before anyone had missed Joe Junior, though of course it wasn't everyone's job to look after the boy. Just hers. Ivy ducked her head with shame. She didn't have to look up to know that Justin was glaring at her accusingly. After this whole week of trying so hard, she'd gone and lost his nephew.

But Joe Junior couldn't be gone. Not really gone, she thought with growing hysteria. She turned to Sophie. "Do you know where Joe Junior went?"

Sophie stared back at her, then slowly lifted her shoulders in a shrug. She might know, but she wasn't going to say a word.

Ivy worried her lower lip as her mind raced frantically. Where would Joe Junior go? Back to Otis? She couldn't imagine anyone homesick for that god-forsaken place! "Where could he be headed?" she heard herself ask aloud.

Arnie shook his head and drained his coffee cup.

"Back in my day, everybody was hotfootin' it to California."

Ivy felt sweat bead on her forehead. California? There were deserts and mountains between here and there!

"But I'd imagine most folks'd head somewheres else nowadays," Arnie continued. "Gold's a bust anyhow. Most adventurous sorts take to the sea."

"The sea!"

"Sure, they got freighters bound for the Orient now," Arnie said.

China?

Wink frowned. "You think they'd let Beulah on a freighter?"

Ivy felt as if she was about to burst. She turned to Linus. "Do you know where your brother went?"

Linus, who was licking butter off his fingers, stopped long enough to answer nonchalantly, "Wishbone, was what he said. Said he was gonna trade Beulah for a horse and get us all outta here."

For a moment Ivy thought she might expire with relief. "Well, why didn't you say so earlier, you scamp?"

"You told us not to speak 'less we was spoke to."

An irritable growl sounded from the other end of the table, and then Justin rose and strode out the kitchen door without saying a word. Ivy jumped out of her chair and ran after him.

She caught up with him halfway to the barn. "What are you doing?" She had difficulty keeping pace with his long strides.

"I'm going after him."

But what would he do if he found him?

Trepidation must have been written all over her face, because Justin glowered at her. "What did you expect? I can't just let him loose on the people of Wishbone. Considering the ruckus he creates here, imagine the damage he could inflict on that unsuspecting town."

She wanted to point out that there hadn't been a ruckus of any kind for days, but she had only to remember the eagerness of the residents of Otis to rid themselves of the Murphy children to know that Justin was right to be worried. But she also feared the havoc Justin could wreak on Joe Junior. If those two butted heads, there would surely be fireworks. "I'm going with you," she said.

"That's not necessary."

She planted her hands on her hips. "You've never spoken two words to that boy. I'm coming along."

"I guess I can't stop you." He nodded toward a stall. "Saddle up Brindle."

Ivy gaped at the horse, then at the wall draped with saddles and bridles and things she had no idea what to do with. *Didn't the man recall that she was from Boston?*

Apparently not.

Ivy again looked uneasily at the horse, an animal she'd seen a dozen times at least. Never before had Brindle seemed so huge. At least twice as big, and with ten times as much pep, as Old Pokey, the horse Wink had given her a riding lesson on.

"Maybe I should take Old Pokey," she said uneasily.

Justin rolled his eyes. "I'd like to get to Wishbone sometime before Christmas."

Seeing her frozen in hesitation and confusion, however, Justin let out an impatient sigh and grabbed a saddle off the tack wall and quickly bridled, blanketed and saddled Brindle. He handed Ivy the reins, saying tersely, "Now see if you can lead her out of the stall and mount up before I'm ready to leave."

Smart aleck! Ivy took the reins from him and led Brindle from the stall. Thanks to that brief riding lesson from Wink, she wasn't completely in the dark about horses. She approached Brindle's left side and doggedly worked her way up the mountain of horseflesh. The beast seemed to be pulsing with energy, but finally Ivy perched uneasily astride in the saddle, her skirts bunching around her. But she was indeed ready when Justin mounted an even larger gray horse.

"Think you can keep up?" he asked.

She answered with a withering look. "I've ridden before."

Once.

"Good." Justin clicked his tongue and he was off. Way off. Ivy gawked in amazement. The man tore across the barnyard and toward the road without so much as a glance back at her. She had no idea how to make a horse go that fast, and she wasn't sure she wanted to. The quickest pace she'd achieved on Old Pokey was a jolting trot, and that had been frightening enough. Nevertheless, she tapped her heels into Brindle's sides and hoped the command would at least result in a walk.

It did better. Brindle executed a short, impatient

dance and then took off. Bolted. Stunned, Ivy grabbed
the reins and then the saddle horn and hunched forward, praying she could just hold on. She had no idea
where the horse was taking her. Corral and house
went by in a breathless blur. She heard hoofbeats and
caught the swishing black tail of Justin's horse and
knew she had made it to the road—and closed the
distance between them.

Then she passed him.

"Ivy, stop!" Justin hollered after her.

How? Ivy wasn't certain how to stop and, furthermore, wasn't sure she even wanted to. She had the
sneaking suspicion that if the horse came to a halt,
she wouldn't. That she would just go shooting off into
the air like a ball launched from a cannon.

Biting the bullet, she gathered the reins more
closely in her white-knuckled fists and searched her
mind for the right words. "Brindle, whoa!" She
wasn't sure whether the command came out as a
whisper or a terrified shriek. Her own body was beyond her control now, lost to wind and speed, and
she had already delivered herself up into the hands of
her maker.

But the words did the trick. Brindle's breakneck
pace slowed to that familiar bone-rattling gate Old
Pokey had executed so expertly, and Ivy jostled
weakly until the horse came to a standstill.

Justin was alongside her in a second, gaping at her
with unchecked surprise. "You really do know how
to ride!"

Now that her horse was still, Ivy felt so light-
headed and trembly that she feared she might just

slither off the animal's back. She had a hard time keeping her hands from shaking, and Lord only knows how she found breath to answer. She could barely draw air into her lungs. ''Of course,'' she said shakily. ''Did you think I was lying?''

He chuckled. ''Not exactly. I just didn't know what a quick trip it would be into town.''

Before she could answer, much less 'fess up to her true equine ignorance, he clicked his tongue and galloped off again. And Brindle, who was apparently just warming up, charged after him.

Though they discovered Beulah tied to a rail by the saloon, Joe Junior was nowhere to be found. A couple of men at the bar recalled having spotted a scraggly youngster and a mule, but that had been hours ago, they said. Justin left the saloon discouraged. He'd known all along that these children would be more trouble than he could contend with, though he had to admit that Ivy *had* kept a tight rein on them. Until now.

But now Ivy had slipped away from him, too. He strode down the street, irritation prickling inside him. He shouldn't have let Ivy out of his sight, but foolishly he hadn't wanted to take her into a saloon, which wasn't a fit place for a decent woman. If Ivy even was decent. How did he know what she'd been back in Boston?

It was a question he'd wondered about more than he cared to admit. In fact, he'd been daydreaming about Ivy entirely too much. The woman was a termagant, and yet there was something about her blunt-

ness that seemed refreshing. No one had spoken to
him like she did. Ever. It took guts, just as it had
taken guts for her to keep her seat on Brindle during
the wild ride into town when she'd only had that one
riding lesson from Wink.

He'd known she was lying. And wasn't it just like
her to stare at him with those green eyes and not
admit it! He'd never met a woman so stubborn, which
was especially surprising given her beauty. She
seemed not to understand how much more easily she
could manipulate him with just a smile than by
launching herself at him and yelling. Because if the
truth be told, despite everything, he was drawn to her.

Sometimes at night it seemed that he'd never get
those green eyes out of his imagination so he could
fall asleep. Or her pert little nose. He'd thought about
her cascades of dark, softly curled hair, her tiny waist,
and how light her step was in the morning as she
helped John Tall Tree by pouring the men's coffee.
He'd even foolishly wondered if she was a good
dancer. He wasn't much of a dancer himself, although
lately, he felt so light of foot sometimes it seemed as
if he were dancing.

He'd also wondered if she'd had a man before,
though the very notion flooded him with foolish jealousy. Was that what she was doing here—running
away from a love affair? A married man who had led
her on? He couldn't imagine. He didn't want to think
about it.

Yet some days, when he should have been concen-
trating on his work, it seemed he could think of nothing else.

As he reached the end of the feed store, he heard voices. Fierce, whispered voices from the alley. One of them was Ivy's. Instinctively he stopped, then ducked against the dark wall.

"You'd better thank God for a roof over your head," Ivy was saying, "and more than that, you'd better behave. You understand me?"

Justin felt his muscles relax. Ivy had found Joe Junior. He was more relieved than he'd expected to be.

In the alley there was a drawn-out silence in which Justin could perfectly picture Joe Junior's sullen face.

"Why?" the boy retorted. "What's gonna happen if I behave?"

"You'll still have a bed to sleep in and food to eat, that's what," Ivy said. "That's nothing to sneeze at."

"But don't you see? He doesn't even like us," Joe Junior said. "He could boot us all out tomorrow 'cause he doesn't like us on account of we remind him of what our ma did to him."

Justin felt the blood drain out of his face, and he closed his eyes. For a moment he felt he was drowning in the dark, the confused silence. He'd never dreamed the children knew about what had happened between him and Josiah and Mary.

"What your ma did to *him?*" Ivy repeated slowly. "I thought it was your uncle who did the terrible thing that caused all the bad blood. That's what you said."

"That's what I let the young 'uns think," Joe Junior admitted. "They don't really remember Ma. But when she used to cry, it wasn't because she hated Uncle Justin. It was on account of she loved him."

Justin clenched his fists. Why didn't the kid be quiet? Why couldn't he—

He sagged against the building, letting it take his weight as if he been a sack of flour someone had kicked over. Mary had loved him, Joe Junior had said. She'd pined for him, cried about jilting him…all those years? Had she really been that unhappy?

Wasn't that what you wanted?

When Mary, his beautiful fiancée, the woman he'd started his ranch for so they could marry and have children, had run off with ne'er-do-well Josiah, he'd let her go, though he'd sworn she'd regret it. He was all wounded pride, and envisioning her potential misery had made him feel better at first. He knew deep down that he would have been the better husband, the better father. Probably she'd come crawling back to him someday.

But after a few years went by and Mary hadn't returned to Wishbone, much less to him, he had been forced to conclude that she'd run off with fast-talking Josiah because she'd just plain loved him more. After that he'd been so consumed by jealousy that he'd finally had to forget, to bury himself in his work. He had single-mindedly avoided thinking about Mary all these years.

Until now.

Now, it turned out, his first impression had been correct, but his heart reaped no satisfaction at the thought.

It was a while before Ivy spoke again, but when she did, her voice was lower, more thoughtful. "I didn't know…"

"She was in love with him all those years." A petulant sigh came from Joe Junior. "Now I supposed *you'll* fall in love with him, too!"

"Me? What nonsense!" Ivy exclaimed.

"You already stare at him all the time," Joe Junior said accusingly.

She did? Justin, who had been lost in thoughts of the past, straightened with interest.

"Fiddlesticks, I don't, either," Ivy said.

"Then what're you hanging around for?"

Money was the obvious answer. But that's not what Ivy said.

"I'm staying to look after you, Joe Junior, and see that you don't grow into a muddleheaded fool like me!"

They rounded the corner and plowed right into Justin. All of them jumped in surprise. Though it was dark, he could see a stain creep into Ivy's cheeks. He felt flushed himself. *Had she really been staring at him?*

The two of them stood glowing at each other like lightning bugs.

"Where have you been?" His tone came out harsher than he'd intended. "I've been looking all over hell and gone for you."

She put her hands on her hips. "Then why didn't you call for me? What were you doing, spying on us?"

"No!" The answer came so quickly, though, it was pretty clear that's exactly what he had been doing.

She tilted a skeptical glance at him, her green eyes shining.

"We'd better get back," he said tightly, then turned and went back to where they'd left their horses. Beulah was still tied in front of the saloon, and they fetched her, too.

For his part, Joe Junior was so happy to be spared a lecture from his formidable uncle that he didn't dare break into the long, awkward silence during the ride home. He simply took the absence of reproach from his uncle as a gift.

More than likely it would be the only one from him he'd ever receive.

Chapter Five

Ivy reached back with a broom handle and gave the braided rug hanging on the clothesline the strongest beating she or it could stand. The old tattered carpet had shed most of its dust already; it was probably cleaner than it had been at any point in its long, much abused life. Trouble was, Ivy's frustrations remained.

Not a word! Not so much as a syllable or a smile had Justin directed at her today. Even his usual growling would have been more welcome than silence. How much of her conversation with Joe Junior last night had he heard? Had he heard Joe Junior tell her the truth about Mary? Or that Ivy was always staring at Justin?

Had she always been staring at Justin?

This had come as a shock to her, but the truth was, in retrospect, she seemed to remember so much of what Justin looked like in certain moments, what his reactions had been to various snippets of conversation, that she wondered if she had actually taken her eyes off the man since coming to Wishbone.

Of course, she wasn't about to go falling in love

with Justin because he had a handsome face. Lord help her, she was immune to that kind of nonsense by now. But ever since last night, it wasn't exactly Justin's handsome face—handsome as ever this morning, she noted as she gave the rug another forceful *whack*—that was plaguing her thoughts. It was that tale Joe Junior had told of his mother. The woman who had loved Justin, then run off with his brother and lived to regret it. Bitterly, apparently.

And on the other side of that tale was Justin—a thirty-five-year-old bachelor, living out on this isolated ranch, all these years, nursing that old wound. She'd been so wrong about him! Called him all sorts of names to his face. She'd thought that he was a man without a heart, when really he was all heart. All broken heart. No wonder Wink had been so certain that there would never be a Mrs. Murphy. She was probably the only woman who'd gotten so much as a toehold on the Bar M in all these years, and she was only tolerated out of dire necessity.

Ivy gave the rug several more slugs before she stopped. Someone was chuckling behind her. She whirled and found herself face-to-face with the object of her thoughts.

Justin was standing just a few feet away from her, rubbing his clean-shaven chin. Her insides did an uneasy flip at the sight of the line of white teeth glinting at her. "What's so funny?"

"You. You're flogging that carpet within an inch of its life," he drawled. "What's the matter with you today? You're jumpier than a cat in a roomful of rocking chairs."

She leaned on the broom handle. My, he was handsome. She *did* want to just stare and stare at him, precisely as Joe Junior had said. "What's the matter with *me?*" She laughed incredulously. "As if I'm the one who's been silent as a tomb all day!"

His smile disappeared. He didn't answer her.

She felt rattled. Didn't he know this tight-lipped-westerner behavior was driving her to distraction? "I don't know how you can try to pretend that nothing happened last night."

"You mean about Joe Junior? Oh, well, the less said about that—"

She huffed in irritation. "I mean about Joe Junior and *everything*. Unless you're not just pretending that you didn't overhear our conversation last night," she said, and by the way his face blanched she could tell that he had indeed overheard every word.

"What do you want me to say?" he asked stiffly.

What, indeed? She didn't have the faintest idea. She only knew that she wanted him to say *something*, to acknowledge how wrong she had been. "I would think you'd want to gloat at me, for one thing. I was so wrong!" She felt a rush of fresh shame at how terribly she'd behaved with him. "I called you Scrooge! A reptile! A fiend!"

"Maybe you were right to."

"I was terrible! But I swear I had no idea…I mean, of course you wouldn't jump at the chance to take care of children who, well, who would be reminders of…" Try as she might, the name wouldn't come out of her mouth.

But he could say it. A dark shadow came over his

face, and his lips were tight, but he spat out the word, his tone terse and pained. "Mary."

She felt her cheeks go red. "You're still in love with her, aren't you?"

"No."

"But you must be, or else why…?"

She couldn't go on. She felt so silly. He obviously didn't want to talk about Mary, but she had been able to think of nothing else since last night. She'd stayed up until the stars began to disappear, wondering whether, after all these years, Justin was still in love with the woman who had jilted him. Oh, he was capable of far more emotion than she had ever given him credit for!

He was also capable of making her feel more for a man than she'd ever dreamed. For weeks she'd been flying at him, huffing and insulting him. Now she felt like flinging herself at him in a completely different, shameless way.

"When you look at me, I know now you're thinking about all the terrible things she did to you," she said.

"You're wrong, Ivy."

She couldn't believe it. She closed the distance between him so that he would have to look her in the eye. "I used to wonder why you were so hostile with me, but now I know. You were thinking of her."

He grabbed her shoulders. "You couldn't be further from the truth."

She wasn't listening to him. "You've been pining for her all this time, so lovesick that you've forgotten how to love. You probably haven't thought of anyone but Mary—or yourself!—in years."

"No, Ivy." He pulled her closer, gruffly, almost as if he were angry. The look in his eyes was heated, intense. "I've thought about you. Some nights it seems as if I think of nothing *but* you." He looked into her eyes, then dashed aside a lock of hair the nippy wind had blown across her cheek. The touch of his hand on her skin made her shudder. Or maybe it was his voice, so rasping it sounded as if every word were being dragged directly from his soul. "I've lain awake nights thinking about those bow lips of yours, and what it would feel like to kiss them."

She could hardly believe his words, yet she clung to them, savoring them. Her? He'd been thinking about her?

"Oh, heaven!" She was unsure whether it was a simple exclamation or an answer to his late-night wondering.

"Yes," he agreed just before his mouth descended on hers.

At the touch of his lips, the whole world seemed to tip crazily. Justin, kissing her. Her, melting against him like butter in July. Nothing was certain anymore; the only thing solid was the feel of Justin against her, holding her to him. She hung on for all she was worth, delighting in the heat of him, the smell of to-bacco and leather and sweat.

She had never felt so full of desire for any man's kiss. Maybe because she realized, as she lifted up on tiptoe to tilt her lips more fully to Justin, that she had never been kissed by a real man before. Zack had not been a man, but an overgrown wiry youth whose usury she'd had foolishly mistaken for passion.

She wondered now, as she felt Justin plunder her lips, how she could have mistaken Zack's immature fondling for the real McCoy. Justin's slightest move felt more sensual, more dangerous than anything she'd experienced. The touch of his tongue awakened her senses in a way that made her feel flushed and weak-kneed yet powerfully alive.

She grabbed onto the lapel of his jacket, knowing what they were doing was a mistake…though a powerfully irresistible one. He anchored her firmly against him right there in broad daylight for anyone to see, and she shamelessly moved against him, testing him, trying to gauge if she really held sway over his imagination as he had claimed.

He let out a groan, and she pushed away, suddenly embarrassed that she could have been so bold, so brazen.

But he held on to her hand, unwilling to let her flee from him.

She pulled back more, surprised that her legs could still hold her up. The world around her was reeling in confusion. *She* was reeling. Justin had kissed her, and she had welcomed his kisses and would have gladly welcomed more if he'd offered. She'd behaved like a wanton, just like those women she'd lived with in prison. The thought filled her with chagrin, made her want to run. What must Justin think of her?

He probably didn't care. No man had ever really cared for her. Maybe he was just kissing her to forget, or because he'd been alone so long. Maybe he was just using her because he sensed that she had a checkered past.

There was nowhere she could escape what she had just done. No escaping the burning, knowing look in Justin's eye.

"I have to leave," she said in a rush.

He laughed softly, a deep sound that sent a shiver right through her. She jerked her hand away and nearly fell backward when he let her go. "Where are you going?"

"Back to Boston!" The words were out before she could think the answer through. But once said, the answer had a comforting effect on her. Home! Someplace at least where the discomforts were all familiar. If she could just get away from here, from those eyes of his, from that haunted look she'd seen on his face last night. From those arms she wanted to leap right back into.

He stepped forward and she jumped back in a dance of wills. "Back to Boston?" He scoffed. "That's the most preposterous thing I've ever heard."

"Why?" she asked.

"You said you wanted to start a brand-new life."

"Well, right now I'll settle for my stale old one!"

"Last night you told Joe Junior you were staying here," he said. "You promised him."

She looked up into his face, her cheeks burning. "So now you admit to having overheard us!"

He ignored her comment. "You *can't* go now. How would you get back to Boston? It's a foolish notion!"

They glared at each other, both building up steam.

She didn't know when, in the past two minutes, Justin's look of heated desire had turned into heated anger, but it certainly had. And frankly, she was relieved. Kisses were perplexing; rage she could handle.

"I have means," she replied, tilting her chin upward. "I've had the means all along, only I didn't want to use it unless it was an emergency."

"What are you talking about?"

She reached into her pocket and proudly pulled out her trump, the ring the odious people of Otis had given her. "This!" she proclaimed proudly, holding up the ring. "I could sell it for train fare. At least it would get me as far as Fort Worth!"

As Justin stared at her prize, he did not seem impressed by her resourcefulness. In fact, his face went white and he staggered back a step. "Where did you get that?"

She looked down at the ring, trying to understand his reaction. "The mayor in Otis gave it to me. He said they found it on Josiah when he died." She frowned as a terrible thought occurred to her. "Did you think I stole it?"

"No!" His voice was ragged. "I just hadn't seen it since…"

Since…?

"It was Mary's," he choked out. "I gave it to her."

The ring suddenly felt like an iron weight in her hand. Mary had kept it all those years, and *she* had been about to pawn it.

Ivy felt remorseful, ashamed. "Take it," she said. "It should be yours."

He stepped away farther, his hands stiffly in front of him. "No, keep it. Use it like you said."

She recoiled. Then he *did* want her to leave. Or did he? She felt more confused than ever, and more trapped. Because she knew that she could never hock the ring now. There was no way out. She would be stuck on this prairie with Justin till the end of time, and right now he looked like he wanted her there less than ever.

She felt ashamed and hurt. He'd been willing to kiss her, but it was obvious he was still pining for Mary.

She shot him a pitying look. "You *have* forgotten how to love," she told him. "You're living in the past and there's no hope for you ever to find comfort or happiness there!"

She turned on her heel and fled inside the house.

Though what they jokingly referred to as the parlor always felt more crowded in the winter than at other times, never before had it felt as crowded as this. The three hands and Ivy pulled the chairs up from the wall and placed them in a semicircle near the stove. On the rug, the children sat at Arnie's feet while he picked at his three-stringed banjo and sang old miner's songs in a croaky but loud voice. Parts of the songs weren't fit for mixed company, not to mention young ears, but Arnie didn't seem to notice, and neither did the kids. Wink, on the other hand, turned purple with discomfort.

Justin barely heard the music, and he really wasn't watching all the people clustered around the stove, either. All he could see, no matter where he looked, was Ivy's face from that afternoon. The hurt she'd showed him, the pity, hadn't left him for a single second. He just couldn't shake that expression.

"Don't sit so close, Linus," Ivy said, dragging the child a safe distance from the hot iron stove.

At her voice, Justin flinched.

Ivy was facing stiffly away from him. He could see only her profile. From the way she refused to meet his eye, he guessed that she couldn't forget their kiss any more than he could.

Justin didn't know how to handle himself now. He fidgeted more than he should have, and fiddled with his pipe while the others listened attentively to Arnie's songs. He wanted to leave but felt as bound to his desk chair as if he had a rope tying him down. He doubted he could have moved if his boots had caught fire. He couldn't force himself away from Ivy.

Still pining for Mary? No, he wasn't, he should have said again. But the ring had startled him. The ring he'd given Mary on the day she'd promised to be his forever.

Forever hadn't lasted past two weeks after his brother had come back from a trip out to Arizona, broker than he'd ever been and ready to leech off Justin's charity. Justin had been willing to give his brother bed and board in exchange for work at the fledgling Bar M. He hadn't bargained on giving his brother his girl as well.

But Josiah had probably been hard for a girl to resist back then. He was tall and dark, with a loud, lusty laugh and eyes that always seemed to shine with some sort of mischief. A girl like Mary probably thought she'd be in for a lifetime of adventure with a man as brash and open as Josiah. Mary had fallen for him, and they had left Justin flat.

He'd never heard from his brother again till after Mary had died. Josiah had written him, asking for money. He'd sent it.

He wished now he'd sent more. And along with the money, he wished he'd sent some forgiveness. Maybe it would have made a difference.

Justin looked at Ivy, who was so different from Mary but who tugged at his heart in the same way Mary had all those years ago. Now *she* wanted to leave him flat, too. The thought made him feel as if an aching canyon had opened in his chest.

It was as if he was in love with her.

Justin frowned. He had to shift in his chair, readjust himself, get used to the odd breathless feeling in his chest. He *was* in love with her.

He was in love with Ivy Ryan.

It wasn't just the kiss that had told him so, either. The feeling went deeper than that, right down to the way he could admire her even when she annoyed the tarnation out of him. Or the way his heart picked up when he heard her laugh or looked into her eyes. It was the caring in her voice when she spoke to Joe Junior, Linus and Sophie. It was the way his feet seemed to dance along instead of trudge as they so often used to.

He was in love. But he was also in trouble. Ivy wouldn't even spare him a glance now. He'd kissed her and her first reaction was to declare she wanted to put half a continent between them.

Then there was that damn ring. Seeing it had surprised the wits out of him. Like a ghost coming back to haunt him. But he wasn't living in the past. Ivy might not believe it, but that part of his life was over.

Maybe he should just drop down on his knee and beg her not to go. He feared, however, that she'd simply laugh in his face. She'd considered him an ogre for so long, a heartless curmudgeon, that she probably wouldn't believe his sincerity. Or maybe she would think that he was using her to forget Mary. But that wasn't true. He loved Ivy for herself. He loved her, and if it took him forever, he was going to find a way to prove it.

He shot to his feet so suddenly that Arnie's fingers stilled. When the music stopped, everybody in the room seemed to gape at him. Expect for Ivy, of course.

"I'm going to bed," he announced awkwardly. "But keep playing as long as you like, Arnie."

"Sure thing," Arnie said with a grin. "I could play all night."

How could he prove to Ivy that he was a changed man?

He pondered this problem as he moved around his room and crawled into bed. Ivy thought he was heartless, which was utterly unfair. Hadn't he taken in the children? Fed them? He hadn't blown his stack at them in days.

But when he pictured them now, trying to prove to himself that he'd done right by them, he saw the three youngsters huddled around that stove. His face felt drawn suddenly, as if all the blood had drained out of his cheeks. Why were they huddled? Because it was freezing outside and they were wearing the patched rags they had been wearing when they came here three weeks ago!

He cringed beneath the covers. He felt ashamed of himself. Truly ashamed.

Ivy was right. All these years, he'd been obsessed with how Mary had hurt him. He had thought about how much better a husband he would have been to her than Josiah. How much better a father he would have been than Josiah. And yet look at what he'd done. Taken in her children, then let them practically freeze to death.

Was it too late now to become that better man he'd always assumed he was? He prayed it wasn't. Desperately.

Most of all he prayed it wasn't too late to prove to Ivy that he wasn't a lost cause after all.

Chapter Six

"Ivy! You'd better get outside, quick!"

Ivy, who was standing in the kitchen, turned to Joe Junior, shocked by his panicky command. "What's the matter?"

"He's sending us back!"

At the back door, Sophie peeked around her brother, aiming an owl-wide gaze at Ivy. Ivy could hear Linus screaming hysterically.

She took off the towel she had pinned to her dress front and wiped her hands on it. Then she ran to fetch her coat. She didn't have to ask who *he* referred to. The same *he* she had been trying unsuccessfully not to think about for an entire day…the same man she had been foolish enough to kiss.

Justin was sending the children back? Back to where?

She hurriedly returned to the kitchen and gave John an exasperated glance as she stormed out the back door. Sure enough, Justin was sitting at the front of his wagon, looking impatient.

He turned his gaze on her, and despite the fact that

she was mightily perturbed at the man, she felt her stomach flip crazily at the sight of his brown eyes. Oh, she was a fool, all right.

"What's going on?" she demanded.

"I told the children to get into the wagon," he informed her. "I'm taking them to town."

She crossed her arms, ready to stand her ground and do battle. "Why? What have they done?"

"Not a thing."

"Then why—?"

His eyes glittered hard at her. "Come to think of it, you'd better come, too."

No doubt! If the children were being packed off, there was absolutely no reason for her to be here. In fact, she half suspected the children were being disposed of so he could get rid of her. "Believe me, Mr. Murphy, there's nothing I'd like better than to get off this confounded ranch of yours, but where are you sending these children?"

"I told you, I'm taking them to town. I'm not saying any more than that."

"Does the stage stop today?" she asked, still trying to puzzle this out. Was he going to trundle them all onto the stage and say good riddance? "Where are you sending us?"

"I didn't mention sending anyone anywhere, did I?" he asked defensively. "Good Lord, Ivy, don't you ever just do what someone asks?"

She fumed silently. He was being evasive, and in her experience, evasions usually meant bad news ahead. "All right, let me get my things!"

"Never mind that, Ivy."

"But my things—"

"Don't worry about *things*."

She swallowed a scream of frustration. Probably her belongings seemed insignificant to him. It was true, she didn't own much. Just a change of dress, the book Carol had given her, and a cheap comb set she'd bought with her first wages as a maid. No, she wasn't going to make a fool of herself by causing a stink about her pitiful possessions. If Justin Murphy was in such an all-fired hurry to get rid of her, she'd oblige him.

She lifted her head proudly and turned to the children. "All right, climb on. We're leaving." She tried to make it sound as if it were her idea.

Joe Junior and Sophie clambered into the wagon wordlessly, but Linus threw himself weeping on John Tall Tree, who looked even more stoic than usual. He plucked Linus off his leg, then placed the boy next to his siblings. "I will see you again, young friends. Very soon, I think."

"Bye, John Tall Tree," Sophie said. Linus howled. Joe Junior's face burned red.

Justin sighed restlessly. "All right, climb up," he told Ivy.

She bridled resentfully and tried to step up. When she fell back, Justin grabbed her upper arm and hauled her up next to him. She landed on the seat with a surprised gasp. She felt amazed anew by the strength in him, and by her reaction to his mere touch. Her cheeks flamed and she faced forward quickly, hoping he wouldn't notice.

Maybe he didn't, because without more ado, he

tapped the reins against his team of sleek mares and they were off. Ivy didn't look back, even though she felt a strange tug of sadness that they might be leaving the Bar M forever. For all its critters and dust and strangeness, the ranch had been the most comfortable home she had ever had. She felt a moment of panic when she realized she was leaving without a word of goodbye to Arnie, Wink and Sam. But she couldn't bring himself to beg Justin for anything just now. She would write the men a letter when she got to where she was going, wherever that was. They would be able to read it by the stove some night.

At the thought of anyone missing her, she sniffed back a wistful tear. Linus was still blubbering behind her, a sound that could be heard over the hollow clop-clop of the horse's hooves against the hard trail.

Justin bristled with astonishment. ''I thought you *wanted* to go back to Boston.''

''I do!'' she insisted. Only her voice didn't have the vehemence of a heartfelt declaration. What had seemed warm and comforting in the spur of the moment a week ago, now made her feel a dull ache inside, as if she would be crawling back in defeat.

''Do you have a sweetheart in Boston?'' Justin asked.

The question was practically the first personal information he'd tried to get out of her. Why would he be curious now, when he was packing her off to God knows where? ''If I had, do you think I would have taken Josiah up on his marriage bargain?''

Justin's expression tightened. ''Some bargain. Why *did* you take him up on it? A pretty gal like you…surely you could have found someone in all of Massachusetts to marry you.''

Pretty? She blushed in confusion. It was the first compliment he'd paid her…only he hadn't actually made it sound like a compliment, somehow. More like a veiled insult for not being able to snag a man despite a certain physical appeal. She detected a hint of suspicion in his tone.

Of course, he had every reason to be suspicious of her. She was a sham, a fraud, a jailbird. Not that it was her fault she'd landed in jail, but she shouldn't have taken up with Zack to begin with.

''I guess I couldn't find any man demented enough to want me,'' she said with forced levity.

Justin didn't laugh at her attempt at a joke. He looked at her again with those dark, glittering eyes of his, and for a moment she felt his raw curiosity. ''So you're Little Miss Innocent, are you?''

She was sure her face was red as a ripe tomato. ''In some ways, yes.''

That, at least, was the truth. She might not have the most sterling character, but when it came to men, she was pure as the driven snow. Well…*mostly*. Certainly she'd let Zack kiss her a little more exuberantly than she should have, and a walk in the park had once turned into a pitched battle. But she certainly wasn't a soiled dove.

Just slightly soiled.

The rest of the trip went faster than she'd remembered it taking even on a runaway horse. Somehow, when she least wanted it to, the landscape slipped away before her, and before she knew it Wishbone was on the horizon and they were rushing toward it. Justin remained silent, but he had an almost gleeful determination about him that provoked Ivy more than anything he could have said.

He stopped the team in front of Tomlin's Mercantile—just where she'd come in, she thought miserably—and turned to her with a smug grin.

"All right, you win," she said. "Do you have to be so happy about it?"

"Why shouldn't I be? I've never done this before," he said.

"Never kicked four human beings out in the cold?" Ivy asked, even though it wasn't actually cold. They would be out in the cool at worst. Still, she wanted to make him sound as much the ogre as she'd always known he was, except for the few days she was foolishly blinded by sympathy for him.

He laughed. Laughed! That took a nerve.

She turned on him in a huff. But before she could speak, Joe Junior piped up from behind them. "I ain't goin' nowheres."

Justin and Ivy turned, surprised by the red look of determination on the young face.

"What?" Ivy asked.

"I ain't goin' back to Otis," Joe Junior said. "I'll work for my keep." His chin stuck up proudly. "I can, too. I won't make trouble. I can ride just as well as…" His boast dissolved unspoken. "Well, I can help out the others, at least. That's got to be worth something to you, Mr. Murphy."

There was a moment of tense silence as Justin

stared at the boy, who despite his big talk seemed younger and more vulnerable than ever.

Justin didn't reach out to Joe Junior, but his voice seemed to. When he spoke, it was in a softer, more kindly tone than Ivy had ever heard from him. "I'm Uncle Justin, Joe, not Mr. Murphy."

In reply, Joe Junior merely shrugged his scrawny shoulders.

"And you won't have time to work," Justin continued. "Not if you're going to school."

Ivy gasped. "Going to school?" She whirled around, flustered. "But I thought..."

Justin beamed a grin as big as the plains at her. "I never said a word about anyone going anywhere! I just brought you all into town for some shopping."

She gazed back in amazement at the store, which seemed a lot less sinister and more welcoming now. Before she could get her head straight, however, Justin had already stepped down, pulled the children out of the back, and handed the reins to Joe Junior for the boy to tie down. "Since you're so eager to work," he quipped to the boy.

Then he stepped over to Ivy and offered her his hand. "Would you care to peruse the offerings with me?"

Ivy laughed. She barely recognized the man with the carefree, flirtatious grin. He looked almost as much a boy as Linus, who was already pressed face to glass against the store's front window, gawking at an elaborately carved rocking horse that was nearly as big as he was.

She felt a silly thrill herself as she walked into the

musty store that smelled of coffee, cinnamon, new muslin and aged cedar shelves.

"Well, well…lookee here!" Hank exclaimed. "It's Justin, with a whole heap of company. What you doin' back so soon?"

Justin hesitated. Then he looked over at Linus on that rocking horse, and a big, beaming smile came over him again. "What do you think I'm here for? It's nearly Christmas, isn't it?"

For a moment it appeared Hank was either going to expire from shock, or gloat, or run outside to call over some witnesses to Justin's transformation. Ivy almost wanted him to, because she herself could hardly believe what she was seeing. But knowing a sale when he had one, Hank's businessman's head soon took over and he rushed out from behind the counter.

Justin was inspecting Linus's rocking horse. "Wouldn't you rather have a real horse?" he asked the little boy.

Linus's face collapsed in disappointment.

"*I* would!" Joe Junior exclaimed. Then, when everyone looked over at him, he blushed. "Someday," he added bashfully.

Linus still clung desperately to the wooden variety. Justin laughed. "Something smaller, maybe," he urged his nephew, pulling him off and distracting him with a shelf lined with toys.

Though, to be honest, Ivy couldn't say who was the most distracted, Justin or his young relatives. For the next thirty minutes, he was completely absorbed in toys—wooden pull toys, colorfully painted tin toys

that had parts that moved when he pushed them along
the shelf, a marionette that he skillfully made dance
almost as if he were a born showman. He decided
nothing would do for Sophie but a doll, even though
the girl protested that she was too old for them. Which
made Ivy wonder if Sophie had ever had one. She
plucked at the rag dolly Hank handed her as if she
didn't know what to do with the thing.

Justin didn't like it anyway. "*That's* not what we
need," he told Hank. "Don't you have one of those
dollies with a pretty dress and a face that's realistic?"

Hank looked at Justin as if he'd grown two heads.
Ivy was beginning to wonder herself. "A china doll,
you mean?"

Justin's face lit up. "That's it! Don't you have one
of those?"

"Well…" Hank rummaged around in back of his
counter and found a flowered box. When he pulled
off the ribboned lid and brought forth a dazzling princess of a doll, with golden blond hair and a delicate
face with blue painted eyes and a dress of white shot
through with gold, they all let out a collective gasp.

"That's just perfect!" Justin exclaimed. He held it
up to Sophie for her approval.

The girl looked numb. "What would I do with it?"

Justin glanced back at the princess in her box and
nodded. "Maybe she's right," he said to Hank with
a meaningful wink. "Now for clothes!"

"What about my horsie?" Linus yelled after him.

Justin laughed. "Some other time, maybe," he said
to Linus, pulling him off the toy. "Right now we've

got to get you suited up. And buy you some new boots!''

And that's what he proceeded to do. Justin bought boots for all of them, and hats and mittens and mufflers. New britches and cotton shirts, coats and woolen socks. When Sophie declared she wouldn't wear a flowered dress, he found a plaid one just right for her, and bought her some velvet ribbons of red and green to wear in her hair.

''Never thought I'd see the day when *you'd* be buying holiday ribbon!'' Hank couldn't help gloating.

Justin took the criticism with a laugh and glanced over at Ivy. ''Well, I've got to buy even more—we haven't started on Miss Ryan.''

Ivy had been happy watching Justin on his spree but felt herself go pale as all the attention turned to her. She was even more appalled when the children jumped up and down in excitement. ''Yea! New clothes for Ivy, too!''

''Oh, no,'' she protested. ''I don't need anything.''

''Nonsense,'' Justin said. ''Do you think we like looking at you in those same two dresses all the time?'' He turned to the children for confirmation. ''Well, do we?''

''No!'' they cried gleefully. And then they were off like racehorses, pawing at bolts of cloth, poring over patterns, pulling bonnets off hat racks and dropping them onto her head. Ivy felt under siege, but of course she was dazzled by the attention. How could she not be? She had never waltzed into a store and simply pointed out what she wanted. In the past, she had usually coveted an item for months, squirreling away pennies till she could afford it, if she ever could. Usually she ended up buying something cheaper, less appealing. But Justin was all generosity, insisting on the finest cloth, the newest pattern, the best stockings.

"And the prettiest hat," he said. He walked over to the display again and picked out a green velvet hat that Ivy had been looking at when she'd first come into the store. She hadn't thought he'd been watching her!

She shook her head. It was such a frivolous item! The lush green velvet was gathered loosely with a brown ribbon at the brim and festooned with a cluster of bright red berries. "I couldn't. Something practical, maybe..." She tried to show enthusiasm for a functional straw bonnet.

Justin's face screwed up in distaste. "You don't want that!"

She laughed. "How do you know?"

"Because you showed up in that silly blue hat—a more impractical object I've never seen."

"Well, I've changed," she declared.

"You'll have to save your own pennies for a granny bonnet, then," he said, and he left her looking longingly at the green velvet, which was really what she'd been hoping for all along. Served her right for not just coming out and saying so!

"All right, Justin," Hank interrupted. "You want that I should wrap all this up now?"

"Not just yet," Justin said. "I forgot the most important purchase."

The children, already dazed from all the attention, looked up at him blankly. Between the clothes and some silly toys and trinkets filling the counter, they seemed to have no concept of what other treats could be in store. Even Ivy couldn't think of one more thing that they could want.

"Candy!" he reminded them.

Linus's face lit up joyfully, and when a full trio of gleeful shouts went up, filling the room with that squealing happiness, Ivy had to bite her lip to hold tears back. They sounded so happy. They really sounded like children. So much so that she was beginning to believe in Christmas miracles.

She smiled as Justin pulled peppermint sticks out of tall jars. Perhaps the turnaround in him was the biggest miracle of all. But would it last?

Christmas Eve was one surprise after another, but perhaps the first big one came when John Tall Tree, after an absence of a few hours, came through the front door hauling a ceiling-high cedar tree.

"Fool white man does not know how to honor one of the oldest traditions of his own people—" John said, displaying his evergreen proudly, "the Christmas tree!" He'd even hammered two crossed boards into the trunk so it would stand proud and straight in the corner of the parlor.

Arnie came in dragging up the rear. "I tried pointing out to John that we'd never had a tree here before," he declared to Ivy almost apologetically. "I don't know how the boss man's gonna take this."

Ivy crossed her arms. "He'll take it and like it!"

In fact, given Justin's jolly mood these days, she was surprised he hadn't thought of a Christmas tree himself. But today he was too busy taking Joe Junior out riding on his new pony, which he had sneaked off and bought from a nearby rancher the day before. Joe Junior, naturally, was over the moon.

When they had carefully placed the tree in the corner, Arnie was still shaking his head, and now Wink joined him. "Never had one of these before," Wink intoned ominously.

"There were never children in the house before," John pointed out in irritation. "*Someone* must teach white children their own customs."

Ivy merely smiled at the men's arguments and showed Linus and Sophie how to string popcorn to make a garland. With the exception of herself, no one seemed truly to have adjusted to the change in Justin. People still looked at him suspiciously when he bellowed with laughter, or blinked in confusion when he spoke eagerly of the Christmas dinner. It was almost as if no one believed a man could change so much.

But she did. Because she'd changed, too. Certainly three weeks ago she had never dreamed she could fall in love with a man she considered a heartless ogre who delighted in his role of her tormenter, but somehow the unthinkable had come to pass. The horrible part now was that he wasn't encouraging her. In the past week he hadn't touched her, certainly not kissed her or even spoken a single flirtatious word. She was in love with Justin all on her own, and every day that passed seemed to intensify her feelings.

When Justin came back into the house with Joe Junior not long before dinner, the two beamed at the

Christmas tree almost conspiratorially. "That's just what we needed, isn't it, Joe?"

Joe Junior shoved his hands into his pockets and turned his red, happy face to Ivy. "Sure is!"

She looked from nephew to uncle suspiciously, wondering what on earth they had up their sleeves now. They were acting like little kids—and only one of them had an excuse!

John managed to stay calm when they showed up late for his dinner, suppressing sly giggles, but Ivy was wary of them all through the meal, which, given the amount of food they had prepared, seemed to last forever. They had a roast beef, a ham and a wonderful stuffed duck. John had cooked up every kind of vegetable he could lay hands on—black-eyed peas, cabbage, carrots and two kinds of potatoes. Plus there was bread, and chocolate cake for dessert. Enough bounty to feed half of Texas.

This was the first instance that there was still food on the table when the meal was over. Ivy stood and started clearing the plates but was stopped by Justin.

"Leave those a while. There's something you'd all better come see."

Everyone tramped into the parlor. A collective cry of delight went up when they saw what he'd led them out for—presents under the tree! Several boxes with ribbons and Linus's rocking horse lay beneath the cedar's lowest boughs. And that was just what was under the tree. On the tree were smaller packages and pouches attached with bows to branches. Everyone crowded around, careful not to have their feet smashed by an exuberantly rocking Linus.

Sam was the first to rip open his gift—a new pair of fine thick leather gloves. Wink got a pipe and a whole pouch of tobacco, which pleased him to no end. "Good quality, too!" he exclaimed excitedly. John received a long box, which he accepted with much grumbling about white man's traditions, until he found himself admiring a sleek new ivory-handled knife. Then his face went especially stern in appreciation. Arnie got banjo strings and a brand-new mouth organ. Within moments, lively music was added to the festive atmosphere.

As Ivy stood back looking at the confused jumble, everyone talking at once, tunes tumbling easily from Arnie, she wondered if this could be the same place she'd entered weeks before. Then she saw Sophie tentatively pull the top of a flowered box and knew the world had changed. Inside was the princess doll, looking even more pristine and out of place among all the cowhands than it had in the store. The girl's pale face froze in disbelief as she gaped at her new treasure.

Wink bent over to compliment her. "Why, that's about the best-looking dolly I've ever seen!" he exclaimed, and everyone agreed as Sophie finally flushed with pleasure. "Would you let me dance with her?"

Sophie clasped her new possession in a panic. "Oh, she doesn't dance, Wink!"

Everyone laughed.

"There's another present there," Justin pointed out to Ivy.

She turned to him, feeling her face go pink, and

looked into his delighted eyes. Some holiday demon must have possessed him.

"No, Justin, you've given me so much already. My new dress…"

His brown eyes took in her wasp-waisted creation from her shoulders to her toes. She'd rushed to finish it for today, and the hands had all complimented her lavishly on her needlework, but she hadn't gone pink from pleasure in the wake of their compliments as she did now as Justin kept staring at her.

"It's very pretty, Ivy. You're almost as good-looking as Sophie's doll."

She laughed self-consciously.

"It'll look even better with what's in that box," he added with a grin.

She couldn't resist going over and opening the box then, though she probably wouldn't have been able to resist in any case. Justin's mood seemed to have infected everyone. She undid the fat velvet ribbon and pulled off the lid to the round box and found herself staring at that coveted green hat. It was elegant and elaborate and impossibly impractical. And she loved it!

She jumped up and modeled her new creation to the delight of everyone. Never in her life had she owned something so frivolous and silly and beautiful. And never had she expected the twinkle in a man's dark eyes to make her want to weep with equal parts joy and longing.

"Thank you, Justin!" She beamed a smile at him, wondering if she could press a kiss to his cheek without the others raising their brows.

But she didn't have the nerve. She just smiled at him, and when he ducked his head and went over to rock Linus on his wooden horse, she felt the unhappy stab of a missed opportunity.

Long past the time when everyone else went to bed, Ivy found herself unable to sleep. Though she was careful not to make a sound, her whole body seemed to hum as she picked up ribbon and rolled the pieces into tidy balls or retied them onto the tree. She could have stayed up forever breathing in the evergreen smell.

There was a chuckle from the doorway. "Do you ever stop working?"

She spun in surprise. She'd thought she was the only one up, but there stood Justin at the kitchen door, his face red from the cold outside. He'd obviously been out in the barn, probably milking early so the men wouldn't have to on Christmas day.

"I couldn't sleep. This was the nicest holiday I've ever spent anywhere," she declared.

His whole face seemed to light up as he stepped closer to her. "I'm glad."

"But you shouldn't have bought me that hat," she said. "It was present enough for me to see everyone so happy."

"That's how I felt watching you opening that hat-box," he replied. "That was all the gift I needed."

She blushed, remembering she had a gift for him, too. "Stay right here," she commanded, then turned and ran back to the little room she shared with Linus and Sophie. Her place in bed now was taken by Princess Cornelia, the name conferred by Sophie on her new friend. She smiled at the children and then reached into her bag for the muffler she'd stayed up nights knitting. It seemed rather homespun to her after the elaborate gifts that he'd given everyone, and she hadn't had time to tie a nice ribbon around it, but she preferred to give it to him now, when no one else was around.

When she came skidding breathlessly back up to him he was still dutifully rooted in the same spot by the Christmas tree. She brought the muffler from behind her back and watched anxiously as he took it from her and unfolded it. In the privacy of her room the scarf had appeared huge, but now, in his big hands, the width seemed barely adequate.

And yet he reacted to the simple gift as if she'd just handed him a gold mine. His eyes shone as he looked up at her. "You made this?" he asked with awe.

Suddenly she felt stupidly proud, but only because his overly impressed expression made her so. "Yes."

He put his hands on her shoulders. "Ivy, it's wonderful." Swiftly he bent and touched his lips to hers.

A quick kiss, a thank-you, was all it was meant to be. She could tell because he immediately pulled back, but only a fraction. For a breathless moment, they stood frozen, their lips only inches apart, the world silent and still around them.

Her eyes flew shut. For an instant it felt as if she were teetering on a precipice, and if he'd lifted his hands from her shoulders she would have collapsed backward, falling into oblivion.

Instead, Justin pulled her forward, drawing her to him. Instinctively she tipped up on her toes and was rewarded by the firm pressure of his mouth on hers. Joy and desire sang through her. She had wanted this so, needed to feel his lips against hers as proof that her longing for him wasn't wrong or misguided. Feeling him against her, she knew that she had been right. That this was right.

He deepened the kiss, plundering her mouth with his tongue, and she reveled in the intimacy. In spite of the dying fire in the stove, a glorious heat built inside her, warming her utterly. She'd never known a mere kiss could make her feel so weightless, so free.

Justin felt it, too. All at once he lifted her into his arms, then twirled in a circle. They were still kissing, their lips inviolably attached, but they chuckled together, giddy with new love.

After a few more turns he finally stepped back and collapsed them into a chair, where they kissed some more then pulled apart ever so slightly. He looked at her, his face lit with emotion—the same strange, exciting brew that was swirling inside her. She wanted to tell him that she loved him, that this was the happiest she had ever been, that she never wanted to leave him. But he stopped her with his own declaration.

"I have something for you."

"Oh, but—"

He reached into his pocket and pulled out a letter. "I picked it up in town today. I hope you don't mind my holding out on you, but I thought you might enjoy it best on Christmas Day."

The envelope made her heart beat double time. Carol! She took the letter from him eagerly and then, as quickly as she could get a glance at the writing, her joy evaporated. The chicken scratch on the envelope was not her sister's round, loopy handwriting.

Seeing her reaction, Justin frowned. "It's from Boston," he said. "I thought it would be your family."

She ripped the missive open, but a quick look at the letter's contents made her feel sick inside. Sick and afraid. It was from Zack.

"My dere Ivy…"

Dear, he had the nerve to call her! After he'd let her go to prison for his crime. After she'd run two thousand miles to get away from him and the blight he'd left on her reputation. She hadn't even known Zack could write, and apparently she wasn't far from the truth, because his unsure scratch was riddled with mistakes.

Yer sis told me you was out in Texas and doin rele well. Im glad for you, Ivy, you know I am. Why did you leve? Carol did not wunt to give me yer adress, only I told her we wuz still engajed I love you as much as ever. You was and are my only girl. Im rele sorry for what happened and that the police pinched you sted of me but you was a brick, Ivy, and Ill never forgit it. Yer a stand up girl. Im glad you got some money now and I intind to cum out for you just as soon as I can so we can mary. Wate for me.

Yer luving husbund to be! Zack

"Ivy, what is it?"

It was only when Justin spoke that she realized her whole body was trembling. To one moment feel so safe and loved in Justin's arms, then feel those icy tentacles of the past get a stranglehold on her was unbearable.

Love her! Zack Hamilton didn't know the meaning of the word. But he probably really *did* intend to come find her. Why not? Con men could prosper anywhere, and here, at least, the police didn't know him!

Justin frowned in concern. "Ivy? You're white as a sheet!"

She didn't know what to say, so she remained silent. The paper had slipped out of her hands, and he snatched it up, glancing at a few lines. Then he darted a dark, confused glance at her. His whole body stiffened.

"Your husband-to-be!"

She shook her head. "No, he's…" What could she say? The man who landed her in prison? Justin didn't even know about her past. He knew nothing about her at all, and if he did, he probably wouldn't have been kissing her like he had. That thought made her feel even more numb.

"You never told me you were engaged."

"I'm not."

"You said you had no sweethearts at all in Boston."

"I didn't have!" Her face burned. "I mean, not really."

"But this man is coming out to join you, he says."

He didn't understand. He didn't see at all. She shook her head frantically. "No, Justin, it's not what you're thinking."

He put her off his lap and stood stiffly. "Is that why you came out here—to get some money so your lover could join you?"

"Justin, no!" She was on her feet now, too. How could such a beautiful moment turn ugly so fast? Her head was spinning from the turnaround.

But Justin seemed to have no problem making the change. His face was red with outrage at her perceived betrayal, yet he already looked fully convinced that she had deceived him. Almost as if he had expected it all along. "What did you intend to do, play Josiah for a fool?"

"I told you, I had already changed my mind about marrying Josiah when I stepped off the train in Otis!"

"So you saw my niece and nephews and decided to follow them to me to see what money you could squeeze out of me."

Her mouth dropped. The man could have been speaking Chinese, for all she understood him. "This is outrageous!"

"I'll say!" he huffed.

"I brought Linus, Sophie and Joe Junior to you, remember? You didn't even want them!"

"You can skip the out-of-the-goodness-of-your-own-heart nonsense," he shot back. "You were looking for payment, as I recall."

Which was true, she was. But she hadn't been as crass as he made it sound.

Had she?

She dropped back into the chair, feeling defensive and angry and beat. It was almost as if he didn't understand her at all, didn't comprehend what these past three weeks had done for her. "I'm not like that," she insisted.

And she wasn't. She was happier, more generous. All this time she thought she was just biding her time, waiting to start a new life, when really she had already begun.

But in a moment, in as much time as it had taken him to flick a gaze over Zack's foolish letter, Justin had changed his mind about her. He was seeing her as someone else entirely. Seeing her as Mary, probably. Zack's letter had opened the same old wounds Justin had been nursing for years and years, the ones Ivy thought had finally managed to heal. It wasn't fair!

"I knew better than to trust you," he said aloud, though she suspected he was speaking mostly to himself. "I was suspicious from the start, figuring you were out for something."

"Well, if it was money I sure didn't get it!" she hurled back at him. Did he really think she was just trying to take him?

His lips thinned into the grim line she hadn't seen for days. Somehow, seeing his old sourpuss expression hurt more than anything. "Not until you started throwing a little romance into the mix," he said, glaring angrily at her dress.

Her whole body flushed with humiliation, and she stood back up again, stiff with angry pride. "If you think that, Justin, then you're not worth my time any more than Zack Hamilton was! She grabbed Zack's letter and flung it toward the stove, then strode angrily from the room, leaving him to stew. But when she came back out a short time later, wrapped in her coat and determined to leave even though she was aching all over from having seen Linus and Sophie snug in their beds and not being able to wake them to say goodbye, the room was empty. Justin was gone. Zack's crumpled-up letter had disappeared, too. Justin had probably wanted to pore over it—the evidence of another woman's duplicity!

Feeling utterly empty inside, she left the house, unaware for the moment that she was being watched.

Chapter Seven

In the kitchen the next morning, Justin could barely hear himself think over Linus's wails of despair. But that was probably just as well. Given the thoughts going through his head, he would have been just as happy not to think at all.

As opposed to the good cheer of the night before, the house this morning had plunged into gloom. The hands, informed by John Tall Tree that Ivy was gone, had quickly eaten their breakfasts and headed out to do chores as if it were any normal day. Justin himself felt he could barely move, and the children were still too shocked to leave the table, though Justin wished they would. It was hard to face them looking so heart-sore and forsaken, especially when he felt much the same way himself.

"Where did she go?" Joe Junior asked.

"I don't know," Justin said honestly. She had simply vanished. On the children's bed, she had left her new dress and hat, Mary's ring and a much-read copy of Charles Dickens.

His older nephew was thunderstruck. "How could

you just let her go? Why didn't she tell me where she was headed?''

''I don't know,'' Justin repeated. It could have been his blanket answer for every question this morning.

Because while everything—Ivy's betrayal, his righteous anger—had seemed crystal clear last night, this morning matters were much fuzzier in his mind. *Had* Ivy really been hanging about the place waiting for her lover? By the clear light of day, that didn't ring true. Especially not when he remembered their kisses. But there had been that letter.

That letter he hadn't been able to find when he'd returned from his walk last night. Probably she'd taken it with her.

Why?

Because it was from Zack, her *husband-to-be*. The term irked him. He had thought he himself was on the verge of being her husband. He'd thought his whole life was about to change. His whole life *had* changed! And now he felt he was being dragged back into a solitary existence he didn't want to return to.

Except now he wasn't exactly solitary. He had three grumpy, upset, devastated kids to deal with. Linus sobbed loudly into his uneaten flapjacks.

''Linus, why don't you go play on your rocking chair?''

The boy rubbed his fists against his red eyes and shrilled, ''I don't wannaaa...'' The bellowed words strung out into a long wail.

Sophie, who had been staring at Justin—those big eyes of hers grating on his nerves as not even Linus's crying could—finally spoke up. "Do you think Ivy left because I let Princess Cornelia take her place in bed?"

The sad little question nearly made him crumble. "No," Justin bit out, then realized he'd answered too harshly. "I mean, you can't blame yourself for this, Sophie. None of you are to blame for Ivy leaving."

Joe Junior shot him a glare. "Then who is?" His glower at Justin, however, seemed to answer his own question.

I am, Justin should have gone ahead and said. *I am completely at fault.*

But part of him chafed at admitting guilt for this. He'd been betrayed by a woman before—with his own brother. And after all, he didn't really know Ivy Ryan, except for three measly weeks. What could twenty-one days teach a man about a woman?

Everything, a voice inside him scolded. Those few days they'd had together had showed him that she had green eyes that could melt his heart, a tumble of red hair he ached to run his hands through; that she had a beautiful smile worth coaxing out of her, and a quick, tough spirit that was as fierce as a bear when it came to something she felt strongly about. Like these kids. Like telling him he was wrong, which he so often was.

Did that man Zack really mean nothing to her? And if he didn't, why had she taken the man's letter with her?

Sophie pushed back her chair and stood. She was glaring at Justin now, too, just like Joe Junior. "Come on, Linus. You and me can go look at that book Ivy left us—that one about Mr. Scrooge!''

After the two had left, Joe Junior asked in a tight, proud voice, ''Is the pony still mine?''

Justin looked up, astounded. ''Of course, he is. That hasn't changed. Nothing has.''

But those last words rang hollow even in his own ears. Everything had changed. Nothing in the house felt right without Ivy.

''I'm going looking for her!'' Joe Junior said, turning and running for the door.

Justin sighed and got up to follow him. He didn't want Joe riding around upset.

But as he reached the door, John Tall Tree stopped him. The cook had been standing in the corner of the kitchen watching them all morning, not saying a word. But now he spoke to Justin directly and forcefully, ''Let the boy go. It would do him good to ride swiftly and get out his anger toward you.''

''Towards *me?*'' Justin said defensively. ''But I didn't do anything!''

John shook his head. ''You have committed the gravest offense to man everywhere.''

''What?''

''You have been an idiot.''

Justin let out a ragged sigh and nearly started yelling in his defense when, as proof of his words, John Tall Tree held up Zack Hamilton's letter.

''Where did you get that?'' Justin asked, shocked. He'd thought Ivy had taken it with her!

''Off the floor in the parlor last night. You argued

loudly, my friend. Naturally I wanted to see what the commotion was about.''

Justin was stunned. ''You shouldn't have read that!''

''That is your opinion,'' John replied. ''My opinion is that you should have read it more carefully. You would see that this relationship is not what you think. That this Zack Who-Cannot-Spell—'' he spoke the name with disdain ''—is not a man a woman like Ivy could love.''

''Ha!'' Justin snapped.

''And if you looked into your own heart more carefully, you would see that it did not matter. Would you spend the next twelve years regretting letting another woman walk out on you for a man who did not deserve her?''

Speechless, Justin snatched the letter out of John's hands. As he read it, he felt his heart sink in his chest. John was correct. There was something suspicious sounding in the man's only contacting Ivy after she had sent money home. And what was this about the police catching her for something he had done? He began to get angry. Was this man really coming after her? No wonder she had run…no wonder…

He looked up at John. ''Wait. *You* picked up this letter?''

John nodded.

''Then Ivy…?''

''She was content to leave the letter for kindling.''

Justin felt panic race through him. What was he going to do?

Fortunately John had a plan. ''The hands have

hitched your wagon," he informed Justin, pulling out his chair. "It is waiting. No doubt Ivy has not left Mrs. Tubbs's boardinghouse in Wishbone."

Justin tilted his head. "How do you know where she is?"

"Because that is where I took her last night." To Justin's surprised glance, he replied, "I could not let her walk all that way, and she would not hear of staying under your roof another night."

The words lit a fire under Justin. He grabbed his hat and coat off the peg by the door, then went back to call the children from their room.

John looked disapproving. "You are taking Sophie and Linus?"

Justin nodded. "Sophie, Linus, the hands, even you!" he replied. "We need to round up Joe Junior. If Ivy won't forgive me and agree to be my wife, then you all are just going to have to help me wrestle her into the wagon and bring her back anyway!"

John considered the matter, then nodded in resignation and turned to the door. "Unfortunately, white men often seem to need help in matters of romance," he agreed sadly.

Ivy stood on the sidewalk, looking into the mercantile, which was now closed. It was late morning, her feet were tired and her head ached, but she didn't know where else to walk. She'd been going crazy in the tiny room at Mrs. Tubbs's house. It was a nice place, but Mrs. Tubbs had stared curiously at the strange young woman who'd arrived at her doorstep so early on a Christmas morning, weeping and dis-

traught. Ivy couldn't blame the woman for thinking
she was peculiar.

So she'd gone out walking—and going over and
over questions she had no answers to. *What was she
going to do?* She said she was waiting for the stage,
but even when it got here she didn't know where she
would go. And how she would pay her way? She
needed to think about how she would get by, but right
now she couldn't concentrate. Once again she seemed
to have hit rock bottom, only she was almost too
stunned, too heartbroken to care.

She was weary and worn-out from spending half
the night bouncing between self-recrimination and
full-out anger at Justin. She was so tired that all she
could do now was peer forlornly into the mercantile,
where she'd been so giddy and joyful just days before, and marvel at how a cup so overflowing with
happiness could be drained dry so quickly.

She heard wagon wheels and hoofbeats behind her,
and when she looked into the glass she saw the Bar
M's wagon driving up—filled to the brim with people!

''Ivy!'' Linus yelled at the top of his little lungs as
the wagon pulled up behind her. The boy looked like
he might jump out of the vehicle, but he was stopped
by John Tall Tree. *Everyone* was crammed into that
wagon!

''Stay here,'' John instructed the fidgeting child.
''Your uncle needs to talk to Ivy alone.''

Ivy simultaneously felt her heart race and her back
stiffen defensively at that prospect. What did Justin
have to say to her? Was he coming here to say he

was sorry, to ask her back? Impossible! She couldn't imagine him apologizing, which would have necessitated admitting he was wrong.

And yet he hadn't been wrong. *She* had also been to blame for not telling him who she was and why she'd come to Texas. She *had* been using him, just not the way he'd said. It hadn't been so intentional, so ugly, as he'd said.

Meeting her eyes, he stepped out of the carriage and approached her cautiously. When he was about a foot away from her, he tilted up his hat brim.

In return, she tilted up her chin. After last night, it was hard to look into those dark eyes and not remember the angry words he'd hurled at her. The accusations.

"Well?" she said. "The store is closed."

"I didn't come here to go to the store and you know it," he said, a little irritation in his voice.

His tone got her ire up. "Then why did you come here?"

"I don't know! You're the prickliest woman I've ever known!"

A loud cough sounded from the wagon, and when they both turned, everyone was peering at them worriedly. John Tall Tree shot Justin a warning glance.

"I'd like to say hello to the children," Ivy said, brushing past Justin.

"Hold your horses," he said, stopping her. He held her arm, and she felt her cheeks glow from the mere touch of his hand. "I've got something to say to you."

She crossed her arms, partly because she was shak-

ing, partly out of shock. He *was* going to apologize!
She could see it in his eyes.

"I—" His face seemed to twist in pain, and his
forehead was creased.

All of the sudden, Ivy felt as if all the anger had
been sucked out of her. He'd come this far, was trying
so hard. She could at least meet him halfway. "No,
I'm sorry," she interrupted. "Last night was as much
my fault as yours. More, even. I should have told you
all about myself from the beginning. Then it would
have been clear that Zack meant nothing to me."

"I know he doesn't," Justin said, stepping closer.

"You do?"

He nodded. "I read the letter more carefully. But
Ivy, I wasn't going to tell you that I was sorry," he
admitted. "I was going to tell you…" His face turned
red and pained again, but before she could interrupt
once more, he blurted out, "I was going to tell you
that I love you and I want you to be my wife."

Ivy felt faint. These were perhaps the last words
she expected to come tumbling off his lips this morning. Or ever! "Your wife!"

He held her arms—heaven knows she needed prop-
ping up—and gently pulled her to him. "I know it's
a leap from Boston to Texas, and that I've been an
old curmudgeon, but I've changed. I swear I have. I'll
try to make your life wonderful."

Wonderful? She couldn't imagine anything more
wonderful than this very moment. She'd never been
so happy. Except…

There was still a cloud hanging over them—the
cloud of her past—and she couldn't ignore it. If she

did, it would surely come back to haunt them later. "But Justin," she said, looking squarely into his eyes even as she felt tears rolling down her own, "there are things you don't know about me."

His expression was impossibly gentle. "It doesn't matter."

"Yes, it does." She gathered courage. "I was in prison, Justin."

It was the first time she had spoken the words aloud.

She expected him to pull away from her, to recoil as she felt herself recoiling from her own admission, but he didn't. He smiled, and lifted a hand to her cheek, where he rubbed away a tear. "So was I, before you came along."

The tears came out full force now. She had never heard such loving words. "Oh, but—"

He put his hand over her lips, and then bent to place a kiss on her forehead. "Enough of that. Are you so mean that you could just leave me dangling here in suspense?"

She blink up at him, sniffing in confusion. "What?"

He grinned. "You never answered my question. Will you marry me?"

"Oh!" For a moment, she instinctively tried to think of the thousands of reasons she should say no, but she couldn't come up with even one. She was being handed the opportunity of a lifetime, a new beginning with a man she loved almost more than life itself. "Oh, yes! Yes, I will!"

The exclamation was rewarded with a kiss. She fell

against him, so relieved and happy and full of joy that she was reeling from it. His mouth tasted hers briefly before he pulled back and whispered, "I don't know if you remember, but we have an audience."

She chuckled and glanced shyly at the wagon full of familiar faces beaming back at them—all except Wink, who was blowing his nose. Why, he was crying! Ivy, who was doing a little crying of her own, laughed in amazement.

"C'mon, Ivy!" Linus bellowed with a four-year-old's impatience. "Let's go!"

"Yeah, Ivy," Joe Junior seconded, "aren't you coming home with us?"

Sophie looked up at her hopefully and Ivy felt her heart fill to brimming with love. Today was Christmas, she remembered. A day when the children should have been loafing about playing with their new treasures. And here they were. For her. But Christmas was also a day commemorating a birth, and that's how Ivy felt—as if she were a new person entering a new life, with love full in her heart.

She turned to Justin, feeling her insides warm as she looked into his brown eyes. "Well?"

He bent down and kissed her again. "Let's go home," he agreed.

Squeezing her hand, he led her to the crowded wagon that would take them all back to the ranch for the best and happiest Christmas day anyone at the Bar M could ever remember.

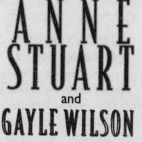

*H*ugh Blake,
soon to become stepfather to
the Maitland clan, has produced three
high-performing offspring of his own. But
at the rate they're going, they're never going to
make him a grandpa!

There's *Suzanne*, a work-obsessed CEO whose Christmas spirit
could use a little topping up....

And *Thomas*, a lawyer whose ability to hold on to the woman
he loves is evaporating by the minute....

And *Diane*, a teacher so dedicated to her teenage students she
hasn't noticed she's put her own life on hold.

But there's a Christmas wake-up call in store
for the Blake siblings. Love *and* Christmas miracles
are in store for all three!

Maitland Maternity Christmas

A collection from three of Harlequin's favorite authors

Muriel Jensen
Judy Christenberry
&Tina Leonard

Look for it in November 2001.

CALL THE ONES YOU LOVE OVER THE HOLIDAYS!

Save $25 off future book purchases when you buy any four Harlequin® or Silhouette® books in October, November and December 2001,

PLUS

receive a phone card good for 15 minutes of long-distance calls to anyone you want in North America!

WHAT AN INCREDIBLE DEAL!

Just fill out this form and attach 4 proofs of purchase (cash register receipts) from October, November and December 2001 books, and Harlequin Books will send you a coupon booklet worth a total savings of $25 off future purchases of Harlequin® and Silhouette® books, AND a 15-minute phone card to call the ones you love, anywhere in North America.

Please send this form, along with your cash register receipts
as proofs of purchase, to:
In the USA: Harlequin Books, P.O. Box 9057, Buffalo, NY 14269-9057
In Canada: Harlequin Books, P.O. Box 622, Fort Erie, Ontario L2A 5X3
Cash register receipts must be dated no later than December 31, 2001.
Limit of 1 coupon booklet and phone card per household.
Please allow 4-6 weeks for delivery.

**I accept your offer! Enclosed are 4 proofs of purchase.
Please send me my coupon booklet
and a 15-minute phone card:**

Name: _____

Address: _____ City: _____

State/Prov.: _____ Zip/Postal Code: _____

Account Number (if available): _____

---

097 KJB DAGL
PHQ4013